The Eternal Forever:
Adam

Andrew Allen Smith

Adam

Book 1 of the Eternal Forever

Copyright © 2021 Andrew Allen Smith

Edited by Jules Nelson

Edited by Pages Promotions

Cover by Germancreative

All rights reserved.

ISBN: **978-1-7373373-2-4**

LOC: On File

DEDICATION

To my daughter who wanted a book with a little more spice in it. To my son who wanted a little more mystery, and to all the people who wanted to see another genre and the strange depths that my mind may take us. I hope you all enjoy the book and can live the adventure I had writing it.

Prologue

I sat looking at the sky. The cool breeze blowing across my face, the thoughts of the last few hours running through my mind.

Her name was Terri. Well, it was Teresa, but she liked to be called Terri. We met at a small get-together between horse enthusiasts. They called us that because we were more than willing to put a lot of money into betting on horses and drinking good bourbon. Teresa was one of those women that you looked at and nearly snapped your neck trying to see again. She was tall. She told me later she was six foot even. She wore a red dress with a slit halfway up the side. With her heels on, she was easily six-four, perhaps more. Her golden hair was long and curled at the end, throwing highlights to anyone who looked. Her pure blue eyes scanned the room, and her perfectly painted red lips smiled as she sipped a martini.

Being older, I glanced at her and then slowly looked away. I knew who I was, and I knew I had a lot to offer, but she would not be interested. I had seen many women like her. They were usually more interested in shallow men with great bodies and greater egos than the wealth of experience I possessed. I had nothing to prove in this world or any other. I knew myself better than anyone in this room ever would.

The bourbon flowed freely, and I mingled with everyone. The senator with the young wife, the actor past his prime, and dozens of men who got their money the old-fashioned way. They inherited it. I laughed, told jokes, and we all had a great time.

I walked to the bar to have another Pappy and waited patiently as the bartender opened another bottle.

"I've been watching you," came a voice from the side.

I turned, and the red dress, perfect lips, and deep blue eyes looked back at me. "That must have been a thrill," I said with a grin. "Nothing like watching the giant from the corner."

At six-eight, I towered over most of the people attending. Sure, a few older University of Kentucky players were there that could look me eye to eye, but age was upon them. I remembered them playing long ago, and they were here trying to get some of their youth back or just to enjoy the thrill of the room.

She filled the room with laughter. The melodic sound was like crystal chimes, swinging in the wind. I smiled at her. She looked deep into my eyes. "I've not been watching like that. I've been watching what you are doing. I don't think any of these people know who the predator really is here, do they?"

"Pardon," I said.

"Oh, don't be coy," she smiled. "I see the way you look at people. I saw you look at me, scanning me and nearly cataloging everything about me, then passing me by. I bet you could tell me my shoe size, right?"

"Ten and a half," I remarked as I sipped my drink but saw her spark of surprise.

"You are right, of course," she looked at me with those eyes again. "And of course, you thought I was one of those shallow twits here for a man with cash and toys and the sense of a boy." The words rolled off her tongue with perfect tone, then she snapped to seriousness. "I don't do boys, Mr. ..." she trailed off, looking for an answer.

"Adam," I said to her.

"Adam," she smiled. "Is that a first name or a last name?"

"Just Adam," I said. "I have a surname, but it means little to me. I decided one day that I just ought to be Adam."

"So, Adam," her eyes had a twinkle in them, "what do you do for a living?"

"I walk around guessing women's shoe sizes, of course," I said to her.

She put her hand on my chest as she laughed. I felt the warmth even through my expensive shirt and undershirt. I felt stirrings I had not felt in countless years as she pushed on me.

"Silly," she giggled. "What do you really do?"

"Mostly, I taste bourbon, enjoy my horses, and visit the cemetery from time to time," I said to her.

"The cemetery? Why on earth would you do that?" she asked with the twinkle in her eye still there.

"I have a lot of friends that have passed, good friends, bad friends, and others that I think about. I just take a few moments to visit. Plus, the cemetery is beautiful here in Lexington," I said to her while sipping my Pappy Van Winkle.

"I see," she said with an inquisitive tone. "War hero?"

"Something like that," I looked down at her. "I have fought in a few wars, people live, and people die." I felt slightly melancholy thinking about the past for a moment. The past was difficult and complicated for me.

"I'm sorry," she said to me, those blue eyes looking through me, "I didn't mean to bring up bad memories."

I shrugged. "I am the one who's sorry. I try not to dwell in the past; there's just too much of it."

"Funny," she said, "I like that."

"You haven't told me your name," I said with a grin. "You know mine now. What shall I call you?"

She reached my shirt and played with my buttons. "I wish you could call me Eve," she brushed her hand up my shirt, and I could feel her warmth. "but my name is Terri." She tapped my drink, and a small sip of bourbon dropped from the glass to my shirt.

"I'm sorry," she said and dabbed at it with her napkin.

"Terri," I said. "I like Terri, but is it short for something?" I continued ignoring her worries about my shirt.

"My name is Teresa Elaine Rose," she smiled and said with measured practice. "I am Teresa from my grandmother, Elaine from my aunt, and Rose because I have thorns."

I chuckled with her for a moment as she poked my chest. She continuously kept a hand on my arms or chest. Occasionally, she would squeeze and feel the tight muscle mass under my shirt or sport coat. I am not small, and I am not weak. Though I have seen many years, I am graced with strength. "Why Terri then?" I asked.

"I started going by Terri so I would not be tied to anyone else's name. It worked well." She smiled as we leaned against the bar. "It also kept my family happy."

I nodded in understanding and turned as another man walked up. "Terri!" he said with near arrogant bravado.

"Hi, Sam," she smiled but was clearly guarded.

"What are you doing at this party?" he asked her to avoid even looking at me. I stood up from leaning at the bar, and he swung to look at me.

"Wow, you like them big now?" Sam said in a tone that reeked of jealousy.

"Sam, this is Adam. I just met Adam a few minutes ago," Terri said with feigned nonchalance.

"Ohhh, just met," Sam said. "Let me tell you a little about Terri, Adam."

I was so tired of these types of people. I counted to ten in my head, trying to stay calm.

"Terri is just here to find people like me and you and take advantage of them. She ..." Sam began.

I leaned into Sam and put my hand on his forearm. The cheap jacket felt just, well, cheap in my hand as I held him. At first, he tried to pull away, but my grip was already tight. He looked into my eyes and I into his, and he saw me differently for a moment. He saw me as I was, not as I am. I felt his bones brittle beneath my grip, the flow of his blood, the feel of his flesh, and squeezed just a little.

"She is just fine," I said. "That is what you were going to say, right?"

His brow furled. He looked at me, trying not to show the inevitable pain but pleading internally as his radius and ulna began to come closer together.

"Yes," Sam said, now showing some duress. "She is perfect."

"I thought so," I said with an easy smile and let go, picking up my bourbon.

Sam looked at me for a moment. "Terri, we will talk later."

I smiled again, looking at Sam. "Can we talk later too?"

Sam looked at me, puzzled, then turned and walked away into the crowd without another word.

Terri leaned into me. "You didn't have to do that."

"Do what?" I asked with near childlike innocence.

"Remember," she said, "I watch people too. I saw how you held him, and I saw him get uncomfortable. I know you were trying to protect me, but hurting people is never an answer."

"It depends on the question," I said with a light smile.

She looked at me, almost pleading, "You know what I mean." She put her hand to the side of my face and stroked it softly. "If we are going to be friends, you can't hurt people."

I smiled and looked into her eyes. Her hand touched the side of my cheek, and I could feel the warmth in her. A tingle of electricity passed from her eyes to mine. No one but me could have felt it, and it flowed through my face then back to her through her hand.

"Not even a little?" I tried to smile as I struggled not to be distracted.

I heard the music in the background start with Louis Armstrong, "All the Time in the World." It was such a good song, full of power and life. She leaned forward and whispered in my ear, "Not even a little. You have to promise."

My body tingled with life as it had not in oh so long. This woman, she had touched something that no one had ever touched. Not in so many years, not in a long, long time, perhaps ever.

"Okay, I promise I will not hurt anyone unless they really deserve it," I said to her.

She bit my earlobe, and I thought the resulting surge could be seen across the room. "Only if I say it's Okay," she said playfully, as I thought I was a mouse being played with by a cat.

"Okay," I said in a hoarse voice. I cleared my throat before continuing more directly, "Okay."

I had never felt so controlled but in control. As Armstrong played, I took her hand, and we started to dance onto the dance floor. It was not forced, nor in any way contrived. We just seemed to flow together. I was impressed as, for her size, she too was lithe and aware of her body. Though thin, she was not lanky. Though tall, she was not overweight. She was the perfect woman bound to human form.

A combination of Julie Newmar and Raquel Welch with the grace of a dancer. I was not sure how well she danced and began a waltz move as the music shifted to "Long Live Forever." I was thrilled as she began to waltz with me in perfect step. As we danced, I felt more alive than I think I ever had. Her movements mirrored mine, and the world seemed to melt behind us. The band shifted to "Por una Cabeza." Terri swung into a tango as we began the dance of frustrated love and passion. The dance was strong and powerful, and I almost wished I had a rose as we took the lead from each other from powerful, to passive, and back again. I felt a drop of sweat on my brow and, for an instant, wondered how long it had been since I had felt sweat from dancing. I saw Terri was sweating as well but smiling and as lost as I was in the pure fury of the dance. As the dance and song ended, I heard applause, and we looked around to see everyone had cleared the dance floor for us. We had been all alone, the center of attention.

Terri beamed. "Oh, aren't you just full of surprises?" A light Kentucky accent passing from her lips.

I bowed to her, and she to me. When she took my arm to exit the dance floor, the crowd parted until we got to the bar.

Several men from the event walked to me and shook my hand. One said, "Wow, Adam, I have never seen you dance. I am impressed."

"I was inspired," I said, looking at Terri.

He smiled. "I bet." Then turned and walked away.

Terri tugged lightly at my arm as she handed me another bourbon. I took the glass and sipped the drink.

"Four Roses," I said. "A good choice."

"What were you drinking?" Terri asked me.

"Pappy," I said as I took another sip.

"Of course. Sorry, I can't afford Pappy as easily," Terri noted with a sigh.

"One of my few vices," I said to her with a smile, "and I will pay."

"Want to take a walk?" Terri asked as I dropped a few bills on the bar.

"Sure," I said. We both downed our drinks almost in unison.

The estate we were at was large, and walking out to the grounds was awe-inspiring. The moon lit up the fields, and you could see a few horses walking in the moonlight in the distance. All around, the smell of grass and flowers was abundant. The night air, though cool, was not cold or crisp, just refreshing. The light breeze reminded me briefly of the woods I walked through so many years ago to find my freedom.

"You aren't like anyone I have ever known," Terri said as we walked near the pristine black fences.

"Really?" I said, chuckling.

"Yeah, I bet you don't feel like anyone else either?" Terri queried.

I turned and leaned my back against the fence, feeling it bow slightly under my weight.

"How many people have you known in your short years?" I asked.

"Probably too many," she said, looking up at the sky. A sorrowful look crossed her face.

I stood and touched her shoulder. "I'm sorry. I'm not sure I understand but are you Okay?" I asked.

"You see the men in there? They all know I am from older money run dry. Sam has told everyone I am sleazy even though I refused him," Terri said, a tear in her eye.

"I'm sorry," I said quietly.

"For what? Making this one of the best days I've had in a while? Please." She feigned a smile and wiped away the tear. "Who are you, Adam-no-name, and what secrets are you holding behind those mysterious grey eyes?"

"I am no one," I said, looking out to the pastures. "I am just someone who lived through a lot of pain and one day came out on top. I am just someone who one day will find purpose in my being."

"Deep," Terri snickered. "That was really deep."

"I'm sorry," I smiled. "I sometimes get lost in the moment." As I finished, a horse walked up to me and nuzzled my shoulder. The beautiful chestnut mare pressed my shoulder again, and I stood and turned to her.

"Oh," Terri gasped. "Never seen that before."

"What?" I asked while absently stroking the horse between the eyes then moving my hand to its long neck. I ran my hands up and down across the mane and methodically rubbed her ears.

"I have never seen one of these horses come up to anyone," Terri explained, reaching up to stroke the stallion.

"Animals seem to like me," I said.

"It seems I do too," Terri said and came close, nuzzling into my shoulder softly. "I'm not sure why, Adam, but you just seem right. I know it's some stupid girl thing, and I know you're older than me, but like I said, you just seem right. I'm thirty-one now, and I've never found anyone who has made me feel like you do in this very short time." She looked up into my eyes, her blue eyes glowing in the moonlight. "Do you understand at all?"

"It's been a long time since I have felt anything, Terri, but yes, I understand," I said, as the horse chuffed and moved back into the pasture.

"What time is it?" Terri asked.

"1:35 AM," I said.

"Really? No watch, and you say 1:35?" She pulled her phone from her purse and looked down at it. "Okay, smarty pants, wanna get some breakfast?"

"Sure," I said, and we walked back toward the house. "You can follow me, or I can follow you somewhere."

"I took an Uber, so if it's not too much trouble, you could drive," she said. "I mean, are you Okay to drive?"

"I'm fine," I said. "Alcohol doesn't seem to bother me much." I considered for a moment how little alcohol bothered me. I tried to get drunk once a long time ago. After a cask of rum, all I had to do was urinate a lot.

We walked to the front of the large barn-style house where the party was still going on, and I reached into my pocket to pull out my keys. I opened the door for Terri as she looked at the car. "1955 or 56?" she asked.

"Good eye. It's a 1955 Corvette. Some of it has been redone, rebuilt to make it better," I said as I slid comfortably into the driver's seat. "As you can guess, there are not a lot of cars I fit into easily to drive."

"I would never have guessed that," Terri grinned. "I have that problem sometimes too. My long legs seem to get in the way of everything."

I looked over and saw the slit of her dress had ridden up, showing her long, well-shaped legs. I sighed lightly to myself.

As I moved on to Versailles Road, I shifted and let the car wind out. My hand still on the stick shift, Terri put hers over mine. I tingled again like never before. When she pulled my hand to her leg, I was enthralled. We were heading into town, and I looked over at her. "Do you mind if I stop by the house for a moment on the way?"

"Sure," she said, squeezing my hand tightly.

I turned on Parkers Mill and drove a short distance until a long drive beckoned. I then turned into the drive where a formidable gate opened before me. "Nice gate," Terri said.

"It is RF-based, and the little keyring I have on my car keys activates it," I said.

We drove down the driveway to my house as the turrets of the side stood out in the powerful moonlight. The grey stone was evident in the Victorian-style home, and as I drove to the side, the garage opened anxiously, allowing me to drive into one of the bays.

"I thought I knew all the houses around here, but I have never seen this one," Terri said. "It's beautiful. Does Dracula live here?" She laughed.

I laughed with her. "Not really, no. Do you want to wait here or come in?"

"I'm coming in. I have to see the inside," she said.

I walked around as she started to open her door. I grabbed it and opened it.

"I could get used to that," she said.

"Manners are important, right?" I told her.

"Not in today's age, but I appreciate them," Terri said, looking at the other bays where unknown cars hid under finely woven car covers.

As we walked into the side door, the garage closed. She startled and turned to look.

"Sensor on my keyring, remember?" I said, laughing.

"Must be nice," she said.

"I used to leave the garage open all the time. This helps me be more mindful."

She grabbed my hand and held it for a moment. "Adam, before we go further, I need you to know," she paused, "Well, I am not the kind of girl that goes home with men blindly. I mean, I like you, and wow, you are more than I can imagine, but I didn't come with you to, umm, well, you know."

I laughed then looked at her, realizing she was feeling embarrassed and excited all at once. "Terri, I am here to get another shirt. Remember." I looked down, and she saw the small stain of bourbon.

"Oh," she said, "I forgot."

We walked through the spacious living room, and she commented on the weapons and artifacts I had there. "Is this a real matchlock?" "What type of sword is this? Why is it paired with an axe?" The questions continued in rapid sequence.

As we walked, we stopped often. It became a history lesson as well as a walk down memory lane for me. So many memories. I explained the different artifacts, the weapons, the china, the collectibles from all over the world. Where they had come from, what they were part of, and why they were important. We talked about the American Civil war, Europe, and both World Wars. She was a sponge and was fascinated with my depth of knowledge. I was equally attracted to her fascination and raw interest. She was like no other I had met. Eventually, we arrived at my bedroom. As I walked in, I looked at her. "You can stay out here. I am just changing my shirt."

"It's Okay," she said. "I was out of line, you are more than a gentleman. I mean, I am so used to men trying to, well, you know, like Sam."

"I am not like Sam," I said slowly, enunciating every word.

"I know," Terri replied and walked into my bedroom with me.

I took off my jacket and laid it on the king-size bed. The bed posts reached toward the ceiling, and the deep cherry furniture made the room seem to glow warmly. I took off my top shirt and walked to a small sink in the bathroom. There I wet down the stain with water. I then walked back to the bedroom to find Terri studying several paintings on the wall.

She turned. "This painting, is it a Van Gogh?"

"It is a reproduction of 'The Crows'," I said. "I always liked it and found it while I was overseas once."

"It's beautiful," she said, then smiled. "Looks like I got your undershirt as well."

I looked down and saw the stain on my undershirt, so I took it off and set it on the bed as well. My body rippled with well-defined musculature and the scars of years past. Terri gasped a little.

"I'm sorry," I said. "I sometimes forget how I affect other people."

"Let me see," she walked over. She looked at me and traced the faint scars on my body. All were not much of a memory for me, but you could still see them in the light. She reached and touched my chest and traced a line on one of the scars that crisscrossed my body. "What happened? Does it hurt?" she asked me in a quizzical tone.

"It used to hurt all the time, but one day they all just healed, and now you can only see them up close. The pain is a memory as well. They took their time; I used to have problems healing, but now, well? I heal pretty quick, and all I have from the past is a few scars." I told her as she traced another scar with her finger.

"An accident?" she asked.

"No, it was on purpose, but that's ancient history," I said.

She looked up into my eyes. Those blue eyes were mesmerizing. She grabbed the back of my head and pulled me down into a kiss. I was hers. I felt the stars move overhead as she kissed me. It was not a kiss of desperation or control. It was a kiss of passion and submission as well as control. The kiss only a few could even begin to understand. Her hand pulled me closer by my head while her other hand roamed across my chest.

I started to pull away, "I thought you…" I paused, not sure if I should continue.

She pulled me back, drawing away for only an instant to say, "Shut up."

She kissed me and moved me toward the bed. As we reached the bed, Terri pushed me down while still kissing. With grace, we rolled on the bed as one. Smiling, she bit my lip as she started kissing me again. I kissed her back, lost in the passion, and felt stirrings that I thought were forever gone.

She began kissing my neck, then my chest, and I thought I would burst, but she quickly worked her way back up to my lips. We were caught in the moment. She slid off the bed and pulled off my black oxfords, then slipped off her heels and came back to me, kissing me passionately again. Her hands were everywhere, and I grasped her and held her tightly as she became even more frenzied. I turned her and held myself over her. As we kissed, I felt her wrap her legs around me and pull me even closer. Even with our clothes on, we were erotically charged. Perhaps even more so than if our clothes had come off.

She felt my hardness beneath my pants with her hand. "Oh, my god," she said, then ground up into me. I pulled her further and kissed her. We writhed together like two teenagers feeling passion for the first time.

Then, it happened. She orgasmed, and I felt the electricity between us even more. It was not through act or kiss, but pure passion that she orgasmed once again. I felt mine brewing. Her hips urged me on, and even with my pants on, I felt her heat. As I felt her tongue going deep into my mouth, I came and nearly screamed with the intensity of the clothed interlude.

I laughed, then smiled.

"What's so funny?" she smiled in return, covered with sweat.

"It's been a long time," I said, smiling wider.

"Maybe it shouldn't have been." Terri reached down and kissed me now gently, cooling from our escapade. "I could be with you forever."

I looked into her eyes deeply. "Forever is a long time."

"No one has ever made me feel like you do, and we haven't done very much," she said to me, kissing me lightly, biting me, and touching me still. "I want you."

"On a first date?" I asked.

"Yeah, you are right," she laughed, "but oh my god, Adam. I never want this moment to end."

I kissed her with a gentleness I did not know I still possessed. "Me either, but we have time."

She got up quickly. "Can I use your bathroom?" she asked. "I bet I look a mess. I don't normally get like that."

"Of course," I said, getting up and going to the large chest of drawers.

She went to the bathroom while I changed my shirt and underwear. Fortunately, my pants were dry. I then picked out a suitable shirt and dressed. When Terri came out of the bathroom, she was a picture of radiant perfection. I straightened the bed and put my clothing in the hampers.

"Wow," she said, "You look great."

"Not really, but you look stunning," I said, looking at her.

"Ready to go eat?" she asked.

"Of course," I said as we walked through the long hall and living areas to the garage.

"It's 4 in the morning. Where do you want to go?" I asked her.

"Well, there's only one place to go at 4 am that has good food," she smiled. "Tolly-Ho."

I laughed, drove out of the garage, and got back onto the road heading to town. A beep in the car let me know the garage was again closed as the road beckoned.

Terri was still full of questions. "How bad were the scars originally?" she asked. "How do you feel? Is the skin ever sore?"

I answered the best I could. "They healed a long time ago. I have been pain-free for a long time as well. The skin feels fine and has actually thickened. When I had the scars originally, I looked almost like a ghost."

She was amazed and truly interested. I talked to her about that and more on the drive downtown, lost in the interactions I had never known. The entire way, she would not let go of my hand and rubbed it on her perfect leg, making it very difficult to drive. I was in what felt like heaven as we pulled into the Tolly-Ho parking lot.

"Do I need anything?" Terri asked as she looked through her purse and put on a small dab of lipstick.

"No," I laughed. "I think I can afford a Ho with Cheese."

"Don't forget fries," she said as she stuffed her purse behind the seat. "I love fries. Oh, and I only share fries if I really like you."

We got out of the car, laughing, and began walking towards the front door.

"Look who it is," I heard the voice from behind, "the big man and his little slut. I guessed you would come here to the 'only place with great food at night.'"

We both turned, but it was Terri who spoke, "Sam, go home. You're drunk."

I saw him and the three other young men with him. I recognized two of them as players in the UK football team. I tensed slightly.

"I guess she was fine enough for you to take to this dive," Sam said in a terse tone. The other men were guarded, and their eyes focused on me.

"It's not a dive, Sam. I like the food," Terri started.

"Shut up, slut," Sam said, walking towards me. "Your boy and I have some pain to discuss. I didn't much like being manhandled, so I picked up a few friends, and maybe we should manhandle you a little."

I tensed, muscles flexing beneath my coat. But Terri held my arm tightly and looked up at me. "Remember you said you would not."

I looked down at her and saw the pleading in her eyes, so I lightly guided her behind me. "I know."

Sam swung and hit me in the face. He pulled back his hand and grabbed it. "Steel?" He shook his hand, I barely moved. He swung again and hit my face, again and again, pulling back his now battered hand.

"I don't want to hurt you," I said to Sam. Then, looking over to the rest, "I don't want to hurt any of you. Just get in your car and go." I added softly as Terri held my arm from behind.

The bat hit me across the stomach and knocked the breath from me for a split second. It cracked, but I grabbed it quickly before the football player could pull away. I held it. He pulled, pulled harder, yanked but the bat did not move. He looked in my eyes with a sense of realization and pulled again harder in desperation. I let go and watched him topple to the ground.

Looking over my shoulder to Terri, I searched her face. "Can I hurt them now?"

Her eyes were full of fire as she said, "Just stop them."

As I turned back, I saw Sam had pulled out a small pistol. He aimed at my chest and fired. I felt the bullet pass through me, and the hands holding my arm went limp. I turned in time to catch Terri before she fell all the way to the ground. Her shoulder was covered with blood, and she gasped slightly.

I felt another bat break over my back, but still, I held her as she gasped. "Guess that didn't work," with a weak voice and an attempt at a smile.

I stood, turning. All four men saw that something was different. Sam was training his gun on me, and I grabbed it by the barrel. He fired, and a hole went through my hand. Blood covered parts of my hand but as Sam watched, the skin folded in upon itself, and my hand was whole. A clean spot in the center of the bloody mass.

"What are you?" Sam asked, looking at me.

"Nothing you could understand." I hit him in the chest in anger. He fell hard to the ground on his face and did not move. One of the boys turned him over. His chest was caved in at a weird angle as he looked up to some unknown destination in the skies, lost forever to this world.

The sun was rising. A blood-red color encrusted the sky above.

The other young men looked at me with both anger and fear. All three rushed me with fire in their eyes. As the first swung at me, I grabbed his arm by the forearm and twisted forcefully. Blood sprayed as his arm came off in my hand. I took the arm and began beating him with it until he fell to the ground. The other two tried to stop me in vain. I reached out and threw one of them. He landed on Sam. I then grabbed the other in the mouth, and with one swift movement, ripped his jaw off.

"You know, you should never attack someone without knowing what you're up against," I said, holding a jaw in one hand and an arm in the other.

The three young men left alive, cowered from me in utter fear. It was a fear I had seen many times in my long life. I looked at them, "Run."

My near-whisper sent them scattering like roaches in the light. The one intact would-be attacker helping his two friends hobble away.

I threw the body parts to the ground like used paper towels and ran back to Terri. She lay there, gasping. Each breath more ragged than the last.

So here I am, cradling her in my arms. The cool breeze blowing across my face. I am looking down at a woman between life and death. I can save her, but at the cost of her being a little of me. I can watch her pass as I have seen so many pass before. The decision is mine. As I wrestle with it, the sirens scream in the background, closer and closer. Just a drop of my electricity-charged, amazing blood will give her life, but how can I decide?

Chapter 1

I drove faster than I normally would have to my home. What would happen next would not be for a hospital, or prying eyes. Prying eyes generated questions. Questions generated fear, distrust, and people that were less than honorable.

As I was driving, I dialed a number. The phone rang and was answered.

"What time is it?" I was asked by a groggy voice.

"Three-thirty in the morning. Three-thirty-six if you want to get particular," I said as I grinned at the phone. I have found that people often imitate their expressions when they are on the phone, and the cellular world has created many people walking around making faces at the ether.

"I should have known it would be you," the voice replied. "Who else is going to be calling, waking me up?"

Captain Shawn Dennis was someone I had known for some time. We intersected at several points because trouble sometimes seemed to follow me. I also assisted him with some rather unique cases that came up in the area. He knew I had a fondness for weapons and tactics. And my mind was often capable of seeing past the obvious, picking out seemingly inconsequential details and seeing them for what they were, facts. "I would say you have a few minutes before your phone starts ringing. I am afraid one of the men is dead, and three others are hurt pretty bad."

"Dead?" Shawn barked at me. "You haven't killed anyone before."

"I would have liked to avoid it," I said to Shawn as Terri stirred next to me. "I will answer any questions, but I am sure the tapes will confirm I was in the right."

"Which bar this time?" Shawn asked.

"I was not at a bar," I said to him. "I was at Tolly-Ho."

"Oh, wow," Shawn said. "Any chance we could say the food killed him?"

I did not laugh. I take life and death very seriously. It may have been funny, but I could not consider it as many would. "I am sorry. I hit him too hard. He shot the woman with me."

"Uh oh," Shawn said. "You told me to expect this someday. I just never did. Should I head over there?"

"No," I told Shawn, "Just take care of things and stop by later. I will be busy for quite a while, perhaps we can talk. I know you will have questions."

"I know you wouldn't lie to me, Adam," Shawn said to me in a lowered voice. "Was there another way?"

"He shot her," I stated. "He shot her and tried to hurt me."

"I am sure it will be an interesting video," Shawn replied. "Do you know who they are?"

"The three that survived are with the football team," I said. "The other I do not know, but I would suspect he is with one of the horse farms. His name was Sam, but I know little more than that. He was at one of the bourbon tastings while I was there tonight."

"I'll find out," Shawn replied. "How bad are the others?"

"I am sorry to say I ripped off portions of their body. I left them there though, so it should be possible to repair them," I said as my car turned onto Parker's Mill, heading towards my house.

Terri began mumbling in the seat next to me; it was starting. I knew the next day would be difficult for her. I saw it only once, but it was enough. I never expected to see it again. I considered and wondered if I should have let her go. I set the thought aside.

As I knelt over Terri in front of Tolly-Ho, I let several droplets of my blood fall into her wound and that had started a process that could not be revoked without great consideration and potentially great effort.

Shawn sighed, and I snapped back to attention. "You know, Adam," he said to me, "I will do everything I can to keep things from getting out of control. I'll try to keep the press out, but you know how they are here. We are a small city. They get tired of the advanced basket weaving classes at the library being a headline."

"It is a much bigger city than it used to be," I said to him. "Thank you for all you can do."

"I want to see this girl today or tomorrow," Shawn said. "I am sure it will be fascinating or interesting, whichever you decide to use. I will have to come take a statement when they call me."

"Probably both," I said to him, "I appreciate all you do. I am more than available for a statement. I am appreciative of your assistance for my unique situations."

"Yeah, yeah," Shawn said to me. "I am sure it will be another day of fun and excitement. We haven't done one in quite a while. It was nice getting calls from you during the day, asking for me to help you drink some Bourbon or go to the Opera for you."

"I am sorry, Shawn. You know I try to avoid trouble and the questions that come with it," I said. "I try very hard to keep to myself."

"This girl must be something special," Shawn laughed. "Do you think she will stick around? I remember you telling me about that other one, Morgan? Is that right? I mean, who calls their kid that? It is like a middle ages thing. But anyway, wasn't that the one who chained you up?"

"Yes," I said, a little uncomfortable that he remembered, "For a few years."

"That would have sworn me off women forever," Shawn said.

"Forever is a long time," I laughed a little. "Forever can be a moment, or it can be eternal. It just depends on how you look at it."

"You are such a doofus," Shawn laughed. "Call coming in; I bet it is about your little escapade."

"Thank you, Shawn," I replied. "I hope to see you soon."

I was glad I called Shawn. I always considered him a good person and saw him grow up from a precocious child to an inquisitive adult. He always had a passion for seeing more. When he uncovered part of my secret, he was more fascinated than concerned. I remembered him asking me, "So are you a witness to some grisly murder? Did you put the mob in jail? Are you hiding from someone?" It was almost cruel, but I delayed telling him anything for many years until one day, when he came to the house, I explained that I was different from most people. He had laughed and accepted my words. But I often wondered what he believed and what he simply thought was bravado or exaggeration.

Terri stirred again as I pulled into my gate. The heavy doors swung open where we had been only a few hours ago, and I pulled around and watched as the garage again opened and beckoned me forward. My car was eager, and in less than a flash, I was parked.

Terri began talking, and she was covered with sweat. The curls in her golden hair were falling out as she became drenched in sweat. Terri's red dress was crusty with blood, but her breathing was now stronger. I was both concerned and alleviated that her condition was improving. I walked to the passenger door of the Corvette and opened it. Terri lay slumped; one of her heels was partially off her foot, her dress was mussed. With great care, I took off both of her shoes and was impressed with her body tone and form.

I have long appreciated the human body and have always been impressed with the female form. There are few women I would not consider beautiful in one way or another. Their form gives them a look all of their own. The unique symmetry makes them attractive, elegant, seductive, hardened or many other looks. Terri was elegant, attractive, and seductive. Even in her current state, the symmetry of her body was able to elicit several random appreciative thoughts, and I wish I could have shared them with her.

With patience and care, I knelt and put my arms under her prone body, then lifted her with no effort. As she rose and I stood, I tilted my arms back, and she slid to my chest. My new shirt was surely ruined by the fight, but I now felt the blood on her dress seep into the fine linen and soak the shirt and my skin. I held Terri close, and as I moved, I closed the car door with one foot as I balanced on the other.

Walking to the house door, I opened it. As I stepped inside, I heard the garage door lumber to a close. I was happy with the technology, and though it had been a fun novelty, this time it was a useful feature. I closed the door, and Terri opened her eyes and looked at me. Her pure blue eyes held an innocence that I do not think anyone but I could understand. I looked into those beautiful eyes, and she looked at me, knowing but confused. "Adam?" she asked. "Adam, it hurts." She was calm and easy, then her face covered with sweat and contorted for a moment as the waves of pain hit her again. "Adam," she cried, "Adam, please no more." As she spoke to me, she turned her head, and her now wet hair fell across her eyes.

I adjusted my arm as I stood there inside the garage door and held her up with one arm. With my right arm, I reached over and brushed the hair from her eyes. "I am here, Terri," I said to her. "I am with you."

I adjusted my arms to hold her in both again and walked to my bedroom. She opened her eyes again, "I know this place." She flailed around a little, looking at the scenes passing by her. "Nice matchlock," she murmured again, repeating her earlier statement. "Taking me to your bedroom?" She said, "All you had to do was ask."

Terri's face contorted again, and this time she threw her head back and screamed. The scream was shrill and powerful, echoing down the hall. I know that the sound cannot escape my home. I made sure no sound can escape my home. I have had many days like hers, screaming with no end in sight. It has been a long time since I have had one, but I know they could come back. I am prepared. Terri screamed again, and I thought of that long-ago time when I was alone, screaming with nothing but rocks and wind to hear my voice. There were no ears to hear my pleas for an end to the suffering.

Again, I balanced Terri with one arm and threw back the sheets on the massive bed. The linen was crisp and inviting, and of course, white. I knew it would be time for new bedding and perhaps even a new mattress after these next few days, but I did not hesitate. I laid Terri on the bed, and she curled instantly into a fetal ball. Her dress was bunched up, and the clothing was a mess.

I went to the bathroom and retrieved three towels and a handful of washcloths. I also reached under the sink to get a small bucket and put warm water in it. I came back out to the bedroom; Terri had not moved. Opening the dresser drawer, I pulled out a small silver knife. It was only six inches long, and it opened to a thin blade with a "snickt" that was usually fun for me. Today, it had no effect. I put the blade on the back of Terri's dress and slid it between her skin and the fabric. With the blade against the fabric, I traced down. The dress seemed to melt away from Terri's body. As the back opened, her bra became visible, the black silk shining in my bedroom's light. The dress continued to fall away as the red fabric was cut cleanly with the razor-sharp knife. The small of Terri's back was indented and one of those that would gain readership in men's magazines. I was mesmerized by her even as I concentrated on my task. As I reached the bottom of her dress, her black silk panties were revealed. The stylish thong did well at accentuating her well-defined buttocks.

I had to work the fabric to not catch on either her wound or any other parts of her body. As I moved the folds of fine clothe aside Terri stirred and looked at me, realizing I was taking off her dress. "You naughty boy," she said. As her eyes began to roll back in her head again, she focused, "My dress, what happened to my dress?"

"I will get you a new one," I reassured her. "It is just a dress."

A look of indignation passed across her brow for a moment, "You're damn right you will."

The pain was back, and I could see it ripple across her face as each nerve in her body fired over and over. She screamed again and passed out. I looked at the wound on her back and took one of the towels, wet it, and cleaned the area. It was caked with blood, and the meat of the wound hung out at odd angles.

Bullets were horrible weapons when they hit you. The weapon that hit Terri would normally have passed straight through her body, but it had gone through me first. In doing so, it lost velocity and began to tumble. That tumble was what caused the odd angles and the excessive damage to her body. That tumble was the reason I was faced with this choice.

I cleaned the area as well as I could and left it unbandaged. For the hours to come, a bandage would be more of a hindrance than any type of help. The wound would seep blood and tissue as it healed and I would have to clean it many times.

I laid Terri on her back for a moment and saw the wound in the front of her chest. The bullet had hit her lung and many organs as it passed through her. I checked the wound then cleaned the front well. The front looked better than the back. The bullet had missed her more than ample breasts. I knew that the tumble wreaked havoc inside, though. It saddened me to consider the pain she was going through now. It gave me hope

Terri opened her eyes as I cleaned the wound.

"You are so sweet," she said to me, smiling, "I am so happy to have found you."

I took one of the washcloths, wet it, and cleaned off her face a little at a time. She watched me as I cleaned her, and her makeup came away on the washcloth.

"I must look a mess," she said and then began to grimace again. I held her hand, feeling her grip tighten as the pain returned. In moments, her back began to arch, and she heaved forward. Her breasts strained against the tight black bra as her face contorted into the look of anguish only those who have known true pain could understand. As the pain began to fade again, she fell into the hands of sleep once more. Her mind and body were exhausted for the moment.

I took my time. Her bra and panties were intact, and the panties were not covered in blood. I cut the bra away in steps. First the straps and then the fabric between her breasts. As the fabric fell away, I was impressed again by her body and the lengths she must have gone to keep it in such good shape. Her breasts were a full D cup, but they did not look huge but instead well proportioned. The pouting nipples stretched upwards. I was at once both aroused and uncomfortable with seeing this woman without her consent. I took the time to clean her skin and covered her in my sheet. I then left a single clean towel and took the rest of the now blood-soaked towels to the laundry room.

Rather than wait, I wanted to start a load of laundry right away. It would be better if the blood did not set in. I laughed at myself a little. I had two linen closets full of towels, I seldom had guests, and I did laundry three times a week. It seemed I was doing busy work to keep my mind off Terri. I did it anyway. I walked to the washer, started a load, pretreated the towels, and threw away Terri's dress. I looked at her bra. It was a Victoria's Secret 32D. I found the tag and noted the style number, then pulled out my phone.

As I dialed the number, I looked at the time and hung up. It was still very early; Micah would not be awake yet.

My phone rang back immediately.

"Did you need me, sir?" Micah asked without hesitation.

"Sorry," I said, "I didn't realize the time. Go back to sleep Micah."

The young man on the other end of the phone laughed, "I was up playing games with friends. We're up `til five or six every night. Did you need something?"

I considered for a moment. It would be hours before any store would be open. The need was not pressing, but I decided to plan ahead. "After the big mall opens, can you go to Victoria's Secret and get a few things for me?"

"Sure," Micah laughed, "I'm not sure they have your size, though."

"Very cute," I said. "Not for me."

"I know, I know," Micah grinned. "Just pullin' your leg, Mister A."

Micah was a good kid. I met him a few years before. He was young and tried to pick my pocket. I remember being aware of him, spinning and picking him up by his arm as he held my wallet in his hand. He kicked and screamed, trying to get away, but then started laughing as I held him, with my arm outstretched. Micah had said, "Okay, you got me."

I retrieved my wallet, then smirking said, "Not big enough to cook; I think I should throw you back." I dropped him on the ground. As I did so, he was still laughing. He asked my name, and I told him, "Adam." At that point, I became Mister A to him.

Micah was smooth and personable, and had a boyish look and charm, even with his large afro. I helped him start a personal shopping business, and he now had six runners working for him. Whenever I called him, only he came, not because I asked for him to do so, but because he was always genuinely curious and more than a little grateful.

"What do you need from Victoria, who has no secrets, by the way?" Micah bubbled.

"Can you get me a selection of ten bras, different types, 32D, and ten pairs of medium underwear? Then some pajamas, three or four pairs. Something nice. Not sexy, just comfortable. Slippers, size ten and a half, and some perfume from there. They have a few nice kinds. Have the women there help you."

"Help me?" Micah said, "We are teaching them how to sell, Mister A. Me and my runners get more calls for them than anywhere else. People are too shy to go into the store, and when they call, we deliver. I may hire this new girl to measure women for a perfect fit at home. I got you covered, Mister A. I will bring you everything by noon. Is that Okay?"

"That will be fine, Micah," I said to him. "Do you still have a credit card for me?"

"I got ya covered, Mister A," Micah said.

"Thank you," I said. "I will see you around noon. We will expand the order then."

"No problem," Micah replied, "See you then. And Mister A?"

"Yes," I asked, wondering his question.

"I am glad you got yourself a gal," Micah said.

"Who said I…" I trailed off. "See you at noon."

Micah laughed and hung up the phone.

I walked back to the bedroom where Terri still lay on her side, curled on the bed. I opened the covers and checked her again, the wounds were seeping, so I cleaned them, but she was not in as much pain, or at least she didn't seem to be. I picked up a new washcloth and walked into the bathroom to get it wet. I took my time and cleaned the wound on her back, then rolled her over and cleaned the front wound. It looked better but still glistened with blood.

Terri opened her eyes and looked at me. "Am I naked?" Her voice was weak and distant, but more coherent than a few minutes before.

"Well, not completely," I said as I smiled at her.

"I remember you, you were shot too," Terri murmured behind the fever, "Are you Okay?"

I was not sure how to approach it all but finally blurted out, "I am fine, Terri. I am sorry about your clothes. They are quite ruined."

Terri winced. I reached out and held her hand. She gripped me with more and more force but did not cry out this time. "Why does it hurt so much?"

"I made a decision, I did so without your consent, for that I am sorry. We are going down a path together now," I said, watching her pure blue eyes. I could tell she was tired and a little confused, but she was not afraid.

"What path is that?" Terri asked.

"Well, I, umm" I stammered for a moment. Why would I feel anything less than empowered? I stopped myself, "We should talk about it when you feel better."

She smiled at me with those eyes. I thought of her at the bar, and here in my bed only a few hours ago. "I can take it," she said. "Just tell me what is going on."

I questioned myself for a moment and paced, walking up and down my bedroom for a minute. "Terri, I was holding you after Sam shot you. I looked down and saw the life running from your body. I felt your heart slow, and slow. You had moments before you would be no more. So, I saved you. Isn't that enough for now?"

"How?" she asked. She was so astute, "How did you save me?"

I looked down. I searched the floor for an answer I would not find. Then I had clarity. The truth was always the best choice. "If I tell you, will you promise to let me explain? Will you promise to let me help you? Will you promise not to get mad?"

"I promise," Terri said.

"When I was holding you in my arms, mere moments from death, I mixed my blood with yours. What you are feeling is your natural cell replication. Your cells are, well, changing. Over the next several days, they will take on new properties and, in the process, you will become like me."

"Like you?" Terri echoed. "What are you? A vampire? A werewolf? Some demon of the night?"

I laughed and Terri smiled even in her pain and weariness. "As far as I know there are no vampires, or demons in the night. I am not certain what I am."

"You forgot werewolves. Are you a werewolf?" This woman in all her splendor was trying to chide me, perhaps charm me in her own little way.

"I am not a werewolf," I said. Then I paused, considered, and stayed close to her. Her breast was still exposed where I cleaned her, so I pulled the sheet and covered her up. She looked down and I could not tell the emotion she had initially, but it was followed with a sincerity I have not felt in so, so long. "I told you my name is Adam. I gave myself that name. As far as I know, I am immortal. Or at least different from other men. I can remember back a long time and with my memories, I am over 4,000 years old. I have not shared this with anyone in centuries, but with my blood in yours, you too will be virtually immortal.

The pain hit again, and I saw Terri wince but ride through wave after wave. She did not cry out this time. She was at least a little in control now. She looked up at me, smiling but exhausted. "I have plenty of time to sleep for a bit?"

I said yes, but she was already sleeping. I looked at her beauty and hoped the pain would lessen. Then pulled up a chair and sat next to her, waiting for her to return.

Chapter 2

I had not moved in over an hour. Terri lie asleep in the bed next to me and with no warning her eyes snapped open.

"Hello?" Terri cried in a terrified voice.

"I am here," I said to her with as much calm as I could muster.

"Who?" Terri demanded as she turned to me with those wide pure blue eyes. "Adam?"

"Yes," I said as I moved to the bed and sat next to her. I saw that the sheet was damp with blood again from he wounds.

"I thought this was a dream," Terri said to me as she pulled the covers tight around her.

"I'm sorry," I replied, "It is not a dream. You were asleep."

"Sam?" Terri asked.

"Dead I am afraid," I said without thinking of the possible effect. "I have a temper, and he hurt you."

Terri closed her eyes for a moment and grimaced only a little.

"Pain?" Adam asked.

"Only a little," Terri said, "Can you tell me what is going on here? I mean this was a perfect first date, and" she looked under the covers, "now I am naked covered with blood and in your bed. I'm not a virgin so something else must have happened."

I laughed a little. "Humor is good," I picked up a washcloth, "Hang on for a second." Walking to the bathroom, I got the washcloth wet with warm water to clean here wounds again. I was not sure how long they would continue to seep. I put a little soap on it and picked up a fresh towel. When I walked back in the room, Terri was trying to sit up.

"Ow, ow, ow," she said as she lay back down.

"It is too early," I said to her. "You were shot."

"That was real?" Terri asked.

"Yes," I peered into those eyes and found no fear. "Yes, that was real. May I?" I said as I reached for her sheet.

"Why not?" Terri laughed, "You've seen it all now, anyway. How did you get my clothes off?"

"Pocket knife," I replied as I pulled down her sheet.

"Damn, I liked that dress," Terri said, "It was a good bra, too. I suppose you cut it up too?"

I began washing her neck and chest where the bullet had entered. The wound was now partially healed but still was wet with blood. "Yes, I cut off the bra too. It was covered in blood."

"You do know blood washes out. They make this stuff called Tide. It works really well. I used it before, you know, like on the bra that you cut up." I was smiling as she continued talking. "Okay, well, I was shot. Why am I not dead? Why is there no hole in me? Why is there blood everywhere?" I lifted her with my arm, noticing her full but pert breasts. "Yes, those are mine. Liking what you see?"

I began to clean the wound on her back. "Yes, I do."

"Yes, I do what?" Terri chortled.

"Yes, I do like what I see," I swabbed her back. The wound was more closed than the front. "I know blood washes out, but your clothes had bullet holes in them. Well, the bra didn't but I cut it off so I wouldn't hurt you. There will be a replacement here today." I laid her back down, walked to my dresser, and picked up a hand mirror. "Here, you can see the hole."

Terri took the mirror and looked in it. "Damn, I like these breasts too. Never get to look at them. Always putting them in the over the shoulder boulder holders."

I laughed hard for a moment, and Terri looked at me with those blue eyes.

"That looks nasty," she said to me. "How is it closed? Can you tell me please what is going on? Why do I feel so tired?"

I considered, for a moment, how to approach this. How to tell her what I had done? Would she hate me now? Had I made a mistake?

"It's Okay," Terri said, "I'm a big girl. Let's be honest, Okay? I like you. I am sure whatever happened will be Okay."

"I am," I began, "different. I did not know how different until very recently, about 10 years ago. I trusted a doctor, and we started trying to understand who, or what I am."

"What?" Terri asked. I looked at her pleading eyes. She was inquisitive, funny, lovely, and all the things I always wanted. What had I done?

"Yes, what." I considered my next words carefully. "I am unlike anyone you have ever met."

"That's for sure," Terri broke in, "I mean, the way you handle yourself. God, you are a good dancer, and the way you make me melt. Oh, and the horse, wow, I had never seen anything like that. You just, well, I just want to be close to you." My eyebrow was raised as I looked at her. She peered up and began laughing. "Sorry, I rattle a little when I get nervous."

"I think you rattle a lot," I was at ease, even smiling as I looked at her and started to cover her back up.

"Can we just put a few bandages on and change these sheets? I mean, I will just get all bloody again."

I was still amazed at the way she handled herself in the face of adversity. "How about I cover you with a towel for now. We let things get a little better before we change the sheets."

"How long am I going to be in bed?" Terri asked.

"I don't know," I put a towel over her body and covered her so she would stay warm. "I have never been through this completely with a person before."

"A person?" Terri said with mock anger. "I am more than a person. How are you unlike anyone I have ever met?"

"I can say honestly that you are unlike anyone I have ever met," I smiled.

"That's for sure," Terri broke in again, "I mean, I am the complete package. All that you know." I stared at her as she talked. "umm, what? Oh, I broke in again."

"Yes," I said, "you broke in again."

"Okay," Terri rolled her eyes. "Your turn. How are you unlike anyone I ever met?" She enunciated the last part with a deeper voice. I suppose she was trying to mock me or make me laugh.

I laughed, and smiled, wiping my face with the bloody towel. Then she laughed. I used a clean corner to get the blood off of me. "Can you trust me?" I asked her.

It was in her eyes. She was thinking, and finally she looked into my eyes. "I do trust you."

"I am unlike anyone you have ever met," I started again.

"This is getting old. Skip to the point," Terri laughed.

"I have memories of life, but none of my childhood. I know I was a child once, but I could not tell you when nor could I tell you of my mother or my father."

"I know the feeling," Terri said, looking at my eyes and stopped. "Oh, sorry. Keep going."

"When I became aware of time, and was taught to speak and read and write, it was a long time ago," I closed my eyes and remembered, "I wandered for a long time until I came to a city. It was cold out and I remember wearing the skins of animals, not any one kind but several kinds. I wandered into the city that is now known as Derbent. I was mostly naked except for draped skins, but I did not know 'naked' or even how I was walking."

"Sounds like a bad deodorant," Terri injected, "Where is that?"

"It is in Russia," I said ignoring the interruption, "I learned their language very fast, actually beginning to have conversations in just a few days."

"You speak Russian?" Terri asked, her eyes were now more inquisitive and showed more of a glow than earlier.

"Yes, I do, but then I learned Farsi," I continued. "When I was there, what would become the Persian empire had control of the city. I remember the fantastic sunrises on the Caspian Sea, and swimming in the waters and how clean they were."

"Persian Empire," Terri asked, "I am sure there is a point here. Can we get to it and then go on with the beautiful fluff? I enjoy your voice and all, but I really would like to know what is going on."

"You said you trusted me," I said looking into her eyes and she nodded. "I became aware and spent my first memories in Derbent around 2200BC."

"Whoa," Terri said. I was not sure how to read her, but she corrected me moments later. "That's a long time ago. You don't look a day over well, 45. Maybe 50."

"You think I'm kidding," I said to her. I was intrigued again by this woman who challenged just about everything I had known about people.

"You know," Terri said, "I have had some pretty interesting days in my life, but I have never heard of someone who is, well what, a few thousand or so years old? You told me 600. Which is it?"

"I wish I knew." My voice trailed off, and I looked down to the ground. "I said *over 600* so it was not as much of a shock."

"You really believe you are that old?" Terri said. "I hear the Ridge has a few openings."

Terri winced and again I could tell the pain was hitting her. It was far more than what she was used to but less than when she had slept.

"Let me look," I stood from the chair next to her and pulled down her covers again. "The wound is mostly healed." I said, nodding.

The mirror was next to her on the bed. She picked it up and looked again at the top of her shoulder and arm. A thin layer of skin was evident across the wound, and instead of bloody red, it was now pink and puffy.

"Well, shit the bed," Terri said.

"I hope not," I smiled as I looked at her breasts.

"What did you do to me?" she asked.

"I was trying to tell you, and you thought I was crazy," I told her. "It will take time, but your cells will eventually be similar to mine. There are things that you will not have. You will get tired when you get hurt, I do not. You will be faster and stronger. You will not be as fast nor as strong as I am, but it will be considerably more than you are now. Life will be different for you. I am sorry. I did not want you to die."

"I'm not sorry for that. It is just this is a bit hard to digest. And what is this story about Derbent? What does it have to do with the price of tea in China?"

I sighed, "You were shot. You didn't see all that happened. I know this will be hard to understand and maybe you can listen if I show you." I walked to the desk on the other side of the room and pulled out a letter opener. I walked back to the side of the bed and looked at Terri in those pure blue eyes. I shoved the letter opener through my hand, handle on one side, blade on the other. There was a little blood but not much. I reached my hand to Terri who now had wide eyes and stared at my hand. "Make sure, I know you will question your senses later."

Terri took my hand with the inquisitive abandon of a new child. She turned it from side to side and touched the knife. She tugged a little on it to which I winced, and she glanced at me with a sorry look and kept studying. She held my hand for a moment more and looked me in the eyes with a softer look. "Okay, that hurts me, but I see you didn't feel much."

"Now watch," I said as I pulled the letter opener from my hand. I held my hand up and I saw the back of my hand as it folded in upon itself. The skin almost seemed to knit before our eyes. Terri was watching my palm with amazement and a sparkle in her eye that could only be described as pure curiosity.

"That is too cool," she said. "Can we do it again?"

"It does hurt," I said to her, "I would rather not unless I have to."

Terri snickered, then snorted. She was sitting up now from where I had checked her before. She was not uncomfortable that she was naked in front of me, nowhere near as uncomfortable as she was making me, as I felt stirrings I had repressed for a long time. "I was just kidding," Terri chided and laid back down but did not cover her bare chest.

I smiled, again. She was a surprise.

"I remember you saying you weren't a vampire, a werewolf or anything like that. What are you?" Terri asked.

I sighed. "It was long ago in Derbent," I began.

"Oh," Terri interrupted, "We are back there again. No easy answer. Okay, I will listen, can I ask questions?"

"I want to say no, but would it matter?" I asked her.

"Nope," Terri said. "You liked me and started this. I guess you are stuck with me."

I looked at my watch, it was just past six now.

"It was long ago in Derbent," I began, "I wandered into the town and it is there my memories start."

Terri was massaging her left nipple and it had grown hard in her hand. I stopped and began looking at her. "What?"

"That is a bit distracting. Remember I was kissing you on this bed a few hours ago," I told her.

"Yeah, I get it. So why haven't you kissed me again while I've been laying here. You have been all concerned and stuff, but where is that passion I saw earlier?"

I stood up from the chair and walked over to her, "I didn't want you to think I was trying anything."

Terri reached up and grabbed the back of my head and pulled me down to her. We kissed. At first it was slow and subtle but then her lips parted, and she began kissing me a little harder. She slowed and then pulled away a little and kissed me again before letting go of my head. "I like you that much. If you like me that much you should show me." As she said the last, I lowered my head and kissed her again. Then I stood and backed up to my chair and sat down.

"Woof," she said. "Let's hear about Derbent." She covered her body with the sheet, looking inquisitive and tired as she waited for me to begin talking again.

"I wandered into town and a woman ran to me. She was older, perhaps 50 years old or more. She ushered me off the road and into a small hut. The hut was, well, a hut. It was stone with a thatched ceiling. It was warm with a fire burning. I was not sure what was going on at the time. You have to understand, I knew things were happening, but I had no language. In reality, I did not even know that I was pulled in by a woman until later. The woman tried to talk to me, but I cannot remember what was said at that time and did not know language anyway. I merely remember trying to mimic the sounds I heard. I was confused and wanted to understand but could not."

"Okay," Terri said, "You were in a house with a strange old woman, long ago in Derbent. I am with you," Terri said with tired eyes. "Does she try to make cookies out of you?"

"The woman gave me food. I remember tasting food as though it were a new experience. It was meat. It was cooked well and made me feel warm inside. I savored the flavor as though I had never eaten before, but I was an adult, barely different than I am now, so now I know I must have eaten."

"A good woman feeds a man well," Terri said with a sly smile. Her eyes were closing now.

"Would you like me to tell you this later?" I asked.

"No," Terri said with quiet grace, "Go ahead, I'm just resting my eyes."

A moment later, I could tell she was fast asleep.

Chapter 3

I picked up around my bedroom. A few towels and washcloths covered in blood were left. I threw these in the hamper then straightened the room the best I could in the situation. I left her covered, checked to see she was asleep, then went to the living room. I had not thought about Derbent actively in a long time. It made me consider my strange life. I looked at some of the artifacts in my curios, considering the past and how incredulous it must sound to someone like Terri. Someone with a life that would be short under normal circumstances.

I walked to the laundry room to check the towels. They were done and surprisingly clean, so I moved them to the dryer. Afterwards, I cleaned up the laundry area. I took the bloody linens I brought in the hamper and started another small load. I laughed to myself as I used Tide, thinking of Terri's bra and her subsequent comments. I knew I would be washing again several times today, but it was Okay. It was good to have company. It was good to have someone to talk to again.

I turned off the light and walked back to the living room. As I did, I called Shawn on my cell phone.

"Hello," came his curt reply.

"How is it going?" I asked him.

"Weird as hell," Shawn stated. "Why can't it ever be easy?"

"What's weird?" I asked, curious.

"Well, we have your body. His name was Sam Caraway. He was a horse farm wannabe with one of the bigger farms in the area. He spent a lot of time spending his father's money. No family, no relatives, just a few friends. Had a girlfriend named Terri Sturgill, but we can't seem to find her. They broke up a few months ago. There wasn't any video on anything last night so right now this is just a hit and run. Looks like a truck hit him and that is what the coroner is saying."

"What is weird?" I asked.

"Well, we also have a severed human arm and a jawbone, but we don't have anyone in a hospital. No calls, no reports, nothing. Just two body parts. Coroner is thinking they may be from the University cadaver freezer, but I bet you are going to tell me they aren't."

I considered for a minute. "Last time I saw them, they were next to the people they belonged to."

"Isn't that just grand? I can deal with the nobody with his chest caved in. But a man with no jaw and a one-armed man that is not a star of 'The Fugitive'? I may have an ulcer within the hour."

"We wouldn't want that," I said, "How can I help?"

"I think you have done enough for now," Shawn said, "Can I come see you at about 11?"

"Of course," I stated, "I am at your service, as always."

"You know I was supposed to be off today," Shawn sighed. "It is my anniversary and I have dinner plans tonight. Malones and dancing."

"Shawn," I said, "I am sure someone else can handle all of this. If the coroner thinks it is a hit and run and there are no complaints, it may not be pressing."

"Since when does anything dealing with you become anything less than pressing?" he snarked.

I was amused by both the accuracy of his statement and the tenacity with which he delivered it. "Of course, you are correct." I thought about my next words carefully for a moment, Shawn was a good person, and I enjoyed talking to him, but he did not know everything, as with Terri it was quite difficult for most to believe. "I will see you at 11?"

"Yeah," Shawn said, "Earlier if I can."

"Of course," I stated again, "As I said, I am at your service."

"Yeah, thanks," Shawn paused for a second as he was not used to people cooperating. "See you soon."

The line went dead.

I thought about the city and how I had come to love Lexington. I liked it since it was small, and I visited the area often. It was a good stop in frontier days because of the active spring. Forty years ago, I came to the city and settled down. I usually stay in an area for about 50 years. With a little anonymity, I could be unburdened by nosiness or suspicion. At some point, I would move to a new area again, and my assets would be liquidated. My trinkets would be moved, and I would establish myself with as little notice as possible. I learned that being known is not the same as being unknown. The best spot was somewhere in between; almost like being enigmatic.

I took a moment in the living room and cleaned. Dust tended to accumulate if I did not wipe things down often. As such, I made it a habit when I was in a room to wipe down at least one piece of furniture. This was not impactful to me and ensured that in a week, most items had been addressed. It also ensured I stayed in touch with the rooms of the house. It was just nicer that way. I developed some odd habits over the years, and this was only one of them. I finished cleaning an end table and walked back to my bedroom.

Terri was still sleeping. It was good that she was sleeping. I did not want to bother her, so I sat down again and thought about the situation. It appeared it had partially resolved itself. Sam was out of the picture and would be little or no trouble. The coroner ruled it a hit and run. With no witnesses or cameras, I would not be put in any uncomfortable situations. Instead, this offered me a pause. I could slow down and pay attention to my decision with Terri and reaffirm that I should control my temper. I learned that over and over, and still, I occasionally ran into issues.

I closed my eyes and tried to sleep. It rarely came but for a moment, this morning, I felt the waves of stress fade away and began to doze off.

"Adam?" I heard and jumped to attention.

"Terri?" I returned the oration. "Are you Okay?"

"My skin is itching really bad," she said.

"Let's take a look," I replied and turned the lights on in the room. I walked over to the bed and lifted the sheets once again exposing her body and, at the same time, causing uncomfortable stretching sensations in my pants. It was different having a woman in the house. I had avoided women for a long time and for good reason. "It is just the healing process," I told her. "Here, use the mirror."

Terri looked into the mirror and saw the wound was almost completely healed. The pink skin was inflamed but was closed and no longer bleeding.

"Oh snap," Terri said. "This is amazing. I do have a problem now."

"There are no problems that cannot be overcome," I said simply.

"I need to pee," Terri laughed.

"Then let's get you up," I laughed.

Terri turned and tried to stand. She wobbled as her legs hit the floor and nearly fell. I caught her and held her up. "What is wrong with me?"

"It will go away," I replied. "You will have to get used to walking again. The cells in your body are having to get used to working differently. I only understand part of the chemistry, but your DNA has, for all intents and purposes, been reorganized. The doctor that was looking at my blood seemed to think a viral adaptation allowed every cell in my body to be purposed as it was intended. More like a blueprint than anything. He was looking for the source when he died in a car accident."

I put my arms under Terri and picked her up with no effort. Well aware of her body, her naked breasts, and her thong next to me. I felt warm. She put her arms around my neck. "You do know you are really handsome?" she said to me as I carried her to the bathroom. She winced again. "When will this pain stop?"

"How bad is it?" I asked her.

"Not as bad as before, but it is annoying."

"I am not sure how long it will take," I said. "This is a first for me. The last time was, well, different."

"That's a sly answer," Terri said to me as she tickled my neck. I held her close as we walked into the bathroom and she abruptly grabbed me, kissing me hard. I kissed her back and her urgency turned into a slow patient battle between us on who felt the most passion. Her lips parted, and she lightly caressed my lips. As I opened my lips ever so slightly, she shuddered a little and then pulled away, looking into my eyes. "Nice," she smiled. Her pure blue eyes were more alive than ever.

As I let her to the floor and steadied her, she looked in the mirror. "Oh my god," she cried out.

"What," I asked.

"I look like I just went through an all-day Aerobics class," she said, "and I smell bad."

I had not lived with a modern woman except for a few housekeepers. This was new to me. I had read numerous books, but they did not adequately prepare me for what I was hearing. "What can I do?"

"Help me get a shower, after I umm, take care of business." Terri said.

I helped her sit down on the toilet only to be shooed out of the room.

I closed the door and waited in my bedroom. While in the bedroom, I went ahead and stripped the bed. The sheets were soaked through. The mattress pad was not. I went ahead and stripped down to the mattress. Holding the linens, I went to the bathroom door. "Are you Okay?"

"I'm busy," Terri said through the door. It made me laugh as it was similar to all the people who had that sing-song type of sarcasm, that well, was just funny. "I'm doing laundry. I will be back in a few minutes."

"That's Clark nice," Terri said through the door.

I laughed again. The reference was from the movie *Superman 2* with Christopher Reeve. Lois Lane was so lost; she said those words mindlessly since she wasn't really interested in what was being said.

I took the linens to the laundry room and examined the sheets. I decided I would try one pass to remove the stains. If that didn't work, I would throw them away. I pretreated each stain and put them all in the oversize washer. As I put the Tide in, I laughed again. I was surprised at how many times I had laughed since I met Terri. I had not felt a great deal in so long this was a refreshing series of moments. I started the washer and opened the linen closet in the laundry room, pulled out new sheets and a new mattress pad, and walked back to the master bedroom.

I walked to the master bath door. "Are you Okay?"

"Why yes," came the reply. "I am ready for some help. I tried to stand up, but I get tired with extreme quickness." I heard a giggle. "Think you can get me in the shower?"

I opened the door. Terri was standing against the wall, with strained difficulty, but she was doing Okay. She looked stunning with no clothes on, but she was disheveled from the last several hours. "Would you like me to carry you?" I asked.

"Nope," Terri said. "How about you help me and let me do it too?"

I reached around her thin waist, supporting her. I felt her hands hold my arm as we limped to the large standup shower stall. I entered with her and she continued to hold me. "You can control both jets with the two knobs on this wall," I told her. "Left is hot, right cold and the center turns them on and off."

Terri giggled, turning the knobs on. She was still in her thong, and I was still fully dressed. The result was expected. We got wet really fast. We were both covered with water as the jets above and to two sides of us pummeled us with hot water.

"Ahh, that feels good," Terri smiled as she started to unbutton my shirt. "Sorry," she continued, "I just didn't want to be without you. Can you take my thong off?"

"I thought you would never ask," I said as I took it off while still holding her up. I then stood and helped Terri take off my clothes. Soon we were naked in the shower with a pile of wet clothes in the corner. I looked at the wound in her chest. It was nearly gone. It was surely tingling or itching, but it was no longer the gaping hole it was several hours ago.

With her arms around my neck steadying her, she looked into my eyes. "You were going to tell me about Derbent and your life before. I am not sure what I believe right now, but I think I need to hear your story to understand what is happening to me."

I lowered my head and kissed her, and there was an rapidly growing reaction below us. "Well," she said, "that's quite a tool you have there?"

I laughed. "Too soon. Sorry."

"We are past that," she said, "I think you have seen the inside of me, quite literally."

I laughed for a moment with her, holding her as we soaped each other in the hot water. I was hard as a rock, but I managed to suppress my desires. Terri was recovering and needed to be taken care of for now. Still, I was amazed at how resilient she had become already. She was fighting the pain as she was standing her own as best she could.

"Okay," I said, "Derbent it is. Let's clean up then you can lay down and listen. This will take a while." I was happy Terri was at least interested. In being interested, she would have a chance of understanding. I needed her to understand what I had done. Whether it was to be positive or negative, it needed to be discussed.

"Okay," Terri replied, "Shampoo?"

"Sure," I reached into the recessed wall and handed her a bottle. I still had one arm around her, holding much of her weight, but I had to be careful as it was both slippery and she was moving a lot.

Terri smiled as she took a small bit of shampoo out and massaged it into her hair. She worked it in well and I was smiling as she did so. "Why the smile?"

"It has been a long time since I was this close to anyone," I held her up as she rinsed, "and you are quite beautiful."

"You keep stabbing me with that thing," Terri laughed. "Do we need to take a cold shower before we get out?"

"Thank you, no," I moved her to the small seat in the shower. She saw what I was doing and sat down. As she did, I stood, rinsed off, and picked up the glob of wet clothes in the corner. When I bent to do so, Terri slapped my butt.

"Nice," she chided.

"Um, thanks," I replied as I got out of the shower and placed the clothes in the laundry basket. I got out two towels and dried myself with exaggerated haste. I then set my towel on the counter and reached into the shower, turning it off. Terri still sat waiting.

"I thought you forgot about me," she laughed, that pixie like glint flashing in her eyes. It seemed she was even more mischievous now, more talkative, but it could just be the nervousness.

"No way." I helped Terri up and we entered the bath area. Holding her with one hand, I helped her dry off. In a matter of minutes, she was dry. As she finished with the towel, she hung it on my still evident erection.

"A good use for that for now," Terri said. "I bet we will work on that thing later." She snickered in amusement. It came out like the happiest sound you would ever want to hear. I picked her up with no effort and carried her to the bedroom. I had not made the bed yet.

"Hmm," I said as I set her down on a Lazy-Boy chair in the corner.

She jumped, and I realized the chair was leather and likely cold. "Warn me next time," she said.

I walked to my closet and pulled out a t-shirt. My shirts were custom made and very long. I went back to her and handed it to her. She responded by putting her arms up. I was quite taken aback by this as it made her breasts point to the air and more to me. My erection pulsed for a moment. When I saw what she was doing, I put the shirt over her head, and she completed by pulling it down.

I could not remember how many times I had made a bed in my life, but I made short work of this. I put the new mattress pad cover on and in a quick motion spread out the fitted sheet. I tightened it so it was crisp then flung the top sheet on. Adding a blanket, I folded neat hospital corners and then put a comforter over the blanket.

"I am impressed," Terri said. "Work in a hotel before?"

"No," I replied, "I was in the service for a while. You would be surprised the focus they have on making your bed. I also worked in a hospital for some time. It was good work, and I learned a lot."

I folded back a corner of the bed, then turned and grabbed underwear out of a drawer. I was quick and methodical as I dressed in jeans and a shirt. I did not put on socks.

"Wow," Terri was watching me great curiosity. "You are quick."

Walking over, I began to pick her up and she held out a hand. "Let me try," she said.

I stepped back.

She used her arms to press up to her knees and stood, then began a slow walk to the bed. I reached out to steady her, but she threw me a sideways glance that said I should let her continue, so I did. It was not as flowing as our dance, nor as perfect as I had seen her walk, but she made it to the bed and sat down. She then swung her legs up and covered up, panting somewhat from the exertion. "Okay, Derbent. Let's hear it."

I walked over to her and leaned in and kissed her forehead. "I am impressed."

"Don't be," she said. "If you are stuck with me, you will get sick of it pretty quick."

"Doubtful," I replied.

She grinned then motioned me with a simple motion as if to tell me to "get on with it".

Chapter 4

It was eight o'clock. I was watching Terri get comfortable, and she finally settled into my bed with several pillows behind her. "Okay," she said, "I am ready. It is long ago, about 2200 BC, and you are in Derbent with some old witch who is trying to make you fat."

"Umm, Okay," I said.

"Readers Digest version," Terri smirked. "You go on."

"Thank you," I said. "I think I will.

Terri smiled at me, then winked. I felt whole inside for the first time in a long time.

"The first several hours were difficult for me. As I said, I had no language, and I was less than able to understand even my basic needs. It made little sense to me. I felt as though I was a child, or at least now how I imagine a child feels. Dependent for everything. There was also the pain. It was difficult, and I remember thinking that was all I could remember. Pain, my entire body racked in pain until the moment this woman found me and took me in. Her small stone hut was sparse and there was little of interest. Somehow, she made me a spot and a makeshift bed and tried to make it so I would lay down. Even that did not register to me at the time. I remember having no concept of what she wanted me to do, but after patting the bedding over and over I finally lay down next to her. She covered me in animal skins, and I felt warm. She was next to me, under the skins looking at me. Her face was gnarled and wrinkled with the hard life she had led. I remember reaching out to touch the wrinkles of her face, then feeling mine and the creases of the scars I carry. I began to feel warmer, near hot. It was curious as I suddenly had a concept of hot and cold, as I lay there. I wonder now if children felt the same or if they feel the same. I looked at her face and did not know what to do. I studied the woman before me and watched her close her eyes. It was then that I closed my eyes and I actually fell asleep. You have to understand that is strange to me. I rarely sleep now and did not know what sleep was then."

"No sleep," Terri said, "We are going to have some fun. I don't sleep much either."

I smiled.

"Don't stop," Terri said. "This is just getting interesting. You are naked with an old woman under a pile of skins."

"I remember my first dream. It was of massive pain and a feeling that I was going through fire, feeling my limbs ache and scream. I remember in my dream I was writhing in pain, and then the pain was less. I do not remember how long I slept, but my pain turned and was no longer there. I woke to a new sensation. I was on my back, and I remember feelings rushing through me. The woman was above me, naked. I remember feeling, well, near short of breath. She had mounted my hard member and was slowly moving up and down on me as I awakened even further. She looked down at me and tilted her body. As she did, I felt even more intensity. I didn't know what I was feeling but her movements were causing me a feeling of urgency and my body was washed with sensations that were overwhelming."

"Let me get this straight, the old woman was raping you?" Terri asked.

"I suppose, but I had no concept of yes or no at the time, so it was nondescript."

"Oh, Okay," Terri said. "I would kick this bitch's ass if she were here now."

I raised an eyebrow.

"Sorry," Terri said. "Keep going, the bitch was wailing on your willy."

I smiled a little and continued, "As she continued to ride me, she would move up and I felt my hardness. I didn't even know it was me really, but then she would slam down on me. This was repeated for some time until it happened."

"What?" Terri asked.

"I came," I said, "I came hard and had no idea what was happening and didn't know what do, so I sat up. She pushed me down softly as my body filled her. A feeling of euphoria came over me, and since the pain was gone for a moment, it was different. She lay next to me with her arms on my chest. I was warm all over and felt good. This is when I determined a difference between pain and not pain."

"I get it. So, she raped you and you liked it," Terri said. "At least you stayed and didn't run out then."

I laughed. "No, I fell asleep again, but this time my dreams were not so fitful. This time I was feeling, well, better. I have no idea how long I slept, but I awoke to the woman still sleeping on me. As I moved, she woke and I felt an urgency I did not understand."

"An urgency?" Terri laughed.

"Well, yes," I smiled, "I really was a blank slate in so many ways. I had virtually no memory except for what had just happened with this woman. Of wandering and being taken in. Of the lines on her face that resembled mine. But it seemed I did not know how to go to the bathroom, specifically I didn't know how to pee. I stood and walked. The woman seemed to understand and led me outside. It was bitter cold and I was naked. I had no idea why I was outside. She pointed but I did not understand. Over and over she pointed, and over and over I did not understand. She seemed to sense my issue at that point."

Terri was smiling, "What did she do?"

"She grabbed my penis and pressed on my stomach. The pain was different, intense, and all of a sudden it let loose. I felt it let loose, and it was the second best feeling in the world. I know it is hard to explain, but as I emptied my bladder a wave of relief flowed over me, and I felt really good. I must have gone for a minute or two. The old woman squatted and peed as well while I did, then watched me as I kept going. I quickly learned the control I needed. I do not know whether it was instinct or blind luck, but I understood now this was a necessity."

Terri was laughing on the bed, "You learned to pee as an adult. Do you think you did before?"

"I am sure now I had, but I had no memory, so it was new to me," I said to her with a grin. "People take the act of taking a leak for granted, and I will tell you it is still an enjoyable pastime for me to this day."

"It was to me when I woke up itching earlier, so I am with you there. Still, was it easier after the first time?"

"Of course," I said, "I understood the urgency of both urination and defecation over the next several days. Still, there was the moment I went back in. It was night outside when I urinated, but the light of the sky was bright enough to see some. As we entered the small hut, the light of the fire lit the woman, and I could see she was different. I had no understanding, but the lines of her face had eased. Her pallor was much healthier, and she seemed to be less haggard. I did not understand how the woman who had lines like me, had less. I stopped and looked at my body. Still the scars remained. I was not any less lined, but this woman was less lined. I walked to her. She was unaware of the change as I touched her face and traced the dim outline of what had been a crease. Her hand held mine and she smiled, perhaps thinking it was an act of affection. She held my hand gently smiling, and then touched her own face as I did. Her expression changed from the smile to what I learned to know as confusion. She touched her face all over, finally running to a bucket filled with water and looking into the bucket, touching her face."

"Wait, wait," Terri stated, "You are saying your orgasm made this woman younger or at least made her look younger?"

"I found later that to be true, though I did not understand at the time," I replied. "It was not necessarily my orgasm, but the semen that gave her some of me."

"Okay, and were you still standing there naked as a jaybird in her hut?" Terri asked.

"I was," I replied.

"Okay," Terri laughed as she adjusted herself in bed, "Just checking."

"I did not really understand naked or not. I may have covered myself with skins out of instinct before she found me, then she had covered me before, but I did not know I needed to be covered. I did not feel cold and still do not like many people." I continued.

"Of course not," Terri laughed. "Continue." She had that twinkle in her eye as though she were caressing my inner mind with her eyes and taunting me in the process. It was hard not to trust her, hard not to feel as I looked at her, but I regained my composure and continued.

"As the woman touched her face, she soon touched other areas of her body, her bottom and breasts, and then legs and arms. She spent some time with her hands and flexed them over and over. As she did so, I mimicked many of her movements. As I said, at the time I was a blank slate, but I was a sponge and learned like a sponge absorbing everything around me."

"You were playing Simon says with no Simon all this time. I bet she was not sure what to do, right?" Terri laughed.

"She made the potential connection faster than I did. She cleaned herself, lead me to the bed area and once again had me."

"Saucy little minx," Terri laughed.

I laughed for a moment at Terri's natural sense of humor. She was so adept and so engaged with my story, but I was not sure if she understood "how" it affected her. I regained my composure and wiped a tear from my eye where I had laughed. "Yes, she was. As I have grown in my language and understanding, I realize she is like most of the human race, lost in their moment without regard to the other moments in the world."

"Well, keep going. The minx mounted you again, then what?" Terri prodded.

"I slept again. I had fitful dreams of a hundred things I did not know. Most of them were odd, strange, and perhaps memories. But now they are elusive. I have often felt that the key to my prior life, however long it was, could have been in those dreams in the first few days with

Morgan. But I cannot remember much of them except to say they were vibrant and fitful."

"Morgan?" Terri asked. "She has a name now?"

"She ended up with many names," I lamented. "After that first day, she had sex with me over 30 times. Each time, my essence had an effect. Each time, she looked younger still until it stopped. As it did, she looked as though she was a young woman of perhaps 25. She actually did a lot for me. She taught me virtually everything. From personal hygiene, such as it was, to how to eat, drink, pee, and so forth. She gave me clothes and began a task to make me more clothes, and she began to teach me how to speak. It was not a horrible existence, and she established a rhythm of ten encounters each day. I had no idea how life was, so it was not strange nor different to me. Everything was new and this became my normal."

"Ten times a day became normal? That's not normal," Terri said. "I mean, I would be all in I suppose if I was an old woman and became a young woman, but otherwise that would have to get a little raw."

I smiled for a moment, "A recognizable side effect is that you heal very rapidly. It is less an issue getting raw and more of consuming time. Still, it became my life. I learned to speak the language very rapidly. As I said, I was a sponge, so language was second nature and soon we were having conversations, Morgan and I. It was almost a week when she and I talked about what I was and where I came from. I was direct, I had no recollection. She was very interested if there were more like me, but that I could not tell. She asked about my scars, and I told her I had no recollection. And then she asked about how I made her young. It was a difficult concept for me, understanding there was age or how I had affected her. She was quite striking now, and in today's world she could have easily been a model. She was of normal height, but had long black hair and her eyes seemed to sparkle."

"Oh, so you traded up," Terri laughed.

I laughed again, "I had no idea what I was doing, but I guess so." The twinkle in Terri's eyes was refreshing, I had not seen it's like in some time. "If it makes you feel better, I was not attracted to her, but she was not repulsive to me. I was learning a lot and starting to understand that I too had emotions."

"No emotions would be better sometimes," Terri said. "Please, go on, this is getting good. You bedded a super model. I got it."

"We talked a lot," I continued. "We talked about concepts and ideas, mainly because I had no concept of concepts or ideas. I learned the basics of life from this woman, Morgan. She asked me about what I liked, how I felt about her, if I was attracted to her, and was not pleased with my answers. I did not understand. Still, I became more and more open to her. She began to teach me about sex, and love. As she did, I began to give her more pleasure, more than just giving her my seed. She was happy with me daily. And as she clothed me, I started understanding more complex emotions. I felt things I did not understand, and a longing returned rather rapidly if we went more than a few hours without our bonding."

"You were becoming a horn dog," Terri interjected.

"I suppose so, but not really," I laughed. "I was starting to understand the chemical attraction of what people call love."

"You should write a few books," Terri laughed again.

"I have," Adam said.

"Okay, Okay," Terri switched again, "We can talk books later. You are getting your rocks off ten times a day with the old woman who became a supermodel, what happened next."

"It was nearly two weeks after I met Morgan when she told me the food was running low. She had planned for the winter, but just for her. I was not part of the plan. She said we had to trade with others, and we would need to go into the town. She asked me to go with her but said I could not talk to others. They would not understand who I was and may become a problem. I had no clue what a problem was, so I said I would be silent. It would be easy. I didn't know what to say anyway. At that time Morgan was my only universe, and because of that, I had no clue how to interact with anyone. We dressed and headed out into the cold. Morgan gave me two bags full of cloth."

"There was snow everywhere, and Morgan and I trudged toward the city. Well, it was a city then, but it really could hardly be considered much of anything. After about an hour, we closed in on a series of huts and stone buildings with one in the center. Morgan explained to me that people traded goods, services, and other people at the main building. She explained that the reason I brought the cloth is she had made them into clothing for people and we would use that to trade for food. I was full of wonder. We walked into the building with stone walls filled with mud and a thatched roof, and I was assailed by scents."

"Mostly good or bad?" Terri asked.

"I am not sure," I replied. "I would be now but as I remembered, they were just new. There were not many traders there, but Morgan walked with purpose to an old woman with masses of food types. There was an argument that brewed quickly as Morgan showed the clothing and the woman balked. I soon understood the woman thought Morgan had stolen the items for it was surely Morgan's work, not some young woman child. Morgan had forgotten her newfound youth, and it was not possible to explain how this had happened. She was spurned. I then learned of anger and saw Morgan raise her voice and begin yelling. Two younger men walked towards the old and young woman, but the older woman waved them off. I did not understand but somehow, she got to sit with the old woman. After talking to her for a while and nodding at me, a deal was soon struck. We left the bags and took a small satchel of food. As we went to the door, the old woman called Magda came with us. Wrapped in skins, she was walking with us. A short hour walk later, the three of us arrived in the hut. I did chores as I had been taught, fed the fire and cleaned up. As I did, the two women watched and talked. The older woman felt Morgan's body all over, and it made me feel a little strange. Still, they stopped, and Morgan called me over."

"Is this going where I think it is going?" Terri asked. "You about to double down?"

Again, I laughed. It was fun knowing that Terri was so easy to talk to. "You could say that. Morgan removed my clothes and then hers. She straddled me but did not let me enter her. I held her as her womanhood rubbed on my stomach and she lowered her mouth to kiss me. I felt the passion I always felt with her, but as I kissed her, I felt my penis enter warm folds of flesh. The older woman, Magda, was behind Morgan riding me. She reached around, held Morgan's breasts, and lowered her to me. I suckled as I had been taught and soon was more and more excited until I came. It was exciting but more for Morgan than the other woman. Morgan lay me back and both women lay next to me, one on either side. And we fell asleep."

"I woke a short time later to feel my penis undergoing a new sensation. The old woman was between my legs and her mouth was around me. The feeling was indescribable, and I felt my orgasm build from the orchestrations of the talented woman. She fondled me all over and it was not long before I exploded into her mouth. My body shuddered differently. I did not understand this new set of feelings, but I liked it."

"Yeah, yeah. A man who likes blowjobs. I get it," Terri laughed.

"I did not know what it was, but the woman came to my side and curled next to me again. Morgan had not moved. I looked at the older woman next to me and the changes had begun. Her body was being modified by whatever was me. She already looked younger, more vibrant, and was changing rapidly. A few hours passed, and Morgan and the woman woke. The woman now easily looked ten years younger. I spoke to them both and then they talked in private for several minutes. The older woman came to me, pinched my face, dressed and left the hut."

"Slam, whir, thank you, sir?" Terri laughed.

"Something like that," I said. "About three hours later, the two men that were with the old woman arrived and brough two carts of food. Morgan was thrilled. We packed the food away in her spots, and the men left."

"Oh, so we have invented the first man-whore house?" Terri laughed.

I grinned for a second, amused at Terri and her views of the world. "Pretty much," I said. "I was traded for a bunch of food. Well, not me, but bedding with me once. I think the woman snuck in the blowjob, but it was not part of the deal. But I knew no better. Morgan nearly attacked me with passion, and we were carnal the rest of the day."

"You have to understand, there was no entertainment. Life was about sex, work, making it through each day alive. The most exciting things to do were work, have sex, and watch the fire. At this time, I started enjoying the idea of having sex, and looking forward to our times. People take so much for granted today, even the ability to find another person. My world was blank except for my experience so far, and it did not consist of much."

I paused for a moment and looked at Terri. She was bright eyed and engaged but her body was still healing. I did not want to overwhelm her. I looked at my watch. It was 10:30. Shawn would be coming soon and there would be some heated discussions, I was sure. I also knew Micah would be here soon, and Micah would want to meet the girl who stole my heart. I would have to defer him to a later time.

"Terri," I said, "we will have company shortly. Would it be Okay if we continued after they left? I want to make sure everything is in order and put on some socks and shoes. "

"Company?" Terri said. "Who is coming?"

"We will be visited by three ghosts," I said.

She giggled. "I want the one who has yet to come."

"You are quick," I said. "A detective will be coming by to talk about Sam and the three others who attacked us. Also, a personal shopper will be here. He is a friend of mine. He will be bringing you some pajamas and some undergarments."

"Undergarments?" Terri laughed. "Who says undergarments. He will be bringing me some bras and panties?"

"Yes," I said. "That too."

"How did he get my size?" Terri asked.

"I am pretty good at guessing. Plus, I saw the tag." I smiled.

"Cheater," Terri said.

"When Micah gets here you can discuss a short wardrobe list, or you can have him go to your place if you like. Either will work." I told her.

"Free stuff?" Terri said, "I am down with that. I will go home when you and I can go together. Besides, I'm not sure I did the dishes."

"I am sure he would do that for you as well," I laughed. "Do you need anything before I go clean up a little more?"

"No, just a kiss. I will nap for a bit," Terri smiled.

I walked to her and kissed her. Her lips felt like silk against mine. I could feel the emotions I had held in check for so long coming out again. Our tongues brushed and I moved away and looked into her eyes.

"Not tired of me yet?" she asked.

"Never," I said and touched her face.

She grabbed my hand and kissed my palm as I stood. "Gonna hold you to that."

I laughed. "Get some rest," I said as she released my hand. "I will be back when Micah gets here.

She smiled and closed her eyes. In a matter of moments, she was asleep.

Chapter 5

It was difficult for me to leave Terri. I considered how I felt for a moment as I walked to the laundry room. I had not considered how lonely I had been for hundreds of years. Unable to share human warmth or comfort, I had buried myself in other activities, and often that was not as positive as it should have been. Still, since moving to Lexington, I had been content. I enjoyed bourbon and the pastimes the area gave and had made friends. True, they would eventually pass, but they were friends none the less. It had been good.

Now I was faced with someone I could talk to, enjoy, and have some semblance of a life with. I struggled with the past and present for only a moment as I mindlessly loaded the washer. I had to stop for a moment to open the fabric softener without spraying it everywhere.

People don't realize sometimes how frustrating it is to open many packages. Blister packs are made to cause most people blisters. The only way to effectively open them is to slowly cut around all the seals and slide the package open. When I had first encountered one it was a package of batteries. I tried to open it carefully to no avail. It was not long after trying I became frustrated and used force, which, of course, opened the package, but sprayed it everywhere in the room. I was careful every time after that incident as I found batteries embedded in the ceiling, wall, and under everything.

Having solved the two-for-one fabric softener blister pack problem, I busied myself with starting the last laundry, cleaning up the area, and then putting everything away. I enjoyed my life. Sometimes order made it better, sometimes chaos made it better, but clean was always nice.

I made my way to the garage to check my car. I opened the garage to a wonderful Kentucky morning. The breeze blew and sweet scents assailed my nostrils. I took a deep breath and felt excited. People would be happier if they just appreciated the fact they can breathe. Breathing is a fantastic center. A great feeling, each and every breath.

I walked to the classic Corvette. There was blood everywhere. It had dried and was the dark red and black that drying blood makes. I knew the seat covers may be difficult to clean. I had faced bloodstains in cars before, and they were not good. Not good at all. I walked to a small cabinet, pulled out some cleaning supplies, and walked back to the car. I took a shop towel and cleaned as much as I could. It was less than productive as usual since the blood began to smear. Still, I used Simple Green and after a few passes, the car was presentable. I was left with a pile of bloody shop towels that I put into a bag to wash. I cleaned my hands with the Simple Green and put that towel in the bag as well. I had learned a long time ago that paper towels and disposable items could sometimes lead to disaster. They created a piece of evidence or an item that could be traced or worse used against me. I had become very careful about cleaning and very careful about everything from trash to towels.

The wind blew and I heard a car door close. I looked out to see the Black Dodge Charger that sometimes frequented my house. The LFUCG police were well funded and one of the few offices I knew of filled with honest law enforcement professionals.

"Adam," Shawn said as he walked into the garage, "Cleaning up a mess?"

"Not a bad one," Adam said. "Just a different one."

"I still love this car," Shawn said. "Not many of them left out in the real world. Even fewer that people actually drive."

"Yeah, it was a find when I got it," I said to him. It would have been hard to explain to him that I bought it when it rolled off the line. The title had transferred twice since then to new versions of me to keep up with the paperwork and not become too suspicious. In the early 1980s I had seen a movie called "Highlander" that would have made my life much easier. It explained a way for an immortal to move assets that did not involve me faking my death and reemerging in another state or country. Funny that someone thought that out.

"We found the jaw and the arm. We still have no takers on it." Shawn said. "The ME is pushing through DNA on them, but it won't match anyone will it?"

"I doubt it. Three football-playing punks that were there with Sam," I said, "I am sorry this caused you a problem. They shot me and would have killed Terri."

"Terri? The ex-girlfriend?" Shawn asked. "Where is she?"

"She is fine," I said, "I bandaged her up and she is going to be Okay." I hated lying to Shawn, but he would never understand.

"You should have told me you knew her." Shawn paused for a second. "The cameras did not help," Shawn said. "Of course, they were all fake or broken. We pulled it and it was snowy. What that gives us is two body parts and a dead body that was ruled a hit and run by the coroner. Any chance there is a dent on the car?"

"Zero," I said and stepped back to let him look.

Shawn walked around the car and looked at all the frame and body. "How do you keep this thing so clean? I would chip all kinds of paint."

"Re Clear Coated a few years ago. It is tough clear coat." I smiled. "I have to have it redone every few years to keep it pristine."

"It sure looked good," Shawn said as he stood. "When can I talk to Terri?"

"Maybe tomorrow," I lied. "She is sleeping."

"Be honest with me, Adam. Tell me what happened."

"It was pretty straightforward, really. I did not want to fight. I didn't want any of it. Sam and I had an altercation out at the King Estate Bourbon tasting," I said. "It is where I met Terri. Apparently, they were an item at one time. He got a little out of hand and I explained to him that he needed to back down. He did. I thought it was a done deal until she and I went to Tolly-Ho and he was there with three guys waiting to get even. Not sure how he even found us."

"Did you threaten him, or did anyone witness this altercation at the farm?" Shawn asked.

"Only Terri as far as I know," I said to him. "As far as I know, we were invisible to most. I had two Pappies, so I was not drunk or out of control at all."

"The two guys you hurt extensively. What did they do?" Shawn asked.

"They tried to hurt us both. I didn't let them," I said. "My goal was to walk away. My goal is to always walk away. Have either of them shown up at the hospital?"

"No, neither," Shawn said. "We really have little to go on. I wanted to be prepared just in case."

"I will help as much as you want me to," I said to him. "I can ask around if you like."

"Don't do anything yet," Shawn said, "I appreciate all your help, but this one is a little too close to home. Why don't you let us handle it? Who knows, it may just fade away."

"Let me know if I can help," I said with all sincerity. "I am responsible, you know."

"If the girl backs you up, it will not be a giant deal anyway," Shawn laughed. "Pretty much a case of walking into the wrong lion's den."

I laughed at the reference. I had been fed to the lions once. It was not a pleasant situation for either me or the lions. "What now, then?" I asked with sincerity.

"My suggestion is you take care of Terri. If I can't talk to her now, we talk tomorrow just to walk through the details, then we put this to rest." Shawn said.

"She is sleeping, but how about we call you later today when she wakes? Then maybe we can sync up tomorrow as well. That work?" I appreciated Shawn a lot and wanted to make this easy for him.

"Sounds good," Shawn said, heading for the open garage door. "Give me a call later. Let me know what is going on, otherwise we will talk tomorrow."

I walked outside with Shawn to his police black charger. "Still can't believe they gave this to you," I laughed. "Pretty snazzy."

Shawn laughed. "It's Okay," he opened the door and it was evident he was distracted. "We'll catch up later."

I nodded, turned, and walked back to the garage. As I reached the bag of rags, I heard a horn beep and saw that Micah was pulling in as Shawn pulled out. Micah drove a bright blue 2015 Lancer Evo. As he pulled up, it purred in predatory anticipation. Micah stepped out with several bags and set them on the ground.

"How many mods have you stuffed into that thing." I laughed.

"It's still street legal," Micah laughed. "It'll rock that poor charger your boy Shawn drives."

I laughed. It was a good laugh. "We both know there are a lot of cars that will rock that poor Charger. It is a cop car. Give him some credit."

Micah laughed. He walked to me and hugged me. I was always impressed with this man. I had known him since he was a kid, and he just kept getting more and more mature. From a life of crime, he had become a good man with great values and a business sense that was past impressive. He also took care of himself. He was about six feet tall, but you could tell he was ripped from daily workouts at multiple gyms. He had found that people in gyms needed people to shop for them, and it was pure salesmanship.

"I filled in some blanks for you. I didn't think any decent girl would want just bras, panties, and pajamas, so I brought some real clothes as well. I also have an assortment of shoes for her to pick from. I have friends at the local Dillard's. They let me run them out, and I bring back the extras. It works out good for me and my runners and works out great for them. Sales at the Fayette mall store are up 15% in shoes just from our people. I just hired a girl that spends all her time doing Ulta runs. She can match a color better than those fancy paint stores. Let's go see your girl, Mister A Damn, Mister A has got himself a girl. I didn't think that would ever happen. All your high and mighty god-like stuff, I thought you was a monk or something. This is just awesome."

"She's asleep," I told Micah and hoped his excitement would not fade.

"Ain't no woman, sleeping or not, ever turned down shopping," Micah said. "She will be flat pissed if you don't wake her up and let me talk at her."

"Don't you mean talk *to her*?" I smiled.

"That's what I said," Micah smiled. His smile was always infectious ever since I knew him. His white smile and his deep chocolate complexion made him wonderfully unique.

"How is your girl?" I asked him.

"My girl? You are tryin' to change the subject. You take these bags. I got some stuff in the trunk." Micah pressed his fob and waited a second as the trunk opened. I picked up the bags on the ground while Micah brought out a thick garment bag and a large box with multiple flaps on it. The box itself looked different than I had seen before.

"What's in the box?" I asked.

"I'll show you when we get inside," Micah said. "This is so cool, Mister A's girl. I blocked my day for this."

"I really think we should let her sleep," I said trying to dissuade this engagement without looking bad.

"Trust me, Mister A. She is gonna like this," Micah said. "You gonna open the door or just try to keep me out here all day?"

I laughed for a moment. He was impulsive and near reckless, but he was probably right. "Let's go see Terri." I said as I opened the door.

We walked through the hall to the spacious living room where Micah set his boxes down. He looked around, "This is such a cool room. I would do it different, ya know. This old stuff would be an accent and not a main focus. You need to add some new stuff, Mister A." He stopped and pulled out a few rods from a bag. "I will set up, and you go get Terri. This is too good. I am dying to meet the girl that could turn your head."

"I hope I live up to expectations," Terri said, emerging from the master bedroom hallway. I smiled as I looked up at her. She was in my T-shirt and had thrown one of my belts on around it. Her body was tight, and all it did was accentuate the curves. Her golden hair hung down and wrapped around to the front. She had brushed her hair and cleaned up even more since I talked to Shawn.

I wondered how long she had been awake. "You're up," I stammered.

"Wow," Micah said, "this is what it must be like to be in heaven. No wonder Mister A is interested in you. You are a total fine goddess. I mean, like you even have Mister A stammering. I ain't never seen anyone be able to make him be anything less than the coolest man on the planet. Aw man, this is rude." Micah stood up and walked to Terri. "My name is Micah. Micah Miles. I own *Shopping by Miles*, a personal concierge company here in Lexington. Mister A helped start the company, but we are autonomous now and kicking butt. I just added a seventh employee who does makeup and color, and we will shop 'til we drop for you as needed. I got some things for you to try on. It looks like Mister A got the sizes about right. He asked for some basics, but I took it to the next level so you would feel at home."

"He is trying to spend all my money," I said to Micah with a smile.

"Oh yeah, I checked. The card you gave me has a five hundred-thousand-dollar limit. We can do some serious shopping on that," Micah laughed. He held Terri's hand in his and led her to a chair. "Damn, you are as tall as me. That will be Okay, but I may have to skip a few things I brought."

"First things first," Micah began and pulled out a familiar pink bag. "Here we have ten pair of Victoria's Secret underwear, and ten Pair of Victoria's Secret thongs. I took the liberty of choosing a few styles. A lot of women are preferring the boy shorts if they don't like thongs, but that is a personal preference. It depends on how you want to wear the panty lines."

Terri looked up at me, standing in the corner like a fifth wheel with a dumb smile on my face. "I can't afford all this. What do you think?"

It was like a slap to my face. I had never had anyone around that care about much more than themselves except maybe Micah, Shawn and a few others. I had not considered this question. "I, umm," I began.

"Wow," Micah said, looking up at me. "You got it bad. This is twice I have seen you stammer. You must think she is *it*."

I was not sure how to react but regained my composure. "Any or all that Micah offers is yours if you want it."

"Girl, we are going to Bora Bora. I always wanted to go there. We will be havin' a fine time dancing, and Mister A can come if he wants." Micah shot in quick. I laughed, but Micah restarted without a pause. "Since we have an open checkbook, per se, which undergarment would you prefer?" Micah winked at me.

"Let's take five thongs and five low cut bikini briefs if you have them," Terri said.

Micah looked in the bags and pulled out an assortment, "You can pick your colors." Terri did so as he held them out, dark colors, mostly blacks and dark blue. He set the ten pair to the side. Terri grabbed one of the black pairs of bikini briefs, slipped them on her legs, and stood, pulling them up.

Micah smiled. "We got the panties, now the bras. I think Mister A got your size right from your bra, but I included a few that were one up and one down since I have seen women go too small to pop 'em out a little and too large when they are modest." Micah pulled out about 20 bras of different colors and a measuring tape. "If you are not sure I can measure you as long as Mister A doesn't throw me around like a ragdoll."

"Like a ragdoll?" Terri laughed, "32D is what I wear. How many do you have of those?"

Micah sorted them all and then smiled, "I would suggest you match the bras. I came prepared to match most every color, knowing that many women like a daily change. It is up to you. If it were me buying for you, I would take these. They match the panties you have and would give you a matching set of undergarments."

Terri took the stack in Micah's hands and stood up. "Tell me how Adam picked you up like a ragdoll," Terri said as she took off the belt around my t-shirt, then pulled off the t-shirt, and took a black bra to put on.

Micah was mesmerized. Terri sat down, now in a bra and panties.

"Umm, oh damn," Micah said, "I am sorry, ma'am. That was so unprofessional. Mister A didn't tell you about when we met? Well, I was a punk, and he was a good mark. I tried to pick his pocket. I was fast, faster than anybody I have ever met. Mister A was faster. I snatched his wallet good, and he grabbed my arm and lifted me clean in the air. I was hanging there in the middle of the sidewalk, wondering what the heck I had just gotten myself into. I didn't know what to do, and I thought it was funny. I mean, here was this big guy, and he was holdin' me up like I was nothin'? Ya know? I gave him his wallet, and he didn't give me to the cops or make me apologize. He just laughed with me. Then he wanted to help me. Yes, help me, a common punk. Now I've been helpin' people too. I will keep growing the business that he helped me start. I mean, he has whatever he wants, and he helps someone like me, you know."

"Now, it's time for some clothes before Mister A and I faint here. Damn, Terri, you are too fine." Micah had hung the garment bag from a rod he had removed from the box he carried in. Inside was a variety of dresses. First though, he reached into a bag and brought out bow wrapped items. "Mister A asked for these. They might be nice, but we can do a little better."

Terri looked at the bow wrapped items and noted they were Victoria's Secret pajamas. "What do you have better? I like these for laying around, but let's see your options."

Micah pulled out two gowns. They were long silk gowns. One was black, and one was white. "These are fitted and should be perfect for you at a 32D. They may be a little short as they are meant to be floor length, but they will look awesome."

Micah hung them back up for a second, "I also have two sundresses. These are knee-length and colorful," he pulled out two dresses with whimsical prints, one yellow, one red. "Two long skirts with peasant tops in case you were a little more that way." He pulled out two patterned, long dresses that would easily be floor length and four tops as he displayed them, I saw that two were "cold shoulder" tops and two were standard peasant tops. Micah set those aside as well, "I also have both medium and large yoga pants and a series of workout shirts. I was not sure on the pant, so I brought both. Seeing you, a medium would work well but the large may give you more length. There are near a dozen shirts to choose from."

Terri was watching closely and not talking. I was the one who asked, "What's in the box?"

"Good eye, Mister A. These are the shoes she has to pick from. You said ten and a half," Micah twisted the box and moved it. The sides and front folded out, showing 16 pair of shoes. "I brought four sets of heels, four sets of sandals, four sets of flats, and four sets of running shoes. Lastly, here is a small section of socks. To get started. Once you are set, I can get you anything you want. We can order online, or you can leave it to me, and I will get you set."

Micah paused, watching Terri.

Terri sat in her bra and panties. There were only bruises where once there were holes in her only a short time ago. She looked perfect and was motionless for a few minutes. Then she looked at me. "I have clothes at home," she said. "This seems like a lot." As I looked at her, I saw Micah behind her mouthing the word "wow" to me.

I was touched and looked at Micah who was smiling. "Go ahead, Micah. Say it."

"I mean, Mister A, she is the whole package. She is sitting half naked and only has eyes for you with my fine body here. She is not wanting to spend your money, and she is almost too pretty to look at. I mean, did you make this girl in a lab? She is nothing less than perfect. She makes you stammer and seem almost normal instead of the ultimate Mister A god-like action figure. Has she got a sister?"

I laughed. Terri turned and smiled at Micah.

"He is the best natural salesman I have ever met," I told Terri. "Whatever you want is yours. I owe you more than that."

"Well," Terri began, "I will take the large yoga pants and all the t-shirts. The black and white gowns, please. Skip the long dresses but leave the cold shoulder tops. I will take these pajamas. They will come in handy for a few days." As she talked, she opened one and put the shirt on then the pants. "The socks for sure to wander around the house in, and I will pick a few pair of shoes." She stood and wavered for a moment.

Micah started to stand, but I was already there, holding her. "I am fine," she said, "Just got up too fast."

"Damn, Mister A, you are just too fast," Micah observed.

Terri leaned down and picked two pairs of heels, black and red, a pair of flats, a pair of sandals, and a pair of tennis shoes.

"Good choices," Micah said, "I can pick up some jeans for you. You look like a four tall, that about right?"

"I'm not sure," Terri said. "I haven't worn jeans in a long time. I usually wear dresses."

"If you change your mind, I will get you some," Micah said, then looked at me.

"Did I do Okay, Mister A?" he asked.

"You did great," Terri said. "Thank you for being so perfect in your assumptions." Micah packed the boxes and put everything together. "That's a well-designed box for displaying shoes, Micah."

"Yeah," Micah said, "Working on several designs. We may try to patent it for concierge services. It is really slick."

"I like the idea," I said, "I know a patent attorney than can help you get started to protect the idea."

"Really?" Micah said, "You think it is that good?"

"I think it is that good," I said as he packed up the last few items and handed Terri a series of bags. She stood up next to me. Micah stood with far less than he came in with. Terri walked to him and hugged him. She stood as tall as he did, and he was star-eyed for a moment. When she stepped back, I walked up and hugged Micah as well.

"You know, usually I feel like the big guy, but damn, I am little next to you. And you got a perfect girl who is my size," he looked at Terri. "If you ever want a fun guy to hang out with, I'm your man." Micah handed her his card. "If you need anything else let me know, Mister A knows I will be here in a flash."

"I do need something else, Micah," I said. "I need the Vette cleaned and the foam in the seats replaced. We had a bit of an accident, and I just want them cleaned completely. Do you know anyone who can do the upholstery and make it perfect?"

"I do," Micah said. "But I am not sure I want them working on your car. Let me check around before I give you to someone. I will have an answer by the end of the day."

"Thanks, Micah. Make sure you give yourself a good tip," I said to him.

"Oh, hell no," Micah said, "I do this for you for free. Damn, you started all this for me. I will just charge cost of goods. I owe you, Mister A. I owe you."

I was stunned again but stated simply, "Thank you." and made a mental note to do something good for this man.

"See ya," Micah said as he headed down the hall.

"Well," Terri said, "I have clothes," she laughed. "I may want to take them off all the time, but I do have clothes."

I laughed, then smiled, and picked up her items. "I have a second empty closet that can be yours."

"I get a closet," Terri exaggerated her excitement, "Let's go see!" and we went into the bedroom.

Chapter 6

Being around Terri was easy. I could tell she was struggling a little as she was still tired. Her body was going through a number of changes. Still, she had a positivity and exuberance that I admired, and it was visible she had won Micah over quite easily. I was feeling more comfortable with my decision and very comfortable with her. It was amazing how quickly I felt at ease with this woman. I had truly only known her a few short hours, though it felt as if she had been part of my life for much longer.

I led her into the bedroom, and we walked down the small hall from the bedroom to the bathroom. Opening the door to the left, I revealed a full walk-in closet that was completely empty.

"Why?" Terri asked.

"I like clothes," I began, "but that doesn't mean I go over the top. I keep my number to a reasonable amount." I turned to the closet facing the empty closet and opened in. A little over half the closet was full, mostly of suits and dress shirts. On the floor was a rack with perhaps ten pair of shoes. "This and my dressers are plenty."

"I have less than that," Terri laughed, "but I am willing to go evensies." She laughed again. It was a melody.

I carried her items into the empty closet and laughed. Reaching up, I touched the one hanger in the closet. "I think you need more than this," I laughed, then went into my closet and brought ten velvet covered hangers. "This should help." I hung the black hangers on the top rod.

"Perfect," Terri said and took the clothes from me and arranged them in the closet. She arranged the shoes on a shelf, then put the dresses and gowns on hangers as well as the shirts. "Can I borrow a drawer?"

"Of course," I said as we walked into the bedroom. "Take any on the left you like." I opened the top left empty drawer. "I doubt anything is in any one of them."

"No one has ever lived with you? Why keep them empty?" Terri asked. "Are you telling me the truth?"

"Of course," I said. "I have no need to lie. It is habit. I never had double-sided furniture until about a hundred years ago. When I did, I wasn't used to the two sides so I just used one, thinking I would eventually have a use for the other side. That day never came, and I kept doing things the same way as a joke more than anything."

"A joke?" Terri asked me.

"Of course," I laughed. "Whenever anyone comes to visit me or I have any type of social life, they tend to snoop. To avoid questions, I can always say I had someone, but they left. And the state of the room always supported that. No more questions. If they press or want to be that person that saves me? I can always say it is too soon after my bad relationship, not pointing out that it was hundreds of years ago."

"That is a bit of a lie," Terri said, looking at me.

"None of it is a lie. It just does not represent the whole truth," I said. "People would not understand if I told them what little I have told you so far."

"I get that," Terri said as she turned to me. She came close and pressed her body near mine. She felt amazing even though she was almost fully dressed. She leaned forward and kissed me. First with soft precision and sensual grace, then with a little more urgency. Without warning, she pulled away. "Promise me you will not manipulate the truth like that with me. I know you are my elder by a ridiculous number of years, and your knowledge of the human psyche is hundreds of times more perceptive than mine. I don't want to be hurt. Not even by you, Adam. You saved me from death. It would be worse than death to know you, with all your morality and higher purpose, misled me for any reason. Even if it was to keep from hurting me."

"I understand, and I promise I will never intentionally lie to you. I will have to be diligent as well. After all, this will be the first time I have been this close to someone in over a thousand years. I doubt I will do everything right, but I will try not to do anything wrong." I said with a solemn voice.

Terri held me. I felt her heartbeat, heard the blood rushing though her veins. "What is it like?" she asked.

I pulled back only a little and looked at her. "What is what like?"

"Living so long. What has it been like for you? I know you will continue the story of you but tell me what it has been like seeing the time of the roman empire, of Christ, of the inquisition, the discovery of America, and so much more." Terri asked, still bright eyed.

"It has been lonely," I said. "I make friends, and then watch them grow old and die. Worse, as some start to ask questions, I have to fake my death and never see them again. You will be the first person I will have been with that knows what I am and will not die as the others do. At least, the first one who was not holding me captive."

"I never thought about lonely," Terri said.

"I have tried pets," I began. "They are a flash except for a giant tortoise I had for about three hundred years. He was killed by a raiding party on the Galápagos islands in the 1600s. I was so distraught I killed all but three sailors on the ship and took it as my own. I sailed for over a hundred years as a pirate and amassed fortune after fortune in the process. I tried people, but until recently they do not live that long. I have tried faith, but no god answers to me even though I have faith. Usually, I sit in limbo as they do, and as of late have watched people believe in nothing, so we are both lost. I have come across some strange things in my life that live a long time, but most are so lost in despair that I steer very clear of them." I paused, thinking of all the years and the pain. "Mostly, I just existed for a long time until I started engaging life and living for what I could."

Terri had finished putting her small wardrobe away and went over and sat on the bed. She smiled at me and I felt all sorts of emotions I had not felt in a long time, if ever.

"I want to hear it all, and know it all, but we can take it slow. I am sure this is hard for you as well. I am sure you feel deeply, or try not to feel just to survive, right?" Terri asked.

"I guess you are right," I said, "It is easier to get lost in a hobby, or pastime, or war, or crusade, than to feel the pain of loneliness that I have felt for oh so long."

Terri looked deep into my eyes; her pure blue eyes seemed to peer into my very soul. It felt good to know that the instant I started liking her she would not be gone. It felt good to know the world would be better with two of us. "Terri," I started, "I know I didn't ask your permission. I know I didn't tell you everything, but are you Okay with this? I never want you to feel the loneliness I have felt. I never want you to have a void to fill as the one I have had."

"It's been one day. Well not even one day," Terri laughed. "Stop being so damn serious. How long do we have to be stuck here? How long until I don't get tired so fast?"

"I really don't know," I said, "I think it is almost over for you. Your body seems to have healed up completely and you have gone through some metabolic and physical changes."

"I know right, my tits and butt feel awesome," Terri said.

I chuckled, "Yeah, they look good too, but it is hard to say with your insides. I don't know how close you were to death. It was close. There may be extensive rework of your inner organs still. Your heart is strong, and you are doing better than I could have dreamed, but I don't know what else is to come."

"Well, that's no help," Terri laughed. "At least it doesn't hurt anymore." She looked around, "If it means something good, I am hungry. I mean really hungry."

"That is good," I said to her, "Hunger means your body needs more fuel to keep repairing. What would you like to eat?"

"Well, are we eating out or eating here?" Terri asked.

"We can do either," I said, "You seem to be good enough to move around, and I can carry you if necessary."

"What a guy," Terri laughed at me. "I am trying to think of what's close."

"I don't want to go too far," I considered. "We could always go to Malones and get a steak."

"Steak," Terri's eyes lit up. "What an awesome idea. They have good salads and appetizers too. I did not realize how hungry I am. You sure I'm not a vampire or something?" she chided.

"No such luck," I laughed. "Just a run of the mill semi-immortal person."

"Semi-immortal?" Terri asked.

"I am not sure," I said, "but I do not know if your body will reproduce the enzymes that make my body work the way it does. I am betting without me you would live a few hundred years, then you would pass away like everyone else. Of course, I have nothing but theories to base that on."

"Theories?" Terri asked.

"Yes, I told you I had been working with a doctor and he had some ideas about how I function that way that I do. He thought my cells cooperate in a different manner than most people, almost like a Jellyfish, but not the same. Anyway, his explanation for how things work led us to consider that what happened with Morgan was temporary at best. That eased my mind at least a little."

"You don't know though, do you?" Terri asked. "Is it possible she could still be out there?"

"No, not her," I replied. "Morgan is gone forever. There are others that may be out there still if the doctor was correct in some of his assumptions."

"That would not be a good thing." Terri said. "How many could be out there?"

"It's hard to say," I considered. "As you are now, and for some time, you will be able to grant people a limited number of additional years. I have often thought some legends were created from offshoots of my blood, but I have yet to come across anyone that was affected by me directly, or that works in a similar way."

"Really? I could go around making little baby clones of me?" Terri considered with a wry smile. "If I were to make a little girl into a *me,* would she grow up or be stuck at the small age? If I were to do a 90-year-old man, how far back would he go?"

I laughed. "I don't know. I am not going to find out. Are you going to wear that out to Malones?"

"Oh crap," Terri said and stood up. It must have been too fast because again she faltered. As I reached for her, she fell into my arms, grabbing me and pulled me down. She smiled, "just kidding, sucker". We kissed, and I held her close for over a minute.

I pulled her to her feet effortlessly and smiled. Already, I was surprised at her recovery and demeanor again. She went into her newfound closet and came out less than two minutes later in leggings and a white cold shoulder top. She looked very put together but walked into the bathroom, worked on her hair, and washed her face.

"Adam," she said, "do you have my purse?"

I had not thought about her purse but realized it may have been in the car all along. "Hang on. Let me check the car."

I walked through the house and out to the car. I was thinking about when I saw Terri's purse last. Honestly, I did not remember immediately. It took me several moments to walk through the chain of events that happened earlier in the morning for me to determine the purse was indeed in the back seat of the car. It was only moments after we exited the car that we suddenly ran into Sam and his compatriots. It was then that we came to the decision that led to this day.

The purse was very evident when I actually looked behind the seat. Frustrated that my earlier focus was so much on the cleaning I did not notice her purse there, I retrieved it and turned to walk inside.

Something felt off. I was not sure what it was. I knew I was forgetting something, something important, but I could not place my finger on it.

I turned off the lights as I went back into the house. As I walked to the master bedroom, I became clearer and once again was nearly infected with the thought of Terri. I felt more liberated and positive than I had in quite some time. As I thought about it, I considered the hundreds of years alone and how this would be a new start to my life.

"Your purse, milady," I said in a nonsensical tone as I walked into the bathroom.

Terri laughed and took her purse, pulling out several makeup items. It was a rapid progression. In the time it had taken me to go to the garage and back, she had brushed her hair and pulled it into a tight ponytail. As I watched, she applied a small amount of makeup and turned to me. "I am starving. You ready to go?"

"Are you sure you are up to this?" I asked. "It is 1:00 now. Eight hours ago, you were near death with a bullet in your body."

She pinched my cheek, "Thanks to you, I am feeling pretty good and want to eat an entire cow. Well, let's go." I chuckled a little as she walked in front of me with her purse in hand. She stopped before we left the bedroom. "Do I need this?" Terri held out her purse.

"No, I can cover it. I think we will be sharing a lot now." I laughed.

Terri put her arms around my neck and kissed me. She pulled me close, and it felt amazing. The kiss held for at least 20 seconds, before she stopped, looking down. "Whoa there, Tiger," she said. "We will take care of that later."

"Funny," I laughed, "I'll hold you to that."

As we walked through the house to the garage, Terri asked, "You have been alone a long time. I have heard you say that, and of course, I understand why you would want to not, well, spread your disease," she looked back at me and I raised an eyebrow, "but don't you like, well, take care of things? Or find someone that is immune or use protection or something?"

"I get by," I said, "If you don't have anything you almost get used to it. I have things to keep me busy, and I enjoy my day-to-day life. Around here, I enjoy spending time with horses or doing little diversions."

"Do you have to work?" Terri asked. "You were flippant about it before."

"I have enough money put away to last a long time," I said. "I invest from time to time and occasionally treasure hunt."

"Treasure hunting sounds awesome," Terri said. "Anywhere exotic?"

"Everywhere exotic," I laughed. "There is no treasure where people are. It is usually where they are not."

"Did you stash things years ago to pick up later?" Terri asked.

"Funny you should say that," I said as we entered the garage. "I did set some things aside from time to time and later have gone back and found them. There were also some things I stashed that were gone, found by treasure hunters or other people." Terri walked to the Corvette passenger door. "Let's take another car. We got the seats a little bloody. I think I have it all clean, but I don't want to take a chance. I talked to Micah, and he is going to see if he knows someone who can break the seats down to redo them."

"We seem to have a lot of time," Terri said, "I can teach you how to do it. I have done a few weird jobs and that was one of them. Not specifically cars, but I have done boats and leather tack."

"Not necessary unless you want to do it," I smiled. "One of the advantages of having some money is the ability to delegate work that isn't any fun."

"Some money?" Terri said as I uncovered a 1964 Corvette coupe. "Geez, a little too much on the Corvettes, huh? I heard your card limit. How do you get a card, anyway? I mean, can't exactly keep a social security number forever, can you?"

I folded the cover into a small square and walked to a cabinet to put it away.

"OCD much?" Terri asked.

"Habit," I said, "I like to keep things neat, sure, but I am not really OCD. Just have habits I have been doing for too long. I am sorry if it seems that way sometimes. I will work on some things but after doing the same things for a long time it just happens. You don't even think about it."

Terri got in the car, and I sat down in the drivers' seat. I like the 1964 model because it too had plenty of room. I backed out of the garage, and once in the drive, stopped, pulled the clips on the roof and dropped the top.

"Ahh, messing up my hair, I see," Terri laughed.

"Worth it," I shot back. "Always fun to drive with the top down when it's warm."

"I suppose," Terri said, "It's a ponytail day, anyway."

I backed up a little further into a turnaround, then shifted and began rolling up to the gate slowly as it opened, then drove out onto the open road. I accelerated, and we were off, heading towards Malones. The drive was only about ten minutes. We laughed in the wind and talked when we could hear each other. Pulling up to the open parking lot, we got out and left the top down on the car.

"Not worried about it?" Terri asked.

"Not really. I love the car, but it is just a car. Most people will just admire it. There is nothing in it of value."

"Except the car," Terri said.

"Yeah. I bought it when it rolled out of the factory. Was one of the first of that year. I have taken it down to Bowling Green before and let the Corvette Museum display it. They take super care of the cars there and except for the sinkhole problem there is no chance it will not be perfect" We walked in and immediately were shown to a table. I was impressed how fast we were seated, but then noticed it was almost 1:30 and the lunch crowd had faded.

Chapter 7

Our seat was not close to anyone. We could talk about almost anything and enjoy ourselves without worrying about bothering people or getting incredulous looks if something strange was said. So, we laughed about everything for a few and placed an order. Both of us got a large filet. If you have not had a filet at Malones, you are missing out. When you add their house salad, you have a meal for most people, and Terri was hungry. Her body had been working overtime adapting and rebuilding cells, and it needed fuel. A lot of fuel.

After our order was placed, Terri looked into my eyes with those amazing blue eyes of hers. "I have not forgotten about your past. It is still a lot to accept, but it is becoming easier by the moment. We left off after she pimped you out, and you got a cart of food. We can wait, but no one is here. It would be good lunch talk."

"Are you sure?" I asked. "Some of it will get brutal."

"Bring it on," Terri said, "I am used to it."

"Okay," I said, "We had just received a cartload of food."

Our salads came first. As is normal with Malones, the staff was attentive and amazing, which made talking for the first few minutes a little difficult. As we began to eat a bit at a time, it became easier.

"After we received the cart of food, Morgan and I spent the rest of the day in bed. It was as though she wanted to have all I could give and more. She taught me so many things on that one day. It seemed the more we did, the more she wanted. And the more she wanted, the more we did." I paused and chewed for a moment.

Terri was silent, eating her salad and watching me, intrigued by the account I was giving.

"Late that night, I fell asleep. We had drunk bottle after bottle of wine, but apparently, Morgan had not drunk as much, or not drunk from the bottle with the sedative in it. I slept soundly while she worked."

"Worked? What do you mean worked?" Terri asked.

"In the morning, I woke, and I was in ropes. My arms and legs were bound. Though I had some freedom of movement, I was not able to get loose. I implored her to release me, but she said she could not. I asked why I was held. She told me I was a treasure, and she could not lose me. I was confused. I was still early to language, but I knew this was not right. It was worse because I did not have a good definition of either right or wrong. I was confused because I was imprisoned by someone who said they cared for me, or at least implied it. I found out I was just a commodity."

"In ropes? I have seen you punch. You could not get out?" Terri asked.

"Apparently, they had considered that. The ropes were counterweighted by me. It was brilliant the way I was bound. If I used my strength, I would use it on myself and cause myself pain or worse. I had no idea at the time how resilient I was, or I would have left immediately. A little after I awoke, the woman who had bedded with me and 11 other women came into the stone hut. Men were outside, and I heard them begin working, even though the season was not the best for it."

"Working?" Terri said as she chewed a piece of bread.

"Yes, they were building onto the stone hut, and it was becoming far more. While the men outside worked, Morgan straddled me naked and forced her breasts on me. Naturally, my body responded, and one by one, the women in the room had their way with me. As I came in each woman, another straddled me. All the while, Morgan kept me excited, and teased me to the edge of sanity. Soon the entire room was filled with pure lust as women began pleasing each other in between turns with me. It truly was a scene out of a horrible book of the damned. I was oblivious. I had not read the book of the damned yet, and I did not understand anything except that my freedom had been taken from me. It is funny. I truly did not understand freedom, but perhaps I just didn't like how it felt."

"Which?" Terri asked, "Being tied up or having women all over your naughty bits?"

"Naughty bits?" I asked. "You must be a Monty Python fan."

"Darn right," Terri laughed. "I mean, wouldn't that be a dream for a lot of men?"

"I am sure it is a lot of men's dreams until they experience it. I will tell you it was not my dream; it was mostly a nightmare." I said, grimacing at the thought.

"Why a nightmare?" Terri asked as she continued eating her salad.

"I had no love," I said, "I had some attraction, but I could not say what it was at all. Remember, I was a blank slate, and because of that, it messed me up for a long time. Here is where I must explain why any of this is important. I suppose I could have just told you what was going to happen to you and leave this all out, but the next parts of my history will help you understand why my decision was so difficult."

The server brought over the steaks. The filets were large for filets, and the smell was intoxicating. Terri got mushrooms on hers, and it was mouthwatering. Malones was known for their steaks, and they were amazing. The server asked both of us to check our steaks for temperatures. We did; it was perfect. The server left, and Terri's first statement was, "Wow, these are so awesome!"

We sat for a few minutes, eating. As was usual, the food was perfect. The company was just as perfect.

"I didn't realize how hungry I was." Terri said, "I usually can't eat this much, but wow, it tastes too good."

"You will have to be careful how you eat. Depending on how much stress your body is under, you will burn calories faster. No diets. You will need food to keep going," I told Terri.

"No issue from me," Terri laughed, "I love food. This is like a dream come true. Instead of watching the cart go by, I can eat. Oh yeah."

"Well, don't overdo it," I said.

"But you just said," Terri began.

"Listen to your body; you will know," I laughed.

We talked about little of nothing and the history of Malones. Other restaurants came up that were in the Lexington area, and we rated them with each other. We even got on a hamburger tour, and we compared hamburger places in Lexington. Tolly-Ho came up as one of the best cheap burgers, and I agreed. After we finished the bulk of the food, we sat, knowing the server would give us some room. I did not order dessert, but Terri did, and we waited for only a few minutes for her Crème Brule.

As she savored the flavor of the unique desert with small bites, she asked, "How long were you tied up?"

"Direct, aren't you," I smiled.

"Well, I knew that was one of the places you were going. It was self-evident that you were an asset. What woman wouldn't want to remain young and beautiful for as long as possible?" Terri said.

"True," I said, "I did not know that at the time, but it is very true. Vanity and greed have been around a long time. I believe that Morgan was fond of me, but I do not think she felt love."

"How long was it? I mean, I know it was a while, but you are avoiding saying, so it was a long while," Terri pressed as she took another bite.

"The days became weeks, the weeks became months, and the months years and far beyond. I was not entirely sure for a long time, but when I escaped and found my way what is now Scotland it was 1439BC. Of course, that is translated to AD and BC, and I am using dates you will understand. With that in mind, it was a little over 700 years."

Terri stared at me wide-eyed and played with a piece of sugar on the top of her dessert. "Are you telling me you were a daily sex toy for a bunch of old women for seven centuries?"

"It was far more than that," I said, "I was a slave to a variety of whims. They started doing odd things after the first few months. They built a complex around me, and I was treated well, fed well, was able to take care of all my needs. I was bathed daily. I was also shaved daily. It became normal for me to have sex with a woman every hour for the 13 hours of the day. Each was given an hour, and each had a diverse approach to how they liked to do things. Between each, I was bathed and cleaned for the next. It was an endless parade of flesh, and I was always excitable and always engaged. After all, it was what I knew. I had no emotional baggage or secondary interest to ruin my libido. I was a sexual machine."

"Odd things?" Terri asked.

"Well, they began experimenting with keeping me excited for longer, trying to see if there were things that would give them more. They skipped a week once, and of course, it did not affect them, but their goal was to see if it was more powerful or fresher. They were unique in their approaches, but they also began experimenting with other things. It is my opinion that the legends of witches and covens originated from the 13 women who held me captive."

"Makes sense," Terri laughed as she took another bite of her dessert. "They certainly were witches, or bitches, or something like that."

I laughed and nodded. "The 13 women became enormously powerful in the area. After a short time, I was moved, then moved again. The fortress of Derbent was a tactical legend, but most of it was originally built to keep me away from the world and prying eyes. I have not gone back but often wonder if the secret underground chambers were ever discovered. They were well-hidden to keep prying eyes from me."

"I would imagine so," Terri laughed. "I am sure it was difficult."

"It was. As the women grew older and stayed young, they became smarter. There were many things they added to the area. They helped the area grow and began becoming more involved in guiding men. They initially only pleasured themselves with me or with each other. One day though, that changed.

Magda was a very pretty woman. I believe she was over 400 years old when she decided she wanted more. She brought one of her guards, a m idle aged man named Conner, into the fold. After he began having sex with her, he, too, was affected. You see, they had the enzymes but to a lesser degree as they were not natural. As she spent more time sexually with the man, she slowly started aging a little. It was barely noticeable, but her solution was to milk my semen and drink it. This worked some, but it was not going directly into the bloodstream, and neither they nor I understood that, so the effect was lessened. The man wanted nothing to do with that, and eventually, she tired of him. Still, he was no longer like anyone else. To fix her mistake, she tried to kill him, which didn't work. It was a brutal battle, and they fought over and over for hours until he fled. That would be the undoing of the 13."

"Really?" Terri asked. "It took one man to bring down 13 women? That's funny."

"Not really. It makes sense." I said, "The 13 women aged themselves and then became their daughters. It was simple, really. With the 13 taking turns, they could transition each other into roles and move things around so they could stay in power. No one suspected that one woman was living for hundreds of years. The man out on his own did not have that benefit. He was eventually found out, and the secret leaked to a select few. Morgan held council with me as though they were wise from their years. I was still a sponge and remembered far more. I had the advantage of being able to see things from many sides, and despite my captivity, I helped Morgan with some tactics."

"I assume you kept learning," Terri said.

"All that I could, but there was not as much at that time to learn," I noted. "As the ages passed the written word became more and more available, but if you consider the time, it was difficult, if available at all, where I was located."

"What happened with you and Morgan?" Terri asked.

"Sometimes, I think she wished she had told no one and never started down this path," I stated. "She would often sit with me when no one else was around. She was the only one who slept with me each night. I believe this made Magda jealous and caused the eventual downfall of the group. Magda longed for the nights with a man, not for the sex, but for the warmth and caring part that was deep inside of her. After Conner left, she became angrier and more frustrated with the situation. She came to me one day and asked me if I wanted to be free. I, of course, said yes, but she asked if she set me free would I stay with her. When I did not answer right away, she walked away angry."

The server brought the check, and I paid with two crisp one hundred dollar bills. It covered the food and a generous tip, since we did not drink. I smiled as the server left the table. When I said, "Keep the change," he skipped a little as he walked away. As we waited, Terri looked forlorn for a moment.

"What's wrong?" I asked.

"I was thinking about how you had most men's dream but were more alone than anyone can imagine. It just made me sad," she said in a soft voice.

We stood. I said nothing and saw the television in the bar area. A story was running about Sam. "Hit and run vehicle still being sought," the tagline scrolled at the bottom. I could not hear the news story, but I am sure it was handled well. Shawn was good about that, and I was sure it would pass rapidly or end up buried as a horrible accident. Moments later, another story began about three missing recruits for the football team. The pictures flashed on the screen, and it was the three men who had been with Sam. None of them had turned up anywhere. There was a plea for information and a phone number. I felt bad for the two, but one of them was not hurt, and I wondered what had happened to him.

We walked outside to the car, and a man and woman were looking at it. "Nice car," they said as we got in.

"Thanks," I replied. "I did a lot of the work myself."

"Nice," the man said, "If you want to sell it, please give me a call." He handed me his card.

"I'll do that," I said. "See ya around." As we got in the car, I started it up and drove out into the parking lot. They watched us the whole way.

"You get that a lot, don't you?" Terri asked.

"You should see it in the DB9," I laughed. "It is why sometimes I drive the Impala. It is pretty plain, and no one looks much at it."

"A little different for you," Terri noted, then smiled at me like a Cheshire cat.

"Well, sometimes I need to be able to adapt and to walk among people without everyone looking at me," I said.

"Fat chance of that happening," Terri replied. "You are a little taller than most, don't you think."

"A little," I laughed. "Still, if you are quiet, people don't notice you. They just let you slide by and ignore you."

"I don't disagree." Terri said, "I can blend if I need to, but it means ponytail and a hat usually."

"Yeah, but I am not as pretty as you," I said, "I always stand out because I am big. But if I sit down or hunch down, I look like a freak, and people don't look because they don't want to see."

"Nice trick," Terri moved her ponytail to the other side as the wind whipped over it. "I can't cut my nose off or anything like that. I look like I look."

"Perfect," I injected.

"Aww, aren't you the sweet one," Terri said.

I laughed and grabbed her hand to kiss it.

"Adam," Terri said with some concern in her voice, "I hate to ask this, and don't get mad, but am I going to be your prisoner now that I am at least a little bit like you?"

I laughed heartily. "No, not happening."

"What if I want to leave in a few hundred years?" Terri asked.

"If you want to leave, at any time, you can leave. I will not stop you. I will just move and disappear after that. It would break my heart, but I would never treat you as I was treated. I want you to believe in us on your terms, not mine. I want you to find happiness. And if it is not with me, then it might be with someone else. Once I am gone, I have no idea how long you would live, but it would be finite, as far as I know. I am not even sure if I am infinite, though." I considered her question for a moment. "Do you think you will want to leave me?"

"No," Terri replied, "I just can't imagine being a prisoner like you were and wanted to know. We haven't really talked about that yet."

"We will get there," I said, "You will have no issues with me."

We pulled into the driveway, and the gate opened. As we passed through, the garage opened, and I maneuvered the car into its bay. "Home sweet home," I said. "Are you sure you are okay with me?" I was concerned, "I have not been scaring you, or have I?"

"No, no," Terri said, "I am not afraid at all. You have just given me a lot to think about."

I looked around the garage. "Why don't you go in? I will cover the car and be in shortly."

Terri looked at me and smiled, "I will go get comfy, and we can take a nap!"

I smiled. "That is perfect. See you in a few minutes.

As Terri went inside, I looked around the garage and closed the garage bay doors.

Chapter 8

It took me a moment to cover the Corvette. I was used to it and easily retrieved the cover, then put it on almost mindlessly. Something was bothering me. It had nothing to do with Terri. I made sure the cover was neat, closed the cabinets, and looked over the cars for a moment.

I was not sure what it was, but I started walking back to the door and stopped. I scanned the garage. The bays with four other cars lay undisturbed. The cars were blanketed with their tight custom covers. The garage was closed even though I was in it now and had my fob. When inside, it was a manual decision on whether to open the garage. I slowed my breathing and listened. Slower. Slower. I closed my eyes. The scratching of the wind on the garage doors was evident, but I felt something else. Then I heard it. A fast heartbeat in the garage.

"Come out now. I will find you," I said.

A younger man stood up behind the Aston Martin. "Don't hurt me," he said, "I," he paused for a moment, "well, please don't hurt me."

"You were there this morning," I said, recognizing the young man. "You helped the other two get away."

"Yeah," he said, "I did; I had to get away from them. I remember the license number of your car. I had a friend look it up. I, well, the police think I am crazy, and I am worried you will kill me, or rip my head off, or bite me, but I had to come."

"What are you talking about?" I asked.

"Cal and Jimmy," the boy said. "You turned them into monsters."

"Monsters?" I repeated, realizing in the back of my mind what may have happened. "How are they monsters?"

"Jimmy," the boy said, shaking, "He has an arm again. He was screaming all morning. But when I came back to his room, he was asleep. And his arm was there. All nice and new, like it had never been ripped off by you."

I realized my horrible mistake. After Sam had shot me, I was covered in my own blood. Fighting with the boys, and letting them live, almost certainly transferred my blood to them. The rest would be a progression. My mind was reeling, considering the possibilities.

The boy shook his head, "Then I went into Cal's room, and his face was whole. The top part was covered with blood, but his whole jaw was clean as a whistle, and he had a face."

"You didn't go to the hospital this morning?" I asked the boy.

"No, they wouldn't go. They were afraid of you, and how you killed Sam without a thought. Then they got all worried because Sam shot you, and it was self-defense. Then, they were worried about going to jail over it. Cal was messed up with his jaw. We wrapped it. Jimmy's bleeding stopped itself almost right away. Then... it got a weird. I watched Jimmy's arm numb out and regrow. It was freaky. They were both in a lot of pain, but they have just been sleeping. Jimmy woke up and ate almost everything we had in the kitchen. It wasn't much, but he was hungry." The boy paused, fumbling. He reached into his pocket and brought out a large crucifix. "I figured if I killed the lead vampire, they might be saved."

I cocked my head at this boy, unsure of whether to be amused or angry. The boy was shaking like a leaf. He held the cross out and pulled a stake out of his coat with the other hand. This was new territory for me. I had been accused of being a lot of things over the years, and vampire had come up many times but having a vampire hunter come after me was something new.

"I am not a vampire," I said.

"That's what a vampire would say," the boy sneered.

"You are probably right there, but I have never met a vampire, so I wouldn't know," I smiled. "Do I need to eat garlic, or go out in the sun, play with your crucifix? How can I prove I am not a vampire?"

"I don't know," the boy replied, "You are something. What did you do to my friends?"

"Well," I said, "I had thought I killed them, but that apparently did not go as planned."

"Why would you kill them if you weren't a vampire?" the boy asked.

"I believe you were trying to kill Terri and me," I said.

"We were just supposed to scare you," the boy pleaded.

"With baseball bats and guns?" I asked.

"I didn't know about any of that," the boy said. "I don't know about anything at all. Now my friends are monsters. You did that to them."

Terri walked out of the door, asking, "Are you coming?"

The boy jumped a foot off the ground, seeing her. "Is she a vampire too? Sam really hated her and you. He wanted us to hurt you bad, but he didn't say anything about killing anyone. My friends are monsters, and if you aren't a vampire, how can I save them?"

He held the crucifix high, and Terri started laughing.

"Should I go see if we can get an Elvira outfit? That might be fun," Terri said with sarcasm and laughter at the same time. "Wait a second. He is one of Sam's, right?"

"Boy, what's your name?" I asked.

"Garret," the boy replied.

"Garret," I said, "We're not vampires. Come inside; let's talk."

"I ain't stupid," Garret said. "Vampires would ask you in so they could eat you."

"What then shall we do? Sit out in the garage all day?" I asked. "I give you my word; I won't hurt you."

"Spawn of Satan, you have no good word to do that," Garret spat.

"Maybe it's you who are, the spawn of Satan. Sent to kill a girl?" Terri said.

Garret glanced at her as I laughed under my breath. "Garret, drop the junk and let's talk. Or keep the junk, I don't care, but you are going to have a heart attack if you keep pushing yourself. You're also sweating all over my garage. Come inside, let's talk. We will figure this out."

"I don't trust you," Garret said.

"Well, you came here to kill me, so I'm not sure I trust you very much either," I laughed. "Truce, just come inside, and we will work this out."

"No," Garret said, "I won't do it."

"Then I guess we will have to fight out here," I said.

I walked over and Garret backed away. "Wait, what?" he said.

"You came here to kill me; let's make this work. One of us should die now," I said.

"That's not fair; nothing will kill you," Garret shrieked.

"Not my fault," I said, "I offered you a way out. You wouldn't take it."

"Wait, wait," Garret scrambled, looking for a way out of the garage.

"You got in when the doors were open. There is no way out except through me," I said, relentlessly walking as Terri looked on from the door.

As Garret walked around one of the cars, he tripped and fell and tried to get up, but I was there. He struggled in my hand as I picked him up and pushed the crucifix to me.

I smiled. "Nope." He swung the stake in his other hand around to stab me, but I grabbed his hand. "That won't work either but let's not and say we did."

"I don't want to die," Garret started crying.

"Stop being a baby and be a man," I said. "Men don't know how to be men anymore. You are a prime example. I have never seen a time when men were as pitiful as they are now, and here you are, being a child when you were trying to be a man. I should kill you to put you out of your own misery. Your lack of any type of self-respect is not only disheartening but also an affront to the humanity men are supposed to have."

Terri was staring at me with a unique expression.

"No, I am not going to kill him," I could tell she sighed a little, "I am just tired of the amazing world of whining wimps."

"Opinionated much," Terri said, watching as Garret shook while I walked him to the door.

"Maybe a little," I replied. "Someday you'll understand, I think. It is unique to see the world from a high-level view and watch how history unfolds." I looked at Garret. "Are you going to be good if I let you go?"

Garret nodded.

"Good. I really don't want to drag you around the house. We are walking to my kitchen. As we do, we will sit down, and I will make us some nice tea."

Garret was more curious now as Terri spoke, "Tea sounds good. I like lots of types of tea."

"As do I," I said. "Garret, what type of tea do you like?" I asked as we walked down the hall.

"I don't know," Garret said. "What kind do you have?"

"How about I make a nice rose tea while you tell me about your friends?" I smiled and tried not to be as scary as I knew I looked.

"Okay," Garret said. "I have never had it."

"I will make it with some wild honey," I said as we reached the kitchen, and Garret sat down at the big table. I pulled out a kettle and filled it with water, and put it on the stove. As I turned the stove on, I moved to the counter and leaned back, giving Garret a lot of room.

"Tell me what happened with your friends," I said.

"You hurt them this morning, and you killed Sam. The police wouldn't even believe that. They said I was crazy. They told me Sam was hit by a car. I saw you hit him, and his chest just caved in." Garret was speeding up.

"Relax, Garret. Did you see Sam shoot me?" I asked calmly so as not to excite him.

"Yeah, I saw Sam shoot you. When he shot you in the hand, you weren't even hurt. You are a monster, and Sam tried to kill you for being a monster."

"I probably am a monster," I said, "but Sam would not have known that. Sam tried to kill me and nearly killed Terri. I lost my temper. I am sorry I lost my temper, Garret."

The teapot started whistling, and Garret jumped.

"It's just the teapot," I said. "I am making you some tea, remember."

Garret nodded slowly. "I remember."

I got out three cups, "Tell me what happened next, Garret."

"We only live a few blocks away from Tolly-Ho. Sam called us because he saw you on Harrodsburg and followed you. He said he knew the girl would want to go there." Garret said. "Sam said we were just going to scare you. He said you embarrassed him, and he was gonna make sure the tables were turned."

Terri shrugged, "So I like their cheeseburgers."

"What happened next," I asked as I filled three tea infusers.

"I helped them back to the house," Garret began, "I wanted to help, but they were in pain. They stopped bleeding, but it was bad. They were awful. I told them I was calling the police and an ambulance, but they both grabbed me. I was terrified; they acted so crazy. They said no. Well, Jimmy said no. Cal just shook his head, and his face was all weird since he had no jaw. He looked horrible. He put a towel on his face, and they both went to their rooms. I started cleaning up the blood, and I couldn't stop crying."

"Why didn't you call the police or ambulance anyway?" I asked as I set the tea in front of him. I also gave Terri a cup, and I took a cup as well. I blew on my tea before taking a sip.

"I wanted to, but Jimmy, well, he said no. So, I didn't," Garret said as he sipped the tea. "It's hot."

I smiled, "Blow on it, Garret. It will cool. It smells good, doesn't it?"

Garret blew on the cup then smelled the tea. "It does smell good."

I took another sip. "Did you clean up the house?"

"Yeah, I cleaned up all the blood, Clorox too. I checked on Jimmy and Garret, but they were just sleeping and moaning. I went back in at about ten, and they were all whole again. It was freaky." Garret said as he sipped the tea. "This is good tea."

"I make it all myself," I said. "I have lots of types of tea. Mine is a chai blend. Terri's is an orange blend with cinnamon. Yours is another special blend. It is good tea. Yours is very rare."

Garret took another sip. "It is really good. Sweet, and it just tastes nice."

"Garret," my voice was low, soothing, "Are Jimmy and Cal still at the house?"

"Yeah," Garret said in a softer voice back to me, "They are home now. They ate a lot but then went back to rest."

"Okay, Garret," I said. "Can you tell me your address?" I whispered.

"Curry Ave, 998..." Garret's voice trailed off.

"Well, that's close," I said.

"What happened?" Terri asked.

"I put him to sleep," I said, "I can't have him running around telling people about me. It would not be good."

"You're going to kill him?" Terri gasped.

"No," I smiled. "The tea he drank is a mild sedative and hallucinogen that has the side effect of wiping about the last two days of memory with what I gave him. It will still be there, but it is like having Rohypnol or Versed. It clouds the memory enough that you just can't seem to pull it up. The difference is this clouds memory based on time and dose and not current memory. I will have someone take him to Cincinnati, and he'll wake up in a nice hotel room. It takes a while to wear off. By the time he is mobile, this should be over. Well, I hope it will be over. But for him, he will have no memory of any of this."

"You can't exactly do that with the other two, can you?" Terri said.

"No," I told her, "I am not sure how this is going to play out." I stopped and picked up Garret and took him to the guest room, with Terri following along.

"My tea is okay isn't it," Terri said, "You're not going to make me forget."

"No," I said, "Not my plan or my desire."

I put Garret on the bed. I turned him a little and pulled out his wallet. Checking his ID, it read 'Garret Mahoney.' The address was in Ohio, as was the ID. I put the wallet back and covered him up, "He will be asleep for at least a day. He is from Ohio. No ID that tells us his local address."

"What are we going to do then?" Terri asked.

"I am going to go find the two boys if I need to go door to door and see how I can approach it. You should stay here and keep an eye on Garret and wait for someone to come take him."

"Trying to get rid of me?" Terri asked.

"You are still a little weak," I said, "and I don't want to strain you."

"What about that bullshit you said earlier? You know, us being together and all and your big decision," Terri said.

"It wasn't bullshit," I replied. "I meant it, every word."

"Then we do this together," Terri said, "I'm a big girl. Who knows, I may even be of help."

"Yes, you might be," I said, "I just don't want you to get hurt."

"I thought I was past that?" Terri replied.

"There are still ways to die. Still ways that you can't come back." I said in a soft voice.

"Well, I will be almost careful then," Terri laughed. "I am learning as I go."

"Yes, you are," I said. "I will need to call Shawn before we go. Then a friend who has taken care of things before."

"How often do you do this?" Terri asked with a prying eye.

"Not very," I said. "The tea is from China, and I am not sure I would ever be able to get more. It is used to cleanse the mind and soul by certain monasteries. I am not even sure they still exist. Unfortunately, it doesn't seem to work on me. I still remember, well, everything."

"We need to continue your story," Terri said.

"We can as we drive," I replied. "There is a lot going on right now, but I can drive and talk after we get the phone calls out of the way."

We walked down the hall. Terri followed me until we got to a door opposite the bedroom. I used a key, and the door opened to a large study. There were numerous bookcases that lined the walls, all were neat and orderly. Beside them were numerous cases with strange items in them. I had collected things for years. Everything from shrunken heads to spears from the bronze age filled the cabinets and shelves in this room. Unlike the living room, each of these items had a unique story. I sat down at a large cherry desk and picked up a phone. I dialed a number I knew all too well.

"Phillip?" I said into the phone.

"Yeah, who is this?" the voice came.

"Adam," I replied.

"Oh, cool," Phillip replied.

"I need you to take someone to Cincinnati," I said.

"Okay, cool," Phillip replied. "They at your house?"

"Guest bedroom," I replied. "Somewhere nice. It's a good kid. He was just in the wrong place."

Phillip chuckled, "Yeah, they always are. We will be there in about an hour. How long 'til he wakes up?"

"Maybe ten hours," I said. "Maybe a few more."

"No issues," Phillip said. "Same fee, no questions?"

"Same fee," I replied. "No questions."

"I will be out. Use the code. Envelope will be on the desk next to the boy," I said. "His name is Garret. Check his wallet for the rest. The address on his ID is for his home, not for his school address. If I get it, I will call you."

"Okay, cool," Phillip said.

"You have such a way with words," I replied.

"Okay, cool," Phillip laughed, hanging up the phone.

"One more," I said.

I hung up the phone and called Shawn. The phone rang only once.

"I thought you might call," Shawn said. "A kid reported the fight you had this morning. He gave a nutty story about his roommates. The officers scared him off before they could get an address."

"Get a phone number or anything?" I asked.

"Let me look into this," Shawn said. "but no, we got nothing."

"No issue," I said, "I will let you handle this. I was just curious. What did he say that was so crazy?"

"He said the boy's arm grew back," Shawn laughed. "Imagine a kid growing his arm back after having it ripped off."

I laughed, "Yeah, that is a little bit out there."

"Anything else I need to worry about?" Shawn asked.

"No," I said, "I was just checking in."

"Give me some time, Adam," Shawn said. "I will work this out, but you need to stay out of this one. You are too close."

"I hear you," I said.

"But you aren't going to listen, are you?" Shawn replied. "I still need to talk to that girl of yours."

"Terri?" I asked. Terri looked over at me. "She is still sleeping; I will call you when she can talk."

"You do that," Shawn laughed. "I am sure she is still sleeping right next to you, huh?"

"Well, she is now," I said. "We did go to Malones to eat, but she was tired again."

"You suck at lying, Adam. Stop doing it." Shawn laughed. "I will be over later to see her."

"That works fine. How about a better idea?" I countered. "How about first thing in the morning? We will get it all sorted out then."

"Promise?" Shawn asked.

"Of course, I do," I said. "I have never broken a promise with you, have I?"

"No," Shawn said. "That much is true. You have bent the truth a little, but never broken a promise, ever. I will see you in the morning at 9:00 AM sharp."

"Got it," I replied, "9:00 AM sharp," I hung up the phone.

"I guess I am talking tomorrow at 9:00 AM?" Terri said.

"You are correct," I replied. "We will get Shawn to a point where he is happy, then move on."

"Don't be so sure," Terri winced a little.

"Pardon?" I asked.

"Shawn Dennis, right?" Terri said.

"Yep, know him?" I asked.

"Yeah, I dated his brother a few years back. His brother talked about him with reverence," Terri said. "Either he will have more questions for me than he would for anyone else, or he won't remember me at all. His brother is quite the player. I found out the hard way."

I shook my head, "It is funny how the eddies of the world bring us all together."

"Yeah," Terri said, "It is funny."

I stood and looked into her eyes. "Tell me the truth," I said, "Is this getting to be too much for you?

"Never," she smiled.

"Well, it seems like a lot for a first day," I stated.

"Well, for our first date, I nearly died, came back, found out I am near-immortal now and not a blood-sucking crazy, and have had to deal with a lot of strange stuff. I did get some new clothes and some nice underwear, so there's that," Terri paused. "Still not my worst date. It has actually been fun, interesting, passionate, and exciting. I would like to stop and spend some quality time with you, but I guess we have nearly forever?"

"As far as I know," I said. "Still, I would rather not put off a single day if I had a choice."

"I am right there with you," Terri said. "Trust me, it is hard to keep my hands off you."

"Ready for another fun time? Curry Avenue isn't that big; we should be able to find them pretty quick," I said.

"Well, let's go so we can get this done," Terri smiled.

I led the way to the garage to go find two boys who could be a problem once they realized what they were.

Chapter 9

We uncovered the jet-black 1996 Impala SS in the garage. Terri got in the passenger seat, I opened the garage, started the car, and backed out. As the garage door closed, Terri looked over at me and was a little concerned.

"Garret will be okay?" she asked.

"Of course," I replied. "I have used Phillip a few times when things got complicated. Nothing like this, but sometimes people at cemeteries or reporters start digging and end up asking me questions that become harder and harder to answer. With few people to corroborate my past and few links to anyone living, it is easy to put the cards together if you are looking for some reason. A few years ago, I invested in a horse that started winning a few races, and reporters started doing what reporters do. Most left me alone, but this one guy, Frances, was just pushing hard. Went after my fake parents that were dead, couldn't find a record of them, and just kept digging. I had Phillip take him to Toronto with no money, no ID, and a few weeks of memory lapses. The result was he was fired. I think he is living up there now, working for a small paper. I visited him once. He has no memory of me."

"Seems a little cruel," Terri said.

"It may be, but I did request my privacy when he and I spoke. It was his choice not to honor my wishes," I replied. "I have learned to avoid anything that may put me in the public eye. It is just too risky."

"That makes sense. With that in mind, the smart move would have been to let me die this morning?" Terri said.

"That would have been the smart move," I said, "but I felt something with you I had not felt," I paused, "well, ever."

"Still," Terri broke in; "The right move would have been to let me die or wipe my memory too."

I was silent as I considered her line of thinking. The car was quiet for a moment as we came to the Versailles Road intersection. "I guess there is no logic in the way I feel," I said as I turned the corner, heading into town. "I struggled with the decision for a few moments when it all happened. After all, I was deciding your life for you as well. I thought you would want to live, and I knew from our short time together that you and I, well, would have a lot of fun together. Was I wrong?"

"No," Terri said. "Don't get me wrong, I am happy for this life. I think my life is going to be interesting now. I am surprised I am not having a nervous breakdown from it all, but still, I want you to be sure, always."

The Impala had a bench seat. It was a big car. I reached over and held her hand. "I am sure."

Terri squeezed my hand back. "Just always talk to me. I don't wanna wake up somewhere not knowing who I am, years from now, wondering about how my life was and why I couldn't remember."

"Won't happen," I said, "I already know I like having you around."

"After one day?" Terri laughed. "You spent way too much time tied up by women. You clearly don't know what it's like to be with one all the time. Tomorrow, I could be a total bitch, and you could be hiding in one of your car covers. Only to be surprised by me, 15 minutes later, as a queen in my own right."

"I have stayed away from women," I said, "You are quite correct. I am no master. I have hundreds of years of experience saying 'no' and walking away from some of the most impressive women in history. I bet you don't know many others who can say that. How many people do you know that met Cleopatra, experienced her unique love of lust and were able to not only turn her down but not get killed in the process?"

Terri laughed. "Was she pretty?"

"She was stunning, but she was not you," I said with all honesty.

"Wow, good answer," Terri replied. "Adam, what are we going to do with these boys when we find them?"

I was sullen for a moment. It was a question I had not considered. "I am not sure," I replied. "There is no reversing my effect on them. It may fade over time but could take hundreds of years. It is in their blood and has changed them now until it wears off, or if it ever wears off. I really have no real data to know for sure. I know the women I was with appeared to age over time, but I wonder if I was deceived, or worse, if it just reset them to a different age. Perhaps the concentration creates a seemingly younger age, but it does not limit the actual in any way," I paused, considering my past. "There is also their maturity. Depending on what they do when they discover this newfound immunity, they could strain themselves and cause themselves harm. Worse, they could do as happened with Morgan and her 12. They could turn to evil, and then it may come down to finding a way to kill them."

"It's not really their fault, though, is it?" Terri asked.

"Well, in a way, it is," I replied. "If they had not decided to hurt you and me this would not have happened. That is my big worry. They are skirting the edge of evil now. They were willing to beat someone up for money, perhaps kill them, and did not consider any of the repercussions of their actions. They just did it. That type of mentality means their moral compass isn't exactly pointing true north."

Terri was silent for a moment. "I get that, but they're just kids, right?"

"I have fought in many wars. I really didn't want to, but I have. Men much younger than these fought valiantly and died for their countries, living for positive ideals. I have buried so many of those men, I can no longer easily keep track. We can't just give everyone a pass when they start making decisions that affect other people. When a child decides their paths are more important than another man's life, the idea that he is a child is gone. They have transcended."

Terri was again quiet as we turned down the Curry Road exchange.

There was a police car in front of a house as we approached 9984. The door to the car on the roadside was cracked open.

"Can I ask you to stay in the car?" I said to Terri.

"You can ask," Terri said, "I may not listen."

I laughed. "Please?" I said as I got out and walked around the car. I looked at the houses in the area. No one came out. Police in the area meant trouble or trouble for you. They hid well. I went to the partly open car door. An officer lay in the front seat, prone. I reached down and felt for a pulse on his neck. He was alive, but his pulse was slow.

"Is he dead?" Terri asked from behind me.

"No," I said, "he is just in the car, where you should be."

"Thought you might be missing me," Terri sighed. "I guess I was wrong."

"Will you stay with him?" I pleaded. "See if you can wake him up. No one in this area is going to help willingly."

"Sure," Terri said as I walked towards the open door of the house.

I watched everything as I walked to the door. I slowed my breathing and extended my senses. I heard Terri slapping the police officer, saying "wake up" repeatedly, and wondered if that was her normal bedside manner. I didn't hear anything from the house. I listened carefully but still could hear nothing. I decided to walk into the house through the open door but was very cautious as I did so. As I glanced inside the door, I saw another police officer laying on the floor. He was prone and face down with his gun to the side of his left hand. The Glock 17 had been fired and was jammed with the ejecting shell casing. My supposition was someone had grabbed the weapon as the officer fired, causing the jam.

I scanned side to side and could neither see nor hear anyone in the front living area. A battered couch sat to the right of the room, and an ancient green Lazy-Boy was to the front of the downed officer. I crouched and eased forward until I was near enough to him to feel for a pulse. Grabbing his left wrist, I felt for a pulse, and nothing was there. I then reached up to his neck and felt for a pulse again. Nothing. This was not good.

I made my way down the hallway, listening carefully and watching for any potential threat. As I passed a small bathroom, I glanced inside and wished I had not. The bathroom looked as though it had not been cleaned in a dozen years. That wasn't so bad. The woman laying prone in the bathtub with her eyes open, staring into a space that only she could see, was not a good thing to find. I was guessing the young lady was about 22, with long dark hair and a tattoo of a butterfly on the back of her hand. Without even checking, I knew her neck was broken from the odd angle her body lay. I could do nothing for her and made my way further down the hall to the first bedroom.

I waited and listened; there was no sound, no heartbeat. I entered the first bedroom. Stacks upon stacks of empty McDonald's bags and a series of video games lay next to a big TV. I knew the boy was a football player, but apparently, things had not been going well. Perhaps he was no longer with the team. It was discernable that he had no respect for himself anymore. Besides the trash, the food, and unused textbooks, there was no one in this room. On the bed was a bloody towel, and there was blood all over the room. This must have been the room of the boy who lost his jaw.

I went down the hallway to a second larger bedroom that had two beds in it. There I found more blood on one of the beds but nothing else. This room was neater. Except for the bed that had blood on it, it was very clean. It was a significant contrast to the first room. Again, there was no one there. I heard a sound behind me and spun to find Terri walking down the hall towards me.

"What are you doing in here?" I asked.

"He wasn't waking up, and I can hear sirens in the distance," Terri said. "Did you find anything?"

I looked around on the desk then around the cleaner room and found nothing. I opened a few drawers with a small handkerchief I had, and again I found nothing. "There's nothing evident of where they've gone," I said. "Let's get out of here and try to figure it out from a safe distance."

"I thought you said you had a friend on the force, you know, Shawn, remember?" Terri said in an inquisitive tone.

"I do have a friend on the force, but I would like to keep it that way. Things like this have a way of creating questions that are hard to answer. It would be better if we were at a distance so we can think, watch, and get an idea of the direction the case is going, rather than being in the middle of an officer-down situation."

"The officer in the front room is dead?" Terri asked.

"Yes. I didn't check to see how he died, but he is quite dead. There will be some major issues from this now," I said.

We walked to the front door and out to the car. After getting in the car, I noticed the officer in the squad car starting to move. I put the Impala in drive, and we drove down the street at a normal rate of speed just as three cars skidded in with lights on and sirens blazing. No one paid us a second glance as we drove out onto the main road and disappeared into traffic.

"That might as well have been from a movie," Terri said. "We drove out as they drove in. I thought that only happened in bad detective movies."

"No, that's just how things happen," I smiled as we drove downtown. As we stopped at a light, I sent a quick text to Shawn. It simply said, "Coffee in 15 with Terri." I put my phone away, and we continued driving.

"Where are we going now?" Terri asked.

"I think it's time you meet Shawn," I said. "At a minimum, it will throw suspicion off from us for a while. It will be assumed that we went down just to see him and meet him for coffee. We can also find out what is going on from him indirectly. Then maybe see where they think these boys are going."

"What am I going to say to Shawn?" Terri asked. "I thought we were going tomorrow?"

"This is speeding things up. It may get bad pretty fast. Just tell him what happened this morning. Don't leave anything out, and be as honest as you can. The truth is always the best course of action because nobody expects it. Police rarely expect the truth, so they're suspicious. But when they encounter it, there is trust. I have told Shawn the truth many times only to have him dismiss it, thinking I am not telling the truth."

"That makes sense. I've told people the truth, sometimes, and they have called me a bold-faced liar. It makes more sense to tell the truth, then you never have to worry about remembering what you've said," Terri noted.

"I think that's a good way to do things simply because telling the truth means never having to make anything up. If you don't know? You don't know. If you do know, you can add it in later, but you better have a good reason for leaving it out. I have found that telling everything sometimes makes people laugh. Like when I cut my finger off accidentally when I was cutting onions a long, long time ago. My finger grew back, so no one believed me, and who knows where my finger ended up. When people ask me why I didn't want to cut onions, I say they make me cry and that I once cut my finger off. It always ended up creating an inordinate amount of laughter," I said. "This will go pretty easy, and Shawn will be very nice to you. Just tell him the truth and be yourself."

"The second part is easy," Terri told me. "But the first part. What if I don't know what to say?"

"Then say it, or don't say it." I replied. "People who rattle are usually guilty of something. People who don't remember exactly, well? They just aren't remembering. Most people don't remember what they did yesterday, let alone last Tuesday or something like that. Trauma puts a lot more stress on the situation."

"Okay," Terri said. "What about the boys?"

"They will turn up," I said. "They always do. Someone makes a mistake. If the police find them first, though, it could be interesting. They may be rather resistant to death. I will have to have all the evidence from the house destroyed. There was blood everywhere. It would be hard to find a correlation, but accidents happen, and it could be a real mess."

"Yeah, I considered both as well," Terri said. "Where will we meet Shawn?"

"I usually meet him at the library. They have quiet rooms that work well and keep me out of the police station. Too many questions come up if you walk in a police station," I explained. "Anyway, the librarians there like me."

"Really?" Terri laughed. "Why would librarians like you?"

"I have a unique view of history and literature and have read a lot of books," I replied as I turned on Vine Street. "Librarians spend most of their time helping people. I have recommended many books to them and had numerous discussions about classical literature as well as many of the new authors who are writing in this era."

"I bet they enjoy the interactions," Terri noted. "Most of the librarians I have known spent all their time telling me to hush."

I looked at Terri, began laughing, then smiled at her. "Are you saying you were loud in the library?"

"I like to talk," Terri said. "I think people should talk to each other. It is better than sitting around looking at a book when you can look at a book and interact. It was more fun reading *20,000 Leagues Under the Sea* and talking to my friends about how awesome it would be to be in a submarine going around the world. Or talking about how Joan of Arc must have felt. Just reading opens the imagination but talking to others opens other viewpoints and a world that is even more awe inspiring!"

I watched as she became even more excited.

"Why just read when you can discuss? Why be quiet when you can interact? I mean, to me, walking around a party is a way to see so many more things than just attending. Walking around a library and asking people what they were reading opened my mind to other books, other ideas, and so much fun. The librarians disagreed, though."

I laughed. "Well, I bet they didn't understand your passion for learning."

"No, not really," Terri said. "They played it safe and asked me to be quiet."

I parked in the parking garage next to the library, and we got out and walked to the stairs. The warm Kentucky air was blowing lazily through the courtyard in front of the library as we walked in. I looked at the huge frame of the library and the wall of marble that had been so controversial for a while. I laughed at the thought of people being up in arms for supporting a third-world group of workers but knew that small minds often made big decisions, and those decisions could change the world. As we walked into the library, we were greeted by volunteers, and I asked if we could use one of the rooms. I got my expected answer, "Ask at the desk."

Hillary Winkel was at the desk today. A woman of about 70 with bright red hair and a still thin figure. Hillary was smart, spunky, and always full of questions. "Adam," she began, "I have missed you so. It has been a while since I have seen you. How are things going? What are you reading this week? Have you written anything yet? I would really like to see one of your amazing stories published. Who is this young lady with you?"

"Hillary," I said, "This is Terri. Terri, this is Hillary." I laughed for a moment. "Hillary and I have known each other for a few years, and she is your main competition at snagging me." I winked at Hillary.

"Really?" Terri said in mock anger, "You bring me to your girlfriend's place?"

"I did see him first," Hillary said, "I will share, though. I just have to hear your story sometime, but I bet you are here to see Shawn. He is already upstairs in Room D. He seems a little on edge. I hope you can help him."

"Me too," I said as we walked up the stairs to the level with the conference rooms.

"Help him? Terri whispered, "You do this often?"

"Sometimes. I see patterns and help the police out, not often, but anytime I see Hillary, they are looking for help. I guess you could say I am a silent consultant. Hillary figured it out, but she jokes about it more than anything. I would come in, and in a few days, there would be a solution." We reached the top of the steps and walked a short path to a small conference room that would fit about eight people comfortably. Inside, with the door open, waiting and looking at his phone, was Shawn Dennis. He turned, stood, and nodded.

"I got here a little early so I could relax for 15 seconds," Shawn said. "We have a bit of a crisis right now. Routine summons delivery and one of my officers was killed. The city is going crazy. A second was injured seriously, and of course, no one saw anything. The three tenants at the rental house are missing. We don't know if it was them or someone else. The whole house looked like a warzone. Two of the beds were soaked in blood, and we don't even know whose blood it is."

"I am sorry, Terri, we haven't met, and I know this may be a shock to you. I am used to ranting around Adam." Shawn said as he held out his hand to Terri.

"It's okay," Terri said, "I'm a big girl. I can handle it. We have met. I dated your brother for a little while. He talked about you a lot. How is he?"

"He is out of touch right now. If you dated him, you know he does that sometimes." Shawn paused for a second. "You seem to look a lot better than Adam described you. How are you feeling?" Shawn asked.

"I am okay, I think," Terri said. "It has been quite the day. I have known Adam less than a full 24 hours, and I already feel like my life has changed."

"For the better, I hope," Shawn said. "Have a seat; this won't take long. I just have a few questions."

"I hope I can answer them," Terri responded.

"I am sure you can," Shawn said. "Tell me about last night?"

"Which part?" Terri said.

"Start wherever and go from there," Shawn replied.

"Well, I met Adam at an event out at a farm last night. You know, the bourbon tasting event? He and I were having a good time, and we left." Shawn glanced at me as Terri continued, "We stopped by Adam's house and changed his shirt because I spilled bourbon on it. Then, we were going out to eat at Tolly-Ho, and that's all I remember."

"That's all?" Shawn said, "What was your next memory?"

"Waking up at Adam's house and him taking care of me," Terri said. "I'm not sure what happened, but I have no memory past that point. I have spent the day with Adam, and he has been nothing but a gentleman."

"Were you given a drink by anyone that could have contained Rohypnol?" Shawn asked.

"No," Terri said, "I would have had to have had it early in the night, and I remember everything else."

"Could you have had too much to drink?" Shawn asked.

"That is possible. I am not used to drinking Pappy," Terri replied.

"You were drinking Pappy?" Shawn asked, "Must have been some rich people there. Do you remember seeing Sam Carraway?"

"Sam," Terri said, "Yes, we saw him at the farm. He and I dated a long time ago, but he left. I didn't see him afterwards."

"Adam tells me you were shot," Shawn stated, "Were you?"

"It turned out to have bounced off my wallet. You know, one of those metal ones. Adam said that too, but I don't remember. It must have knocked me out." Terri replied.

"Last question," Shawn said, "Are you in danger now? Do you feel unsafe in any way?" Shawn again glanced at me.

"Not at all," Terri said, "With you two around, I feel nothing could get to me."

"Are you sure?" Shawn asked Terri again.

"Absolutely," Terri replied. "I have never felt better in my entire life."

"All right," Shawn said, "I will assume this is closed, and I have a cop killer to find," Shawn said as he stood. "Adam, it is always a pleasure, but this was a little more awkward, and I'm sorry for that. Some weird things happened today, and I'll get to the bottom of it one way or another."

"I am sure you will," Adam said. "Any leads on your cop killer?"

"None so far," Shawn said, "but we are looking and looking for the three boys who live in the house where the officer was killed."

"Are the boys suspects?" Adam asked.

"Not really," Shawn said, "Coroner says the force used to kill Rodriguez was almost mechanical. We may be looking for someone who is either really big or is carrying something like a hammer or bat. I expect they'll turn up, maybe even turn themselves in."

"It happens that way sometimes?" Terri asked.

"Yep," Shawn said, "A lot of people can't live with themselves when they do something as horrible as murder. Then there are others who don't feel a thing and still others that can rationalize it out. It's why so many soldiers get PTSD. They just can't handle knowing they've killed someone, and it causes a bit of a problem in their mind."

"I have a lot of friends that couldn't handle it," Adam said, "It eats you up inside."

"How'd you do?" Shawn asked.

"I flew the medivac chopper. I still think about all the people I brought back, but I didn't have to fight." I said truthfully. In Iraq, I had flown a medivac helicopter, and as such, everything I said was true. Unfortunately, it was not the only war I had fought.

"Took the easy way," Shawn said.

"Easy?" I replied, "You try flying 20 missions a day in the heat of it all with a big cross that looks like a target to Taliban."

"I suppose so," Shawn said.

Shawn was different this time. I wasn't sure what he thought he knew, but his body language was different with me. At first, I thought it was Terri, but I soon realized it was not. It was something else. Something was bugging him, so I walked out as he did and waved Terri back.

"Shawn," I said as we entered the atrium, "Are you okay? You seem angry with me."

"Adam, I have known you for quite a while, but someone saw your car in the Curry area where everything happened. Does this have anything to do with you?" Shawn asked. "Don't fuck with me right now. I have a bunch of officers who want justice, and I need to know. When one of the cars was coming in, they saw you at the light next to Speedway."

"I got gas at Speedway today," I said, knowing I could not back it up. "Well, I was going to get gas but realized I only had cash with me and didn't want to go in. I'm at half a tank now. I'm sure their cameras could see me pull in and out."

"I doubt it," Shawn said, "They are still using VHS recorders from the 90s. We have pulled tapes before, and the snow is so thick you would think you were in Alaska."

"Do you think I would hurt a cop?" I asked.

Shawn looked at me, shook his head again, then sighed. "No, you would never. I'm just tired. We'll catch this guy and have no more problems."

"I am yours if you need me," I said, "If you need anything, just let me know. If you need to talk, I will be there for you, and I will nose around and see if I see anything."

"Don't get too involved," Shawn said, "Let me look into everything. It would be better if you took Terri home and took a few days off."

"I may just do that," I said.

"It would really be a good idea, Adam. The best thing right now is to let us take care of everything. We are more equipped to find whoever this is and handle it. I don't know for sure what happened with you this morning, but I'm hopeful it doesn't have anything to do with what's going on right now." Shawn said.

"I understand," I replied. "Terri's a little afraid to stay at home right now. She and I are going to hang out for a little while and try to enjoy the rest of the evening. The biggest trouble we will get into is deciding which wine to drink and what pizza parlor to order from. Will that be okay?"

"That would be perfect," Shawn said. "Thanks for coming down with her, glad she wasn't shot. Did you take her to the hospital?"

"No, I didn't take her to the hospital. When I found out it was just a ricochet, I left it alone. She didn't want to go to the hospital either, and I can respect that. I really hate hospitals," I said.

"Well, you should consider getting her checked out," Shawn said. "You never know if there's any type of internal damage. I would hate for you to be responsible for such a pretty woman having problems."

"Speaking of pretty women, how is your wife?" I asked.

"She is doing okay, now," Shawn said with a little remorse, "We were having some serious problems after her mom died, but somehow things just worked their way out. It's amazing how sometimes things like that happen."

"If you ever need help with anything, you know I would be there," I said.

"How can you say that after I just treated you the way that I did?" Shawn said, "With all the help you've given me already, it was horrible for me to assume you could have anything to do with a cop getting hurt, let alone killed."

"You have to go where the evidence leads you, Shawn," I said. "If I was in the wrong place at the wrong time, I would fully expect you to investigate me completely. After all, I would do the same thing if it were you, and probably a little more so, just to prove your innocence."

"That means a lot coming from you, Adam," Shawn said, "We'll keep in touch with you as this unfolds; still, you should stay out of it."

"I'll do my best," I smiled.

Shawn shook his head and turned and walked down the stairs, shaking his head all the way. I turned and walked back into the room with Terri. She was sitting there looking at me, smiling. I felt good about it. I was a little concerned because I had never felt this good in my entire life. I was worried that something would take it away from me or that this was some cruel dream that I would wake up from and find she was no longer there. I walked up to her and held her. It felt good. It was nice to have someone tall give me a hug and nice to have someone who cared to be there with me. I sincerely hoped that this was the beginning of a long time of happiness. I knew I had no reason to expect happiness in the world. In fact, I knew the world was full of sadness, but for now, my goal was to enjoy all the time that I had with Terri, however long or short it was.

"How did that go?" Terri asked.

"It went pretty well," I said, "Someone saw my car leaving the Speedway near Curry, and Shawn was concerned why I would be there. I explained that I stopped to get gas but didn't have anything but cash on me and left. He was satisfied with it, and there is no way to verify it, so it won't be a big deal. I hate lying to Shawn, even though it is to protect him. He has suggested that you and I go home and stay out of everything. Obviously, right now, it is getting late, so part of that is a good idea, but I will have to listen close and determine if I have to get involved, if the boys show up again."

"What are we going to do right now?" Terri asked.

I looked at my phone and checked the text messages. I got three. The first one was an alert that the garage opened. The second was an alert the garage had closed, and the third was a text from Phillip stating that my issue was being taken care of right then. With the house empty again, I knew it was time to go home and wait. I suppose if Terri wasn't there, I would have gone searching for the boys. From the police perspective, Garret would turn up later and would not be an issue as he had an ironclad alibi in Cincinnati. I didn't know what was going to happen with the other two boys, but I was concerned that it was about to become a difficult situation.

"We'll go to the house and see what happens," I said.

"Sounds good," Terri said as she skipped down the stairs.

I followed her, considering all the permutations of this moment and all the complexities that could follow. It was like some ridiculous math problem with sides changing every instant, and I knew there was a solution; I just had to find it.

Chapter 10

As we left the parking lot, traffic was a bit heavier. This was the second time I had been in Lexington in the last 100 years. I had always liked Lexington because it was busy enough that I could get anything but small enough that I could easily get anywhere. Being larger also had the side effect of allowing me to fade into the crowd as people were not paying a ton of attention like they would in a smaller town. I had found though, that since about the year 2000, the city had boomed and traffic and had become a big issue. A trip that normally would have taken 5 minutes could now take 15 to 20, and where I used to be able to go from downtown to my home near New Circle in under 10 minutes, it sometimes could take an hour. As I pulled out to Main Street from the alternate entrance of the parking garage, I knew today would be one of those days. Main Street was backed up solid, and it was plain that Broadway would be as difficult.

"Traffic really sucks," Terri said, "there really is no way around it anymore. I liked it a lot better when the town was a little smaller."

I reached over for a moment and squeezed Terri's hand, "It's funny, I was thinking exactly the same thing."

Terri laughed as we started inching forward, "Why don't you tell me more about Derbent."

"Yes, you will need to know all of this at some point, so good idea," I considered where I had left off when we were last talking. "As I was saying at the restaurant, Magda was very jealous. Morgan was there and sat with me a lot. It seemed to bother Magda. I was still having sex between 20 and 40 times a day with the 13 women, but Morgan and Magda were noticeably vying for my affections. I really didn't understand any of this at the time. I had amassed a great deal of knowledge, but I had very little practical application and virtually nothing of what people refer to as "street smarts." Instead, I made assumptions based on what I knew, and both women tried to explain to me how much I meant to them. Looking back on it, I can easily see that both wanted what I gave them, eternal youth and eternal life. Neither of them really loved me or cared about me instead, they coveted me for what I gave them. With the news of Connor and his strange affliction that allowed him to live far too long, our small area was being assailed. Fortunately, Magda was no fool and had never given Connor easy access to my chambers. Questions were being asked that were becoming more and more difficult to deal with. The women, all 13 of them, decided that it was time to move so that we could no longer be easily found. I remember the day that all of them, except Morgan and Magda, left. They had amassed many fortunes as they all were easily able to understand and manipulate people with their constantly growing knowledge and wisdom. I was actually impressed at how well they had done, or at least I would be later when I understood everything that happened."

We finally turned on South Broadway, and the traffic was just as bad. People were in foul moods, but it didn't matter to either Terri or me. She looked at me with an inquisitive nature that I had never seen, and I was enjoying her attentive personality.

I continued, "Morgan and Magda became increasingly antagonistic towards each other. It was then, on an evening I will never forget, that Magda came to me while Morgan was out in the city. She asked me an easy question that I had no good answer for. She asked me if she was able to kill Morgan. If you think about it, it was kind of funny to me. I had no real concept of death as I had not died. Since I walked into Morgan's life, all I had experienced was eating, drinking, having sex, and taking care of basic bodily functions. I could defend myself and didn't like pain. I had not felt pain since those first few weeks when Morgan found me. I was fascinated by Magda's curiosity about how to kill someone. She was kind to me. She was also observably angry. Because I was just with her and Morgan, they had far more time with me, and Magda was more attentive. It was during this time that Magda tried to teach me love. She said to me often that love was a deep feeling that bound two people together. I didn't understand anything about being bound except that I was tied at almost all times. Magda spent significant time finding the different things that caused me pleasure. She took me to the edge of orgasm and held me there as long as she could, and then as I went over, I was lost in the sensations. She tried other things, and all of them were attempting to get me to have a longing for her."

I kept driving, and we were getting close to the less-busy areas. It was nice to see us moving, but it was still slow going.

I continued explaining my past, "Morgan was more attentive as well. She was not competing as Magda was and seemed oblivious to Magda's need to destroy her. Instead, she tried to treat me far nicer than I had been treated before. We still had servants there, and they would bring in hot water that was boiled on fires outside of the chamber. We would take long hot baths together and then spend time in bed for hours with no apparent rhyme or reason except for me to fill her with more of my seed. Where Magda was competing, Morgan was enjoying the time. Perhaps it was because Morgan was older when all of this started, or she just understood a little more. Both women were now over 700 years old, and both women had amassed great respect and massive fortunes.

The 11 women that were sent out were supposed to build another area and then come back for us. I was unaware of this at the time, though. It's a funny thing when you have unlimited time. The passing of it just doesn't seem very important. One day, Morgan and Magda both came to me and said it had been 10 years since the others left, and they were concerned that they would never be back. Both of them asked if I was ready to go out into the world with them and find a new home."

"They were trying to be nice to you now?" Terri asked.

"No, this was to be the day that changed everything. They were not asking for me to go with both of them; they were asking which one I was going to go with. Like you, I didn't understand the question at first. I told them the three of us could go anywhere, but I asked if they could set me free. At that point, Magda and Morgan began fighting. Since I was tied up, I could not interfere. I watched as the two women fought. It looked like something out of a really bad movie in today's cinema. As each woman would draw blood or cause pain to the other it would nearly instantly heal. Not as fast as I can heal, but enough that they could have fought forever, and nothing would have changed. It progressed from knife to sword, then sword to axe, then axe to hammer, and still neither could gain an advantage. Their clothes were ripped and shredded, but their bodies were perfectly intact. There was blood on the floor of the chambers pooling in places." I paused for a moment, thinking about that night.

I continued as I saw Terri hungrily waiting for more, "After what I now know was about six hours, the two women stopped, looked at each other, and laughed. I was confused at first at how they were so angry and then began laughing at each other. I soon realized the complexities of the two women were far beyond my imagination of the time. For a very ancient person, I was still very naïve. As Magda and Morgan hugged each other, I realized Morgan had another intention. Morgan picked up one of the swords laying to the side of their fight, and as Magda walked towards me, Morgan decapitated her. At the time, I did not understand what was going on. I knew something was wrong. Magda's body was still moving, and her head was looking around, amazingly still alive. Morgan had other ideas and had apparently thought more about Magda's question to me and came up with her own answers.

She picked up Magda's head and looked into her eyes. I could see the look of fury that Magda gave her as Morgan tossed her into the fire pit. Morgan was not done. Using the sword, she hacked off Magda's arms and legs and threw them into the fire as well. She then took her time and sliced through Magda's torso, quartering it. With little care, she removed each of Magda's organs and threw them into the fire individually. Finally, she threw the remaining four quarters of her torso into the fire and tossed the blade into the edge of the fire as well. It was evident Morgan had considered blood as a potential vector. She poured oil on all of Magda's blood on the stone floor and then lit that on fire. I remember the room smelled like barbeque or some fantastic animal being cooked to eat. I knew it was Magda and had no appetite, and I didn't know why. I had little concept of right or wrong, but I had just watched Morgan kill someone who was practically immortal, and all I felt was a slight thought about missing being with Magda. It was not love or anything similar; it was just knowing that she would never be there again."

"Now it was just you and Morgan alone with whatever servants she had, right?" Terri asked.

"That's right," I replied, "Morgan now had me to herself. As it had begun, so it was again, and Morgan clearly had a plan. She lay with me once more, and then she had servants come in and bathe and clothe me. I was dressed in slave clothing, but it was clean. I waited alone in the room that had been my home for over 700 years until finally, Morgan and the servants came back and let me out into the air."

"What was that like?" Terri asked.

"If you remember, the last time I was outside, it was cold and winter. As I was let out into the bright sunlight, it was warm in the height of summer. I can remember, as if it was yesterday, the smell of flowers. Roses and honeysuckle filled the air, and so much more. There were animals making noises all around, and the smell of people and animals was both pleasant and foul. I was ushered into a wagon drawn by several animals. I had no issues, and though I was still tied, I was enjoying being outside. I am sure I looked strange surveying all of the sights for the first time. I was still a child in many ways, even as old as I was since I had never really experienced anything. I did have the gift of language, and I could understand many of the people around me. I listened as I do now and heard people talking about their family or trading or their animals and most of it made no sense to me. As I listened, a few people talked about Morgan and the 13 families of witches who lived in the area. I had no concept of the word 'witch' and asked the servant who was sitting next to me. I had never really interacted with the servants before, and it was then that I realized that the woman next to me had no tongue. Later I learned the 13 women had servants but always made sure they could tell no one of what was happening inside my chambers. The woman looked at me with pleading eyes, and it was unmistakable that she too was as much of a prisoner as I was. "

"Wow," Terri exclaimed. "What a way to ensure control."

We passed the hospital, and traffic began to pick up again. We were soon coming up on Alexandria Drive, and I turned there to get back to Parkers Mill and my house. I was glad to be almost home.

"We can continue when we get to the house if you like," I said.

"Maybe," Terri said, "I think I want to nap again; should I be tired again?"

"I am sure you should," I said. "We have pushed pretty hard today. We can take it easy at the house."

"That sounds like the best idea ever," Terri said as we turned down Parkers Mill.

We talked about the drive and the horse farms in the area, and soon we were pulling into my garage. As we got out of the car, Terri grabbed the cover.

"Just leave it, we may go out later," I said.

"Sounds good to me," Terri smiled and came to me. Grabbing my hand, she led me towards the house. It felt good to be home with Terri. As I closed the garage, I felt a little bit of happiness. It was a good feeling that would not last.

Chapter 11

I paused for a moment, frustrated that Garret had been able to get in without my detecting him. I opened the door again for a moment and looked around the pristine garage with the covered cars and the uncovered Impala until I was satisfied that we were alone.

"Garret got you a little spooked, didn't he?" Terri asked.

"It's usually pretty hard to sneak up on me," I said. "I've been paying attention to everything around me for so long that anything out of place automatically makes me a little antsy."

"I bet it's pretty easy to get into the habit of not having anyone around, isn't it?" Terri said.

"It's also pretty lonely not having anyone around. I know. I've been used to it for longer than anyone should have been used to it, but that doesn't make it easy," I said. "After I ended up alone the first time, I wandered for years, wondering if I had done the right thing."

"Are you telling me that you got away after being chained or roped up or whatever for 700 plus years, and you missed it?" Terri asked.

"Of course not," I said. "I'm just noting that I, at least, had human company around, and I, at least, had someone to pass the time with. A great many authors have written about it, but none have really hit the mark. To put it simply, even a tormentor is a person who is spending time with you; and it is far better than the torment you instill upon yourself when you are alone."

"Yeah, that makes sense," Terri smiled. "I've been alone before as well, and since I was alone, I went out with some pretty stupid guys just to have somebody around."

"Same thing," I said. "I've known a lot of women that are the same way. They get into a relationship that is very difficult, but they don't want to leave because it's better than being alone. I often wonder if these women started supporting each other instead of looking for some man if things would change. They might eliminate most of the men in the world. After all, that was one of the goals of the 13 women holding me captive.

They had far more reason to dislike men in their time than women do in this time, and still they ended up making bad decisions and ending up in worse situations."

"I stopped you from talking, but I feel a little better for moving around," Terri said, "Why don't we go in the bedroom and lie down? You can keep talking for a while. I think I'm okay to listen."

We walked down the long hallway to the master bedroom. I had not made the bed since Terri was there before, and she climbed under the covers as if it was her own with clothes on. Her right hand was out, and she patted the bed next to her, beckoning me to come lay there.

"I'm in," I said.

"Not yet," Terri giggled with a wry smile and an air of suggestion.

"Maybe I should be," I said.

Terri smiled as I moved to the bed, then got in next to her. We were facing each other eye to eye, and I peered into her eyes for several moments while she looked at me with that near-mystical twinkle.

We kissed. It was slow, almost experimental. Our breath was light, as though we were holding on to our air, fearing it would be taken away. I kissed her again and felt her lips part. The tip of her tongue barely brushed my inner lips. I gasped ever so quietly. It had been so long. The kiss was always the part that took my breath away. I held her face and brushed her hair aside so that I could kiss her with more passion. In a matter of moments, we went from soft and sensual to needy and powerful. I held her tight and realized she was holding me just as tight. Our kiss had such urgency as though we needed each other and could not get enough. As our tongues intertwined, she became more aggressive and forced her tongue upon me. I was lost in the moment. Over thousands of years, very few had kissed me as this woman was, and it was urging me to do more and more.

My hands were everywhere but nowhere. I caressed the small of her back and held her as I kissed her neck. I felt her body stiffen as I slowly worked my way down to her shoulder. It was evident that she was lost in the moment as much as I was. I was so excited it felt like I had been drinking alcohol. My mind was everywhere but always focused on her. I slowly lifted her shirt and began kissing her tight stomach, rubbing her shoulders, and occasionally touching her face. Each time I touched her face, she would kiss my hand and shake near uncontrollably. She seemingly wanted more and more.

I took her shirt off in one motion, she removed her bra, and her breasts stood near perfect in front of me. I felt as though I were once again an animal. I knew what I wanted. I would please her, not as I was taught but as I knew she would want to be pleased. I spent time paying attention to her every move, down to the quivers in her body and the movements at every angle. I quickly learned what she needed and gave all I could to give her more sensations and greater pleasure until she had a massive uncontrollable orgasm.

"Oh, my god," Terri panted. "That was, well, unexpected."

I smiled and held her tight. "I'm glad," I said. "I never want to be predictable."

"That was definitely unpredictable," Terri replied.

Terri caught her breath rapidly and turned her attention to me. She mounted me as our bodies were soaked in sweat, and I was lost in the sensations she gave me. She was slow and easy, paying close attention to me as I had to her. After what felt like forever, I started to build until I could no longer hold my orgasm. I felt much different. For 700 years, I came dozens of times a day, and it had never been like this. I gasped for a moment and screamed lightly, then slowly sunk towards the bed. Terri fell upon me. We were both drenched with sweat.

I held her in my arms and never wanted to let go. I looked at her and she looked back at me, her golden hair wet with sweat but a smile upon her face.

"You are amazing," I said.

"So are you," Terri replied.

It was as though a door had opened. As she lay curled inside my arm, I was at peace and felt better than I had felt for as long as I could remember. My breathing slowed. I held Terri while I pulled the sheet over both of us. We lay there. As I caressed her shoulder and moved her hair away from her face, she put her hand on my chest and held it there. Her heart rate slowed as her breathing slowed. I could hear it and feel it, and I felt as though my senses were even more acute than normal. In a few moments, she was asleep on me.

I thought about the past, the present, and the future. As I did, hope sparked. I felt as though the future may well be brighter than I could have ever known. I lived the equivalent of a hundred lives, but now I had an opportunity for more than ever. Now, I had an opportunity to truly live.

As I pondered my old life and my new life with Terri, my mind drifted. In a matter of moments, I too was asleep.

Chapter 12

I dreamed.

I had not dreamed in so long with any clarity that it was a new feeling for me. Many of my dreams were fraught with the horrors of war and all of the things that I had done in my past that were less than positive. In many ways, I was a monster. At least, many people thought me one. My time with the 13 women taught me not to trust. Each time they dangled things over my head to keep me under control, only to eliminate them at the last moment. I grew used to this disappointment, even though I didn't know what disappointment was really. To me, it was the way of things. As the days turned into years, my trust faded away. I simply stopped asking.

Terri asked me why I didn't escape. As much as I was imprisoned by the 13 women, their servants, and their small army, I was more a prisoner of myself. In my dream, I remembered feeling angry one day when they took away one of my rewards. Honestly, as I dreamed, I remembered that it was not so much malicious as they simply didn't remember promising me extra time to talk. Instead, as were most days, I was used and then left by one woman after another. I was well aware that these women had beauty in some way or form, but it really didn't affect me. After all, there were 13 women, and each of these 13 women had their selfish needs for me.

In between two of the women, when I did not get my extra time, I pulled on the ropes, perhaps for the first time in many years. When I did so, the rope snapped under the strain of my muscles, and I was free. I had tested these ropes early on, but between the sweat, the oils, and everything else, the rope simply degraded. Either that or my constant exercise in between women had made me even stronger. I often realized how much stronger I was than everyone, but I was a prisoner of my own mind. In my dream, that realization was pointed out to me very clearly.

The dream took an interesting turn, though. As I lay in chains, not ropes, Terri walked into the room. She walked up to me, her dress dropping to the floor, and she was naked. She kissed me lightly and then touched the chains on my legs and arms. Suddenly the chains were gone.

I was free. As I stood, she embraced me and, in my dream, I felt the warmth of her body.

I woke with a start. The room was dark. I could see the outlines of everything. Terri was still asleep, her shoulder between my arm and body. Her hand was on my chest. Her leg was draped over the top of mine. I slowed my breath to listen and could hear her heartbeat ever so rhythmically. This was like a dream come true. I leaned in to kiss her forehead, smiling to myself.

"You're up again?" Terri asked.

"I had a dream," I said.

"Feeling a lot like Martin Luther King, now?" Terri asked.

"No," I said. "It was not that kind of dream. I dreamed of you, and you would set me free. You were naked, and you set me free. I was my own prisoner by my own hand, and you set me free."

"Nice dream," Terri said.

"It was even nicer than that because you were in it," I replied.

"Was I better than your 13 women?" Terri asked.

"I know it will seem like a line, but there is no comparison. In all the years that I remember, I have never felt the pure passion that I feel for you. Nor have I ever had anyone pay such close attention to me that I could lose control," I said.

"Thank you," Terri said. "That means a lot to me."

"Thank you," I said; "for changing my view of the world in a matter of minutes."

"Tell me about them," Terri said.

"About who?" I asked.

"Tell me about the 13 women. You have said a little about Morgan and Magda, but you have left out details. What were they like?" Terri prodded.

"I didn't think you'd want to hear about that," I said as I considered Terri's request, "It was a long time ago, and I am not sure what happened to all of them."

"I'd really like to know," Terri stared at me in the dim light. "Call it morbid curiosity, but I would like to know what type of women would keep a man hostage for so long."

"After living for as long as I have, I believe just about anyone would have done the same thing," I said. "After all, if given the promise of eternal life, how many people would sacrifice someone else? Think about it. The whole basis of Christianity is built on one person's sacrifice to give a great number of people eternal life. How many Christians truly think about that gift?"

"I understand," Terri said, "I also understand that if you don't want to tell me, that would be okay. After all, it's in the past."

"No, I'll tell you," I said. "I was getting to that point anyway. Where it would make sense, and where you would understand more about me and more about the decision that I made with you."

"I know it's difficult," Terri said, "but I appreciate it. I truly appreciate what you've done for me even though I still don't fully understand it."

"Well, this will take a little bit," I said. "Let me start by saying that I knew each of these women, their wants, their desires, and more. I will stay relatively high level, but if you would like more information, just let me know. There's still a lot to tell after I left Derbent, but I think this is a good way to introduce you to the next stages that I faced."

I paused and took a deep breath. I usually tried to put these 13 women out of my mind, but of course, they invaded from time to time. They had all shaped who I became and how I felt about the world. I considered how I wanted to start then thought the best way was from the beginning.

"The first woman I met was, of course, Morgan," I began. "When I met her, as you know, she was an older woman. She told me many times that she was preparing to die before that day that I happened upon her hut. She lived a good life, loved one man, and was childless. The man she loved was killed in a scuffle between two tribes. After spending time with me and becoming younger, Morgan had long dark hair and a dark complexion on an oval face. Her eyes were a beautiful blue, and they gave her an exotic quality that most men would be drawn to without question. She was very thin but had ample bosoms, and her thighs were well-shaped. She would have borne children easily if only she had been able. One thing I have not mentioned is after all the time I spent with these women, not one ever became pregnant. It seems whatever made me made it impossible for me to give children to most women, or at least all I have come into contact with so far. Morgan really loved life and enjoyed learning and talking to other people. She spent a significant amount of time during our time together learning about herbs and other healing methods from the Far East, what is now China. Many people would come to her for her simple cures, and she enjoyed helping people, which is what started the entire ordeal. I often wonder how things would have gone if we had not traded my services for a few carts of food."

"Magda was the second woman I met," I continued. "She was the older woman at the bazaar that traded food for a chance to be young again. By the standards of the times, Magda was quite educated and had sufficient power because of her husband and his stature to be a great trader. She continued to trade even after she looked far younger. Where Morgan wanted to help people, Magda had no use for people. Magda was used to getting her way in any situation, and no matter how difficult the decision, Magda was willing to make it. It was Magda that brokered the deal with the additional 11 women to create the group. Her thought was the group of 13 women with the gift that I gave them would be able to manipulate the world. Magda had great vision but did not realize how big the world was or how difficult it would be even over the span of several lifetimes. Magda was a tall woman for the time, about 5'10". She had flowing chestnut hair and deep dark eyes. Even though her eyes were brown, they often looked black as night. Magda was constantly looking for affirmation of who she was. I believe it is partly why she wanted first another man, and then me, to herself. It was Magda who decided to remove the tongues of the servants. It was also Magda who would have killed anyone to protect the secret of me. There were hundreds of years that I thought Morgan was softer of heart and Magda a tyrant. I realized that was wrong as the years moved forward."

"Magda's sister was Tina. I had a difficult time with her real name, so everyone began calling her that. At first, Tina was a shy woman. When I met her, she was plump and aged with faded red hair and lifeless grey eyes. After being with me for a few days, she became younger with bright red hair and vibrant blue eyes. Over the span of a few weeks, she began losing weight and, by the end of six months, she was thin and beautiful with flowing red hair and a white complexion similar to that of a porcelain doll. When she went outside, she would often come back in with a sunburn which would heal almost immediately. I would say that prior to me, she had trouble with her skin in the sun. Tina was always very kind to me but kept her distance because she seemed to understand the evil inside of her sister. It was always noticeable that Tina was afraid of Magda, as many of the women were. Only Morgan had no fear of Magda, and it was Morgan that always stood up for me and made certain I was well taken care of each day. Tina had a voice like a siren, and as she sang, you could do nothing but stop and listen. In my later life, when I read mythology, I often wondered if Tina had survived, and her voice had lured sailors to the rocks, and their deaths, as she sang to them."

"Nya was a younger woman when she first joined the group. She was a fur trader and knew Magda, and Magda ended up bringing her to the group. I would say most of the women were in their 50s or 60s, or at least looked like that by modern standards when they first came to me. I could not be sure as I have realized the lifespan of the human race has changed over the years, and not only do people live longer, but they also look younger. I would guess Nya was in her 20s or 30s. Nya did not change significantly when we were together, except that over time, she became exotically beautiful. When I first met Nya, she had short hair that was cut as though someone hacked it off. Over time, her hair grew out and was jet black, glistening like morning fire. She had olive skin and could have been from China or somewhere else in the Far East. Most striking about Nya was her emerald-green eyes. To this day, I have never found anyone with eyes so bright and so inquisitive. Of all of the women, Nya was the most experimental with me. She took her time and tried to find more and more ways of pushing me to an orgasm. I am told she was a brilliant negotiator, but I never saw that part of her as it happened outside of the room."

"Maura," I continued, "was a beautiful woman even when she looked older. Maura was originally in charge of a small cooperative at the edge of town. She and Morgan were acquainted, and Morgan brought her into the group. Maura had a vibrance about her and was very talkative. She taught me diction in the language and was constantly trying to help me remember who I was. After she spent time with me, her auburn hair shone in almost any light. Her massive breasts turned the guards' heads whenever they came in. Of all of the women of the 13, I expected her to be the easiest to deal with. After only a few weeks, I found that she could go from perfectly nice to horridly awful in a matter of seconds. She often threw clay pots in her anger, and I watched her kill one of the servants for spilling her food on the floor as if it was nothing. Although I did not fear her, nor have I really feared anyone, I always kept a watchful eye on where she was and what she was doing."

"I bet she was bipolar," Terri said.

"I'm sure you're right," I said. "Of course, there was no way to diagnose anything like that at that time. The herbs and simple tonics that Morgan learned were often considered like magic. Any type of real medicine or psychiatry would have had you stoned."

"Did she continue being nice to you or was Maura a problem?" Terri asked.

"I was always safe," I replied. "Like I said, Morgan was constantly protecting me from anything that could have happened. It was undeniable to all of the women that Morgan was in charge of me, even though Magda could easily have been considered the leader of the group."

"This makes me want to go back to where you left off, leaving Derbent," Terri said.

"I can do either," I said. "Which would you like to do?"

"Will you introduce the rest as you tell the rest of what you need to tell me?" Terri asked.

"Of course, I will," I said. "They're all part of what you need to know. If not in my story, then later as we talk. We have time."

"Then start where you were in the back of the cart with the girl with no tongue leaving the city with Morgan," Terri said with wide eyes. "Magda had just been cut to pieces and burned."

"As I said, I discovered the woman with me had no tongue," I continued, "She was a woman of about 30 and worn by a hard life. She wore peasant's clothes, and I didn't know how long she had been there. Servants came and left a lot. I did not have time to get to know any of them. In fact, it was strongly discouraged that I spend any time with them. If you think about it, it made good sense. The servants and guards were rotated. None of them realized all of the things that were going on, or how the 13 women and I did not age at all. The woman with no tongue helped me get situated and sat next to me. Two guards drove the cart. Morgan followed to the side of us on horseback. Another cart followed us that I later found had tradeable goods inside of it. The women had amassed quite a fortune, but the 11 who left took most of it to establish a new colony. Morgan now knew, as did I, that we would not likely see them again. Since I have grown older, I feel that their betrayal made Morgan even more cruel, and she was not going to allow it to happen again."

I took a deep breath and looked at Terri for a moment before I continued. "I do not know how long we were in the cart. We stopped many times for food and water and to take care of basic needs. At night, we would sleep, and Morgan would have me several times. She was far gentler now that it was only her. In the mornings, when we woke, she would take me again. I was no longer in ropes, chains, nor held at all, but I had nowhere to go, so I stayed with her. There were several times that we would camp for days. As we neared mountains, Morgan rode ahead with one of the guards while the rest stayed with me. I didn't think anything of this but looking back now, this was very out of character for her. Before she left each time, she told me she was going to negotiate our passage. I understood the words but didn't understand why we would have to negotiate going anywhere. Every moment I was outside in the cart or walking alongside it I was taking in all the wonders of the world. It seemed as though new, strange, and fascinating were now my norm. I found later that we were approaching several larger cities that would become the beginnings of the Roman Empire. That would not be for hundreds of years. After many days of travel, we finally stopped. While we waited for Morgan and the guards to return, two of the guards began sparring. They used staffs and would fight until one of them was knocked to the ground. I was fascinated with this type of interaction. I had never seen anything like it."

"You had never really fought anyone at that time, right?" Terri asked.

"No, I had never fought anyone," I said, "but I heard them talk of it. The women mumbled about it often. Of course, I saw the women fight. I also saw the fight between Magda and Morgan. It's kind of funny. If you put 13 women in close quarters, there will eventually be fights."

"If you put two women in a room with a man there will eventually be fights," Terri said.

I laughed hard. Terri was good at making me laugh. It was a pleasant change from my normally boring nights, reading another book or writing some poem in my journal. "I agree with you. At the time, I didn't know I would agree with you, but I absolutely do now. Over the years since then, I have found that being in the proximity of several women or several men can be entertaining. Men have a different code, apparently, and are quick to forgive, but I have seen women with a tenacity that would terrify a tiger."

"I know a few of them," Terri said.

I laughed again. "As I sat watching these men spar, I was fascinated by their movements. After about 30 minutes, one of the men fell again and laughed. Both men saw me watching, and both men had kept their distance. Knowing how the servants were treated, they did not want to lose their tongues. Still, they saw my curiosity. The man who was laughing held out his staff to me. I was curious, curiosity seemed to drive me at every turn, so I walked to him and took the staff. I really didn't know what to do with it, but the man seemed to understand that. He took the staff back and showed me how to hold it, twisting it in his hand easily. I was amazed at how easy he made it look, moving the staff backward and forward to strike or parry. He handed the staff back to me and pointed to the other man."

"Just handed it right to you?" Terri said. "It was a trick, wasn't it?"

"You are, of course, correct," I said. "The two men apparently had intended to humiliate me or to take out some frustrations on someone besides themselves. Still, I held the staff as he showed me with one palm up and one palm down, equally spaced across the staff. I should note, I have since learned that that is not optimal, but it definitely works. I squared off with the man, and he smiled at me as he walked up with another staff. It started out easy. He knocked his staff at the center to mine. I felt the weight and, as I did, started feeling more comfortable with the weapon. He started swinging a little faster. The hits became more and more intense. The bad part was he was swinging the same way each time, straight down upon the staff, and my hands would sting each time he did it. When I started pushing back just a little, he swung underneath and pulled the staff from my hands. Then he turned and swung under my legs, easily knocking me to the ground. I didn't really know how to feel, but for some reason, I was annoyed. I felt something akin to anger. Looking back at it now, it wasn't really anger because I didn't feel the overwhelming urge to destroy everything, but it was difficult. I stood almost immediately, picked up the staff, and challenged again. Both men were laughing at me, and that felt uncomfortable as well.

The slave girl who rode in the back of the cart with me walked up to me and brushed me off a little. As I said, I was perturbed or angry or something. The man composed himself held his staff and walked to me again. Once again, he started easily tapping my staff with his, working up to a higher and higher speed until, once again, he was swinging down upon my staff, hard. I was paying attention this time, and as he swung up, I took a step back. He missed, but as he realized his mistake, he corrected, and as I was off-balance again, I was once more knocked on my butt."

"I bet that made you really mad," Terri said.

"You're of course right," I said. "I was actually angrier with myself. It was after that second hit that I realized I saw it all coming. It was as though it was in slow motion. Here I was, letting it happen. I stood again, picked up my staff, and readied it again, as I had been shown. This time I changed the position. Instead of leaving the staff at a horizontal position, I moved it to a vertical, and I held it in a spaced grip, leaving a significant amount of the staff above me. The guard was openly confused. He stepped up with his staff at the horizontal, and as he pushed forward to tap my staff, I pushed down, forcing him backwards. He swung his staff to the side and came at me from an angle, but I slid my staff with his, and this time I saw the thrust coming. I blocked his attack then waited. He swung again at me, and I stepped back. This time, he missed me completely. His face changed, and he stepped into the swing aiming harder at my legs. Now I pivoted the staff down, and it blocked my leg. His staff hit mine with a resounding knock.

The woman who rode in the cart with me watched intently as the guard began speeding up his attacks. Instead of moving forward or trying to attack, I simply paid attention to the vector of his staff and blocked each time. Soon the man was sweating. He turned to swing again, and this time feigned the swing. I had no concept of deceit, making it much harder for me to see the next hit coming. At the last moment, he shifted. I did not have time to compensate. He struck me on the side of the face, hitting hard and making my lip immediately swell. That brief shock allowed him to once again sweep my legs and watch me fall to the ground. I stood and looked at him, still not angry. He was unmistakably worn. His friend, the other guard, nodded his head as though accepting that I had done better than they expected."

"I stood up again, holding the staff vertically again. Before I could move, the woman came to me. She wiped my face and the bit of blood that was upon it. She straightened me, brushed me off, and then brushed her hands on her dress and brushed her hands together. As she stepped away, I saw her stick her fingers in her mouth to clean off the blood on her hand. I had no idea then what that single action had set in motion, because at that moment, it was me, the staff, and the guard. I was standing there, waiting for him. He, too, waited for me. Neither of us moved. He was still breathing a little hard, I was not. I moved forward, and this time it was obvious he was tired of the game. He swung hard to my head. I blocked, but he parried immediately to the opposite side of my head. I swung back quickly, and he landed on air. He swung at my legs. I stepped back out of the way, and again he missed. He forced himself upon me over and over, trying to land a blow. No matter what he did he could not land a single hit on anything but my staff. Finally, he feigned a move again, and this time I saw it. I was pretty sure I knew what he was going to do and prepared myself. As he swung, I stepped to the side. He missed while I turned and caught him on the shoulder with my staff. He swung again. I was ready and again blocked, this time seeing my opening. He had overextended and was off-balance, allowing me to step past him. I swung at his legs and knocked him to the ground. As soon as he fell, I stepped backwards and stayed there."

"Three times and you finally won," Terri said, "that's pretty good."

"Looking at it now, it was amazing but apparently my senses were much sharper than his." I smiled. "His friends started laughing at him, and the man jumped up. I could see the fury in his eyes. At the time, it reminded me of what I often saw in the 13 women's eyes. After all, anger and passion are not so different. He did not wait this time to line up with me or give me any pause but instead swung directly at me. I blocked. He swung at me again, and I blocked. You could tell his anger was growing exponentially. He was full of fury as he swung and connected with my staff, then swung over and over as if to pound me into submission. He moved back and used one hand to swing. When I blocked, he used his other hand to push me. I was off balance for only a moment, but he swung again and came down hard upon my staff. I was only able to block him at the last second. As I did, he tried to push at me again. This time, I began to understand what he was doing. As he reached for me, I simply grabbed his hand and pulled him past me. The guard fell to the ground, hitting hard. This infuriated him even more. Standing, he grabbed his staff and came at me at full speed. That was when his friend finally stepped in and stopped him. His friend was still laughing and told him to cool off. The friend walked to me and held out his hand. I didn't know what he wanted at first, but then reluctantly, I handed him the staff. His friend chuckled for just a moment, then walked over to the man I had just knocked down, sitting with him on the other side of the camp."

"I'm surprised they didn't go to town on you," Terri said. "I know how men can get. They sometimes go a little crazy if they don't get their way."

"I'm kind of surprised about that too, but they must have been men with some honor. I never gave them the chance because that was the last time I would see them. I walked back to the cart with the woman who rode with me. She was waiting and smiling but also sweating profusely. I was unsure what was wrong with her but told her to lie down. I would watch as we knew it would be at least another day before Morgan returned. I walked around the camp and checked on the woman often. She shivered and quaked, sweating hard. I took her some water. It was then that I noticed her hair was darker than before. Over the years, I learned the effect that sex had on women with me. It did not make sense to me, but this woman was going through the same change, only faster. The men had no clue and paid no attention to either of us. Several other servants milled around the area. They paid no attention to us either. I shook the woman and told her to not make any noise. I said to her that we needed to find a way to leave. As naive as I was, I knew Morgan would kill this woman if she knew what happened. After Magda's dismemberment, I knew Morgan's potential for violence had no bounds. I don't know what I was thinking, but I felt that without being bound, the best solution was for us to leave. I looked around the camp.

As darkness fell, I thought over options and our only hope was to leave during the night. Perhaps we would travel enough distance to stay safe and be outside of Morgan's wrath. The woman was still shaking. I could tell she was not feeling well, but I knew I couldn't wait for her to be better. I whispered to her that it was time to go, and she whispered back that she was ready."

"She whispered back?" Terri asked. "I'm betting the woman has a tongue now?"

"Yes," I said. "During the time that I had been there, from afternoon until evening, he tongue grew back. I don't know why it surprised me, because my face had been hit hard and didn't hurt at all 30 seconds after I was struck. I just never put all the pieces together. After all, I spent 700 years being pampered by women and servants in the middle of nowhere. Getting hit by a staff had never have been part of their plan. Nor would taking any chances with potentially hurting me. As it stood now, I realized that this was not just something that kept people alive. Whatever was within me did far more. It was apparent the woman was surprised as well. She put her fingers in her mouth and explored her partially regrown tongue. As she stood, I noticed she was a very pretty middle-aged woman. I knew that as the night went on, more years may fall off of her features. I grabbed some water in a skin and moved around where the guards didn't see me. They were busy playing some game with rocks that was similar to modern-day craps. The woman and I walked off into the night.

We soon were further and further from the camp, and now the sky grew darker and darker. The moon was in the sky, but it was only a quarter moon. With only a little light, it did not light up our path well. I could not see well, but I could still see. I could hear everything. Even in this stressful situation, I was listening to nature and was fascinated by the new sounds. We wandered forward into the night, heading away from Morgan, away from all I knew or at least all I could remember. I was naive but not stupid. Every once in a while, I would stop and erase our tracks. My goal was to keep us from being followed long enough for us to find the distance we needed. Normally, I did not get tired. That night was no different, but the surprise was that the woman kept up with me well. After a time, when there was no sight of the fire or the camp, I turned to her and asked her name."

"Asked her name, huh?" Terri said. "Did she remember how to talk or just how to whisper?"

"Actually, it may have been a mistake asking her name," I laughed. "When I did so, she told me her name was Ariana. The revelation that she could now talk opened the floodgate that could only be described as biblical. I think she did not realize when she whispered previously, and of course, the escape was definitely tense. Ariana explained to me how she had become a slave. She told me how her house had been taken from her because she was not paying taxes. How she lost her husband years before from a raid. She told me about her daughter who died in childbirth and her son who died with her. She explained that her younger son and daughter had been together in the womb. That took me some time to understand. As happened often during that age, the daughter was stillborn. The son, born minutes later, lived for a few hours then died as well. She explained she had another son a year later, and that son lived and was healthy. She told me of her eventual spiral to servitude. She entered into an agreement to work for the 13 women, and in exchange, they allowed her son to live. She told me how it felt to have her tongue cut out. Then she told me how it felt for her tongue to grow back. She asked about me. Why I had sex with the women so often. She told me that Morgan and Magda were both cruel women, and how both of them beat her continuously. Ariana continued talking. Even when she asked me questions, she answered them herself. I didn't need to speak."

"The gates were open, eh?" Terri laughed.

"You could say that. After she started talking, I don't think I got a word in for over an hour." I paused for a second before continuing. "It was a unique series of conversations. It was undeniable that the combination of not being able to talk for so long and her newly restored tongue, plus the invigorating nature of her body going through changes, was making her more than a little hyper. After about two hours, she started letting me get words in."

"How is this happening to me?" she asked.

"I don't know," I answered.

"Are you a demon?" she asked.

"No, I am not a demon," I replied.

"Are you a god?" she asked.

"No, I am not a god" I replied.

"Are you evil?" she asked.

"I don't think so," I replied.

"That's what evil would say," she eyed me suspiciously.

"Why do you sleep with the women all the time?" she asked.

"When they have sex with me, they get younger and live as I do," I replied. "It is like what has happened to you."

"Did you have sex with me, and I did not know it?" she asked.

"No, I did not have sex with you," I replied.

"How did this happen to me then?" she asked.

"I am assuming my blood has the same effect," I said to her, "When the guard hit me you tasted my blood. It is all I can think of right now."

"Are you sure you didn't have sex with me?" she asked.

"Yes, I am sure I did not have sex with you," I replied.

"Did you love those women?" she asked.

"I am not sure what you mean. Magda spoke of love, but I am not sure I feel what she wanted. I am not sure I feel what anyone wanted." I replied. "The idea of love does not make sense to me. A feeling that has no real basis in anything but thought? How can this be?"

"Do you miss any of the women you have left?" she asked.

"I do not miss any of them," I said, and she nodded as though she understood.

"What did you do before you were a slave?" she asked.

"I am not sure I was a slave. I understand the word, but I had nowhere to go. I could have easily left as the ropes were not so strong, I could not have broken them. I was apathetic, and perhaps I was just comfortable, I am not sure. I had no real desire to leave until I knew what they would do to you if we stayed. I had no memory before the moment I met Morgan except I was cold." I told her.

"How long were you there?" Ariana asked.

"I am not sure, I understand how the women talked of time, and aging. I just don't know. As far as I know it was forever."

This made her laugh, and she laughed hard, "Most men would have loved to have 13 beautiful women forever. Why would you ever want to leave."

I remember being confused. I laughed but I wasn't sure what I was laughing at.

"How long will you live?" she questioned with a somber face.

"I have no idea," I replied truthfully.

"We walked and were quiet except for small questions. They were nondescript and I think Ariana was just enjoying having someone to talk to and being able to talk at all. Then Ariana began talking to me about time, and how seasons were measured. I knew that the year went through four seasons, but I had never thought about the crops, or the seasons of vegetables or flowers. Ariana explained how in the spring she cut flowers and how over time crops came in and left and were harvested in late summer and fall. As we talked, she gave me clear ideas that I had not been told before. The 13 women gave me language and a good base to work with, but they left key elements out of life. I realized that I did not have many concepts down.

As we walked, I started understanding how time was measured more effectively. At once, I told her after running calculations in my head that I had been there probably around 700 seasons. I explained that the Lily's had been brought to the great room 700 times. Ariana was stunned. She looked at me with pleading eyes and asked a simple question.

"How long will I live now?" she asked with those eyes that begged for an answer.

"I don't know," I replied. "I am assuming my blood changed you, it is all I understand. I don't know how long it will last."

"I'm betting it could be a hard thing to deal with, right?" Terri asked me.

"I think you will understand as I progress just a little further," I replied. "Ariana and I walked all night. As the sun rose, we knew we were going in the right direction, heading east. She was savvy about the world, and understood where we were, easily far better than me. After all, this was my first trip anywhere. Ariana began telling me about all the tribes to the east and about the wonders of Egypt. As we walked, I was impressed with Ariana's wealth of knowledge and how willing she was to share it with me. She knew a lot about the world. Far more than I had ever been told. Her knowledge was limited. At that time her entire world was only the size of what is now Texas."

"I know this is off subject, but I have seen the world go from the size of a room with 13 women to space and beyond and been fascinated with how the human race has progressed." I considered.

"This may be a dumb question, but do you think you're human?" Terri asked.

"It's not a dumb question," I said. "I have considered that possibility for a while. When the ideas about UFOs came out, it started making sense. I dismissed it though, when no credible evidence was presented. That theory might explain many things. It would not explain why my organs, muscles, bones, and DNA are all human. As I have said, I really don't know what I am, just that I am different."

"I have had many names, but I took Adam from a series of places. Mostly, I like the name Adam, because according to the Bible, he was the first of his kind. According to Mary Shelley, the monster took the name Adam for the same reason. I really can't say if I am a monster, an alien, or a human with strange blood coursing through my veins. I am fairly certain I am the first of my kind, and I may be the last."

"That sounds pretty lonely," Terri said. "You said you tried to have children but have never had any."

"I'm not sure I tried to have children. I did do the things that would cause children and never have had any. I'm not sure what that means. It could be that most of the women had already gone through menopause and been rendered sterile, but I doubt it. Each had their period monthly while with me. This is one of the reasons I considered the idea of being alien. If I was, my sperm may not be compatible with a human egg. Then again, there could be other reasons. Perhaps my sperm haven't found the right egg. Perhaps I have very selective sperm, I don't know."

"That in itself is a pretty funny idea," Terri said. "You could do a casting call for a new show, *Find the Right Egg,* and invite women to donate their eggs and let you try to fertilize them. Maybe even do it the old-fashioned way."

"Already went down that path," I said. "I told you there was a doctor that was interested. He and I discussed why I might be sterile. We were supposed to test it at some point but didn't get a chance. Since he is dead now, we never will."

"Wow," Terri said, "we went down a rabbit hole. So, the sun was rising on you and Ariana. What happened next?"

I smiled at Terri's curiosity. I took a breath and continued. "After the revelation about how long she could live, Ariana was very quiet. Sure, she still talked some. Of course, she was still very fascinated by the fact that she had regrown a tongue, but there was something else on her mind. As the sun continued to rise, we saw little but desolation before us. There were no cities or people, just rolling hills and meadows. We continued walking. It was quiet for a long time. Only the morning calls of birds could be heard.

"What is your name?" Ariana asked.

"I have only been called Hantezzija," I replied, "It is all I know."

"I will call you Hante. Hantezzija, is far too long to be a name," Ariana said.

"What did that mean," Terri asked.

"The closest thing it comes to in English would be 'prime'" I told Terri.

"Hante, will you leave me?" Ariana asked next.

"I do not expect to," I replied.

"You left Morgan," Ariana stated, "Will you not tire of me and leave the same way?"

"I left Morgan to save your life," I replied, "If she had returned and you were whole again, she would have killed you to protect our secret. I did not want you to die."

Ariana smiled for a moment. Ariana stopped me by walking in front then hugged me, holding me for a moment. She looked up at me and said, 'Thank you for saving my life. Promise if you have to leave me, you will kill me. I cannot imagine another lifetime alone.'"

"I thought about that for a while as she continued to hold me, and finally, said, 'I will, but I do not intend to leave you.' I had no idea how I would kill her, or if we would ever be separated, or if she would ever change her mind, but I understood what she wanted and why she wanted it." I explained.

"I think I can understand how she felt," Terri said as she touched my face. "I can't imagine being alone for an eternity. I'm sure it's been horrible for you."

"Not horrible, just lonely," I said.

"Well, you don't have to be lonely anymore," Terri said as she reached up and grabbed my head. She pulled me close for a kiss that I could not resist, and our naked bodies intertwined once more. We held the kiss and were lost in the feelings that were growing for each other. We broke the kiss, and Terri nestled her head into my chest. She held me and caressed my arm with tender strokes. I held her and caressed the small of her back. Her breathing slowed, and soon Terri was asleep next to me.

Chapter 13

I fell asleep, and again I dreamed.

I realized I was asleep very rapidly as the sounds and smells were not exactly correct. I was inside the chamber where I was a prisoner of for so long. There was no one in the room save me. I looked down at my arms, and I was not restrained. Nor was the room covered by guards as it usually was. There I was again, in that room that had been my home for so long, and for once, I was not a prisoner. Realizing it was a dream, I looked around and explored. I stood and walked to the walls. Their rough-cut stone mortared together and was still tight with the mason work of the time. I wandered around the edge of the room and felt the walls; much of it was familiar.

I had been given freedom from time to time to wander the room like this but only when all 13 women were present. I looked around, and still, it was just me. I walked to the large fireplace and saw that inside it, the bones of Magda were still there. It was as though she had just been thrown to the fire. Her quartered body smoldered slightly as the flames licked across the edges of each rib and each piece of her body. The skeleton looked back at me and seemed to smile like all skeletons do with their teeth locked into an evil grimace or a cunning grin. Fire lashed out in the eye sockets, and it looked as though Magda's once beautiful eyes were now dancing with hellfire.

I turned to explore the rest of the room and saw the ornate tapestries covering so many areas of the room. As I scanned the room, I heard a sound behind me; it was the crinkling and crunching of something sinister.

I turned back to the fireplace again, and now Magda's skeleton was nearly complete. As I watched in fascination, the skeleton body attached itself to the head, and each piece I thought lost in the fire bound to another until it was once again whole. It sat in the fireplace, then stood and walked out of the hearth. I watched as the bone slowly morphed and flesh formed. I knew this was a dream, but a dream I relived for centuries.

I watched as tendon and muscle bound to the skeleton and as the abdomen and chest cavity filled with organs. Intestines writhed like unchained snakes, struggling to be free until they were encased in sinew and the beginnings of flesh. With patient persistence, the body began to look like a woman. The face was covered first with tendon and scalp and then more tendon. As dermis and epidermis filled in, it began to look like the Magda who had been my warden for too many years. The skin gained pigment and became a normal color. I watched as eyes formed, expanded, and grew into the piercing eyes that Magda had looked at me with for so long. The rest of the body was covered with skin and then a light smattering of hair. Magda's perfect breasts were formed. The pert nipples stood out in the air of the chamber.

I still knew this was a dream, but it felt real as Magda began walking towards me. I did not move. I was not afraid, but instead, I was curious about the entire transformation and how it happened. Behind Magda, the fireplace roared in anger, having dispensed its prisoner and wanting more. Magda reached for me. Ropes bound her arms and legs as they had bound me for so long. Behind her, the fiery growl intensified. The look in her eyes was no longer powerfully confident, but now desperately pleading. She struggled forward still. In spite of the bounds, she had nearly reached me with her hand towards my heart when all of the ropes became taut. I looked at her, and I did not see the woman who tried so hard to conquer me, but instead, I saw a woman begging for something I could not have given at the time.

As I looked at her, her face changed, her hair changed, and her body changed. Instead of Magda, Terri was bound before me. I reached for her, but as I did, she was pulled away with fiery indignation as the fireplace maw opened and took her like a morsel in a buffet. I heard crunching and the sickening sound of bones splintering and popping as fire and brick worked as powerful teeth upon Terri's body. In a matter of moments, the fire died, and before me again lay the skeleton in the fireplace.

I realized I was inside of a dream. I also realized that my mind was trying to work something out. Perhaps it was something I did not consider. Maybe something I missed. I was not sure, but I knew it meant something. Maybe everything I was telling Terri, trying to explain the difficult decision of what I had done, was not what I should have done.

Maybe my mind was trying to tell me I should have let death close its icy hand upon Terri's soul. The decisions and the issues weighed upon me like a world on the shoulders of Atlas. I struggled to remember what I was missing or what I was trying to tell myself. Nothing came.

As I stood staring at the fire in my dream and the skeleton of Magda, or Terri, or whoever it may be, I felt my arms grabbed from both sides. I looked to my right and to my left. The two football players, whom I had fought with only a day ago, were wearing the garb of the guards. They held me tight. I could not move. I tried to wrench free to no avail. They were impossibly strong as though they had the strength I possessed. I could not move and found that I was being carried towards the fire. Closer and closer, until I could feel the fire scorching the clothes from my body. As I was nearing the edge of the flames, in unison, the two boys said, "Do you see now?" Then they threw me into the flames. I struggled and tried to break free as I felt my body burning and recreating over and over. Each second, I knew that if there was a hell, I was there now, doomed to feel the fire for all time.

I woke with a start. There was no fireplace, no football players, no skeletons, just the safety of my home. I looked around the room, and it was peaceful. I felt better. Terri was still curled up in my arms, facing me. I felt her warmth before me, and listening, I heard her heart beating ever so rhythmically. Her face was unlike any other woman I had known. I longed to share time with her. I reached out and touched her face ever so carefully and felt each pore underneath my fingertips. She slept with the peace that only good sleep can bring. Paying close attention to every breath she took and every beat of her heart, I fell back to sleep.

Chapter 14

I woke up early and realized that I had slept more than I usually do. Terri still lay in the bed, sleeping deeply. Rather than wake her up, I decided to get up and check the morning news. Things have changed a lot over my lifetime or at least the lifetime I remembered. Where once things were done by word of mouth, then by song, and eventually by writing and criers spouting the news of the day, now television, and finally the internet gave news so rapidly that it was almost precognitive.

As I walked into my office, I turned on the computers that were there. Normally, I turned them off all the time as I didn't want any possibility of took a digital footprint someone could detect or invade. I took the time to study security in the early 2000s and kept my skills well-honed simply because of the amount of information that could be mined so quickly. I was always concerned someone would find me. I knew once found I would be unable to stop the flow of information and would have to spend the rest of my life running from who I was.

First, I logged on to the newsgroups. Newsgroups were old-school ways of sending information around on the internet, but they were also full of truths and data that weren't scanned by social media platforms attempting to press their control on people's buying dollars and social habits. Instead, newsgroups just put the news out or at least some semblance of news. There were no verifications for anything, but there was a lot that could be reviewed as potential fact or fallacy very rapidly.

As usual, I looked at the groups that had to do with the paranormal and oddities around the world. There were the usual stories of werewolves, vampires, ghosts, and much more. Nothing struck me as out of the ordinary. I moved to another group. Looking over the sightings of Bigfoot and the Loch Ness Monster, I still saw nothing that stood out as important to me.

I looked at other paranormal areas and scanned the headers, looking for anything of interest. There were, of course, many things for sale about eternal life, but most of them involved buying some water or becoming a flesh-eating zombie. Again, nothing I needed to worry about.

I switched to modern news outlets and looked over the local television stations. Overnight, there was very little going on. As I scanned, the biggest news was still the police murder yesterday and a fringe story about a hit-and-run in front of Tolly-Ho. Nothing new came up. I looked over other stories. There were random stories about shootings and corruption, but these were things that were common.

I went on to some fringe sites and found a lot of chatter about the far right, the far left, and of course, the mysterious, silent center. I laughed to myself about how cyclic history had been. As the great empires rose and fell, I traveled many of them and saw great similarity with the world today just on a much smaller scale. There would always be people controlling others from places of power, and those people pushed everyone to either the far right, the far left, or the mysterious, silent center.

I then went to my least favorite place to review: social media. As I looked over the social media sites, the continuing mindless ponderings of people was very evident. I was disgusted at the name-calling and trite musings of people who could not form a sentence in public. They were attempting to sway people to their argument by something as meaningless as 'unfriending' someone. It was sickening to think that in the life of man, we had been reduced to creatures affected by a simple binary decision: *Are you my friend or not?* I finished looking through some of the headlines and a few select groups in about 15 minutes. I slid my chair back just a little and stood, still looking at the screens before me. I shook my head in disbelief but knew that the machine in front of me was what would control mankind from now on. Men thought computers were built to serve, but as algorithms determined behaviors, and behaviors built algorithms, the only outcome was man serving the needs of these complex machines built of sand.

I heard the toilet flush in the master bedroom and knew that Terri was awake and moving around. I went through the master bedroom and then into the master bathroom, where I found her staring at herself in the mirror. She had on one of my shirts which looked like a dress on her. She was looking at her face, her eyes, and her skin very carefully. She glanced over at me and smiled.

"I think I look pretty darn good now," she said.

"I thought you looked pretty darn good before," I replied.

"Flattery will get you everywhere with me," Terri replied as she looked at herself in the mirror some more. "I don't think I've ever looked this good. Every time I thought my skin was this clean, I would get a pimple usually right in between my eyes so I would look like some cyclops waiting to spray its juice upon an unsuspecting group of individuals."

I laughed pretty hard for a minute. "Thank you," I said with a smile.

"For what?" Terri asked.

"For making me smile, of course. I don't think there are a lot of people in the world that realize how important it is to laugh with someone. I think there are fewer people in the world that actually do it. I am just excited and impressed with you and your amusing wit."

"Are you calling me a nitwit?" Terri asked.

"Of course not. I'm not calling you anything. I'm just saying how wonderful you are. Now, I have two very important questions. The first question is the easy one. How did you sleep?"

"I slept really good," Terri said. "It was as though I had a long day fighting between life and death and then was reborn and had some big guy have his way with me. All the while, he made me feel like I was the most important woman in the world. If you think about all of that, I was kind of worn out, and sleeping was pretty amazing."

"I like that. I'm glad you slept well and even happier that we had a wonderful time together," I smiled. "Second question, maybe a little harder. Are you hungry?"

"Hungry?" Terri repeated with extra emphasis. "Do you mean you have food, and we can eat? Of course, I'm hungry. I feel like I could eat just about anything. I realized we didn't eat after Malone's yesterday."

"That's my fault," I said. "I usually only eat a few meals a day and didn't think about it after we got you the one big meal. We had so much going on, and everything just fell into place that it felt good to be close to you. Would you like to go out, or would you like me to make you something to eat?"

"We can do either," Terri said. "I could eat anything that you have here, or if you don't want to cook, we can go anywhere that you want. I don't feel hungry in the normal way; I just feel like I should eat. My stomach isn't growling and grinding like it usually is."

"There's a reason for that," I said. "Now, when you get hungry, and your stomach lining starts to erode, your body repairs it so fast that you don't feel the minor pain that everyone else feels when they're hungry. Instead, you will feel more, I guess, empty, and you will know you have to eat."

Terri laughed. "After last night, I could be called a lot of things, but empty isn't one of them. Why don't you decide if you want to make something or if you want to go out, Okay? I'm going to take a shower. If you have a toothbrush, it would be really nice. Toothpaste would help too."

I opened the drawer to the right of the sink, and inside were several new toothbrushes and toothpaste. There was also a Sonicare toothbrush. "There are new toothbrushes here. Some of them are older, but they're all still sealed. I bought them in case I ever had company, but as you can guess, I've never had company. Whatever you need should be in either this drawer or the three underneath it. I believe there are some generic deodorants in there as well if you need them, and of course, you have the things that Micah brought from Victoria's Secret."

"That's perfect," Terri said. "You could, of course, join me."

The shower in the house had four heads that were set very tall so that I could be covered with water instead of having to duck as I did in earlier houses. A control on the wall turned on each head individually, and each head could be a different temperature. Terri used the shower the day before and had rapidly gotten used to the controls as she stepped in and turned it on to exactly where she needed to be. Steam rose as the instant hot water heaters came up to speed, and the pressure of the heads sprayed water everywhere. Terri took off the shirt, threw it outside the glass door of the shower, and stepped into the four streams of hot water. The steam obscured my view of her only slightly, and rivulets of water dripped down her tight body and into the drain beneath her. I shook myself as I realized I was staring at her breasts and stomach, mesmerized by having a woman so near me again. I took off my clothes without a thought and set them inside the hamper next to the shower. I opened the glass door, stepped in, and closed it behind me as the fan pulled the steam to the ceiling. I touched Terri, and she turned to me and smiled. She put her arms around my neck, locking them at the wrist, and pulled me close. It felt good to be close to her.

Terri picked up a bottle of soap, squeezed out a generous amount, and smeared it all over my body. I laughed a little as she lathered it up and then rubbed her body and breasts against mine. She kept rubbing, grabbing suds, and massaging them across her body. It was the most unique way I had ever experienced getting clean. I was literally being washed by this woman's body. She grabbed more soap, rubbed it through her hair, and then took the suds from her hair and rubbed it on mine. I was in heaven having her near me. She took a little more soap to rub against my back and, without warning, slapped me on the bottom. I turned rapidly with the slight sting, and she laughed before moving on to my arms. She continued rubbing her body against mine like a female car wash.

I picked up some of the soap and began washing her back. When I reached her buttocks, I spent extra time cleaning every inch of them. I also spent time massaging the small of her back. It felt good to touch her everywhere. I got a little more soap and crouched to my knees to clean her legs, knees, and the tops of her feet. She grabbed my shoulder as I picked her foot up and massaged it with soapy suds. As I let her foot down and grabbed the other, she shifted her weight. I massaged her other foot with equal vigor. As I did this, she rubbed my hair, holding my head close to her body. I was intoxicated by her scent and the feel of her skin next to mine. I knew I had all the time in the world, so I stood and looked into her amazing blue eyes and kissed her softly.

We stood there for a few minutes as the water rushed across us and then finally broke the kiss. I stepped back. Terri looked down and laughed. She grabbed my penis that was hard from our interactions. "Hasn't been feeding you enough for a long time, has he?"

I laughed at her interaction with my penis. "I'm sure that we'll have plenty of time to feed him again."

"Did any of those 13 sluts give your penis a name?" Terri asked me.

"No, I have not been blessed by anyone naming my penis," I said.

"I think we need to think up a name for your penis right now," Terri laughed.

"How about we skip that part and just move on," I laughed.

"Don't worry," Terri said, "I will think of a good name sometime in the future. I think we can come up with something proud and manly."

"I used to laugh when I thought people did stuff like that, but then found years ago that they do," I said. "I always thought it was a joke or something to make conversation between people. Obviously, it isn't."

We stepped out of the shower, and I pulled the towels from either side of the door. They were very fluffy and very soft. Over the years, I found that textures meant a lot to me. My heightened senses picked up imperfections in just about anything. My sense of touch allowed me to discern incredibly small differences in texture. Almost all people have that ability, but few people pay attention to how sensitive they are to the world around them. As I picked clothing and towels and really just about anything, the tactile quality was as important, if not more important, than things like color or type. Instead, I focused on the feel of all the things around me. Micah thought of me as far too picky when I asked him to purchase towels for me once. It took five trips for him to finally find a set of towels that I considered soft enough. Over time, Micah got used to this eccentricity, and even in the clothing he brought, he started to consider the type of silk and the different types of cloth used to make them.

"I love these towels, they are so soft," Terri said. "Where did you get them?"

"I'm really not sure," I said. "Micah got these for me years ago as a gift. I never asked where he got them. He knows that I like things soft and smooth. He's developed a habit of purchasing things for me that just fit."

"He's a good kid," Terri said. "You're very fond of him."

"It's rare that I meet someone very young and get to interact with them through more stages in life. It used to be that I would be part of small communities, and there would be children, and I would see them grow up. Depending on how far back they remember, I could only stay with people for perhaps 20 or 30 years. Maybe a little more sometimes if they weren't noticing me. Otherwise, as they aged, and I did not, it became an issue."

"I can see where that would be hard," Terri said. "I'm just glad you have Micah and that he has actually adapted to your needs. I'll have to ask him what I should get you for your birthday. Of course, I don't think they have enough fire trucks to put out the candles on the cake."

"Somehow, I think you're right," I laughed.

"Does Micah suspect anything?" Terri asked.

"I don't think so," I said. "Micah is a very observant young man, but we've only known each other about ten years or so. He asks few questions and I offer few answers. As he becomes more and more of an adult and loses the childlike innocence that makes him who he is, he'll begin questioning more. It's true that I changed my hair some and cut it shorter or let it grow longer, but in the end, I'll never age like all the other people that he knows. Someday, something will happen, and I'll be gone. He'll be left with the entire company. I staked his company, but I immediately put in a provision that if anything ever happened to me, all shares would transfer to him. The company isn't worth very much in the grand scheme of things, but it is doing well. It will give him a good life."

"You old softy," Terri said; "thinking about this young man means a lot. I'm impressed with you every time I learn something more about you."

We both finished drying off before walking back through the master bedroom together and into the two walk-in closets. Terri did not have the selection that I did, but it was only the second day. She created another outfit with the choices that Micah had provided for her. I dressed casually in jeans and a long sleeve white collared shirt.

"You know it's warm enough to be in short sleeves?" Terri laughed.

"It avoids questions about the scars," I said. "Sometimes it's easier to just blend in and not have those questions swirling around." I paused, then said, "We haven't decided what we're going to eat yet."

"I'm expecting we may have another busy day," Terri stated. "I am assuming you're going to want to try to find the boys."

"You assume correctly. I made this mess; I'll need to fix it before they hurt more people," I said with a solemn tone.

"I understand," Terri said, "but am I part of that mess?"

I walked over to Terri and put my arms around her, holding her. "You are nothing but amazing, and I've only just started getting to know you. You are not a mess nor problem nor anything except a fantastic addition to my life."

"I bet you say that to all the girls," Terri laughed.

"There are no other girls. No other women. No one but you," I whispered.

"You do know that sounds pretty corny," Terri smirked and slipped out from under me.

I laughed at this woman who was handling her transition better than I could have ever hoped.

"We need to get back to your history lesson for me," Terri said. "I need to know what happened to Ariana and Morgan, and the other 11 that seemed to have disappeared from your radar."

"How about I make breakfast, and I'll talk as I cook?" I asked.

"Sounds good to me. I'd like to say I'm hungry, but I actually feel empty. Think you can fill me up?" Terri laughed and ran toward the kitchen.

I was laughing hard as I entered the kitchen and found her sitting on one of my stools at the kitchen counter, waiting for me. She smiled as I entered the kitchen. I stopped by her stool and kissed her again. It was going to be a fun breakfast.

Chapter 15

My kitchen was full of stainless steel. Both new and old utensils were hanging from different areas or stored in unique displays. The center island where Terri sat had a granite top that was a deep dark obsidian. A stainless-steel sink lay on one side, while a bar was on the other. Terri sat bouncing her leg like a child waiting for something fun. Around the island with a significant amount of room was a stainless-steel refrigerator, dual stainless stove, stainless microwave, and stainless dishwasher. This was all surrounded by antique white cabinets with frosted glass and wood doors. The overhead lights were a combination of Edison lights and can-lights. It gave me the ability to make the room very antique or modern, depending on the amount of light I used.

I reached into the refrigerator and pulled out eggs, bacon, and cheese. I looked over at Terri and asked, "How do you like your eggs?"

She smiled and said, "Fertile?"

I took out a single egg and looked at it, turning it over and over. "How do I tell?" We both laughed for a moment.

"Whatever is easiest," Terri said. "I would be fine with scrambled eggs, and you can put a little of that cheese in them."

I set everything down next to the stove. Reaching to the left of the stove, I pulled out two small frying pans. They were made to make omelets or other small dishes. I enjoyed the pans because I didn't need to have too much or waste any food. I also reached to the top left cabinet and pulled out a small bowl, then grabbed the whisk from a stainless-steel container in front of me. I broke the eggs into the bowl and whisked them to a froth. Turning on the stove, I heated both pans. I went to the right of the stove and opened the cabinet that seemed to have every spice that had ever been discovered. Over the years, I found that there was a spice for everything, and not having a spice could often be the difference between a culinary masterpiece and a bland dinner.

I didn't want to make things too complicated and was enjoying my time with Terri, so I grabbed, from a very high shelf, just a few spices to jazz up the eggs a little.

"I don't know if you're aware of this, but you're not talking right now," Terri said, "I thought you were going to continue where you and Ariana were escaping."

"I was just trying to get started," I said as I laughed a little and scraped the eggs with a spatula while the bacon cooked in another pan. I folded in the cheese simply because I like it to be a little crunchy and mixed in with the eggs and hoped that was okay with Terri.

I recalled for a moment where I left off when I was telling my story to Terri. I never told anyone the story the way she was being told, but I had a purpose for it and wanted to make sure I didn't miss anything. "We were in the wilderness somewhere to the west of the Caspian Sea, slowly putting distance between Morgan, her guards, and the two of us. I continued to take the time to mess up our trail as we walked, making sure that it would not be easy to follow. I had not thought about it until I started telling you the story, but I had no real tracking knowledge, only instinct. Perhaps if I did not have that instinct, we would have been caught. I am sure that Morgan was behind us somewhere, desperately looking for me and wondering why I left with the servant girl."

Our bacon finished fairly rapidly, and the eggs were done in short order afterwards. It was a simple meal. I walked to my left and pulled out two plates and laid out our breakfast. I set one before Terri and one next to her, then went to a drawer and got two forks. I also reached to the counter and got the salt and pepper and set them before Terri, in case she wanted it. Then I sat down next to her, and she began to eat.

I took a few bites, chewed, swallowed, and continued talking. "Arianna continued to be a wealth of information. I was learning more about the outside world than I ever knew possible. Many of the things that she explained simply made sense; I just hadn't considered them before. Something as simple as caravan trade made sense from the point of view that people came and went to where I had been. I had never been exposed to it previously, as the 13 women kept me from interacting with other people. Ariana told of the wars and the death and the hunger all over the world. Many of her friends and family died from raiding parties that came in the night to steal goods and women. As we continued walking and occasionally jogging, the day looked bright, and eventually, we came to a series of bushes that were bearing fruit. Ariana showed me how to if tell the fruit was poison or not poison. I now know that the poison affects me and would have affected her, but it would not have killed either one of us. Instead, we would have both felt very bad while the poison worked through our system, but it would have been short-lived. I was poisoned once by a man who thought I was trying to steal his business, and I did not understand why I felt so bad. Later, he confessed to poisoning me and attempted to blackmail me, stating I practiced witchcraft. I asked him if he was sure the poison was actually poison. He doubted himself and tested the poison on himself. That solved both problems."

"You let a man kill himself?" Terri asked.

"I had no idea that it would kill him," I said, "but I would not save him as I have you. As he lay dying, I did not feel good about it. I really didn't feel bad about it either. After all, he tried to kill me."

"I suppose that's right," Terri said as she finished her eggs. "So back to Ariana."

"We ate some apples and worked our way East. I asked Ariana if she knew where we were going or what was to the East, and she had no idea. We had already gone farther than she had, and she did not know the area well. All she knew were the tales of the evil sea and the nomadic tribes that constantly warred on its coast. As we walked, I came across a series of sticks and branches. Eventually, picked up a long stick and thought of my recent interactions with my guards. I wondered what it would be like to be as they were, trained to fight. I remembered how he showed me to hold the staff and I walked with it while Ariana looked at me and smiled. Time continued to pass, and we continued walking to the East with Ariana talking almost nonstop. We found a stream, and the cool water quenched our thirst and, of course, gave Ariana the ability to talk more. During the days while I had been held captive a significant amount of the time, I was on my bed alone. I was not used to someone interacting with me anywhere near as much as I was getting now, and I was finding it a little exhausting while at the same time exhilarating. Over the 700 years, I was taught language and actually found that I had been taught several languages, but I found myself asking Ariana for clarification on many words that I didn't recognize. She was patient and explained the words the best she could, and I added them to my vocabulary."

I took a few more bites as Terri finished her breakfast. She finished first, stood up, and carried her plate to the sink. She placed the plate in the sink and also cleared the stove. "I would think that cooking as much as you have over the years, you'd invent something to keep bacon from spraying all over the stovetop when it cooked." She did not ask but instead, looked under the sink, found some towelettes, and cleaned the mess. She then looked around and finally found the trash can to the right of the sink.

"Making yourself at home?" I asked.

"Just trying to help," Terri laughed.

As Terri started the dishes, I finished my plate, handed it to her, and then continued to talk. "The day passed, and twilight came. I looked at the sky, fascinated by the color changes. I did not look away until the cool blues of night had intruded on the landscape. Ariana suggested that we stop and camp. I asked her if she was tired. She said no, however, there were wolves and bears in the area, and it may not be good to challenge them at night. I had no idea what a wolf or a bear was, so I was not sure why we were stopping. I conceded she had more knowledge of the outside, and I had no reason not to trust her. We did not have significant clothing either and she noted we may get cold. I noted the evening was not so cool as to be uncomfortable.

As we settled in, Ariana cuddled very close to me. I felt her warmth, and we shared our heat for the night. We were against a tree on the edge of a large field. The tree was aged and over 100 feet tall. A warm breeze blew in the night, and it was almost comfortable lying next to the tree with Ariana nestled in my arm. I laid with women dozens of times a day for hundreds of years, and as we lay next to each other, I felt the stirring and the need for a woman but I also, for once, felt free to choose. This would be the second night that I would not be with a woman, and it felt good to have the choice."

"I was doing some math inside my head, and in the time that you were with the women, if you averaged about 20 times a day and 365 days a year, you are the most oversexed person in the world. I mean, based on that, you had sex over 5 million times in those 700 years. You would think you would have gotten sick of it. I mean, even something as great as sex gets old, doesn't it?"

I looked at Terri for a moment and kind of cocked my head to the side. "Then, to depress you, you should consider the other side of the equation. For over 3,000 years, I have been mostly celibate. Those first 700 were, of course, filled with sex, passion, and debauchery. These last 3,000 or so have been filled with anger and uncontrollable undirected passion, with me doing hundreds of things that I would never do again. Of course, I learned how to masturbate with minimal success. That's not like having sex. I may have been the most oversexed person ever during that time, but it's only because of the length of my life. Does that make me the most celibate person you have ever known, considering how long I had to wait in between? Of course, there were times that I took chances, and I had to be very careful. Would it have been better if I had never had sex at all those first 700 years and never missed it, or is it better knowing what I know and not being able to be with anyone?"

"I hadn't really thought of it that way," Terri said. "After all, this is a pretty unique situation, and I'm surprised I'm accepting it all."

"Honestly, so am I. It's hard for me to accept if I think about it but it is my life, and it's interesting how it is going. I sometimes consider what the next 1,000 years will bring. Will I one day be walking alone on this planet as radiation tries to kill me and my body regenerates as fast as it does? Will I get to see a world with flying cars and teleportation? Will there be a time that I will see other worlds and beyond?"

"No," Terri said; "you're not going to be walking alone. I'm going to be right there with you."

"It's only been one day," I said; "you may tire of me and this life someday. You may want to move on somewhere else without me. Something else may happen that could tear you away from me. The biggest thing I've learned over the years is that there are patterns everywhere if we want to look at them. In spite of those patterns, nothing is for sure."

"That makes sense," Terri said, "but I will still be standing there right next to you. Kind of a depressing thought, though, to be the only ones left in a radiation-filled world. I can't believe you're such a downer this morning. You really should have come up with something better like being in another Ice Age; that wouldn't be so bad. Maybe you could have made it an alien invasion, and the two of us were fighting with energy weapons side by side, terrifying the aliens with our regenerative powers. Maybe you could have made it the return of the dinosaurs who had just been sleeping for a long time and now had a taste for crunchy humans. There are so many options that are just kind of bad but not so alone, and you had to pick the radiation-filled dystopia. You know, maybe we'll get 100 acres in the middle of nowhere and start our own nudist sex colony with just you and me and keep it that way forever. Come up with some positives and stop killing off the world."

I was laughing at Terri as she went through the possibilities. "I get it," I said. "Point taken. I will work on it. As it was back then, Ariana and I woke the next morning, and it was a beautiful day again as the sun rose in the eastern sky. We began walking and heading towards another day. I watched behind us consistently but was now paying less and less attention. I was sure Morgan was looking for us, but we now had several days start, and each day put us farther away. I knew enough about the sun to fill a thimble. Over the years, I picked up that the sun rose and set in the same place every day. As we walked, I remembered all of the things I had been taught and kept moving in the same direction. I was betting Morgan didn't realize how much I retained over the years as they talked around me. I am nearly sure she thought of me as just a toy without the intelligence I possessed. Still, I had no idea where we were going, and Ariana was little help. We were now outside of her knowledge by quite a bit.

By midday, Ariana's incessant talking was once again almost becoming an irritant. I interacted as best I could and laughed as she talked as I did not understand most of her references. Ariana seemed to talk a lot about death and loss as if it was the largest part of her life. When you think about it, the 13 women were around me always, and the guards and servants were changed consistently. I had no concept of the idea of death or anything similar to it. Except for the brutal death of Magda, I had not seen death since from the time I came to Morgan till the time just a few days ago. It had been explained that most people grew old and died, but even the idea of growing old and dying seemed foreign and unreal. Now here we were, and I began to understand that a lot of Ariana's life was punctuated by gaining people and losing people."

I paused for just a moment as Terri finished the dishes. She had paid attention to everything she had seen and put everything back exactly where I had taken it from. She then wiped out the sink and threw away the small towelette that she was using. "I agree with what you saw," Terri said, "All of my life, the thing that I knew most of all was that eventually, it would end. My grandparents died, my parents died, and I have had no one. I have seen friends pass away and people that weren't friends go, and perhaps we could best say that people are like spices. They make our days a little better, but eventually, they're gone."

"That is one of the biggest concepts that Ariana taught me. That and never start a conversation with a woman who hasn't talked for years."

Terri laughed.

"I was incredibly curious about death and how it worked. We ended up talking for most of the day as we continued walking to the East. Ariana told me about the fevers that took away children. She told me about the pets that she had and how their lives were so short compared to our own. She told me about her family and how her father and mother had died, and each of the family members she had previously. As the day passed, I became more and more sensitized to death and what it meant to the people around me. As we talked about how long I had been alive and my life with the 13, Ariana was equally fascinated and appalled. She asked if it was right to cheat death. She had been worried earlier about being alone, and she was frustrated with the thought, but she could never be alone now and felt how lonely I had been. As we continued talking, the statement came up numerous times that she felt it would be better to die 100 deaths than to be alone without love or companionship."

"It's easy to say that if you're not dead," Terri laughed.

"Actually, that's where the conversation went. Ariana began talking about the afterlife and how I would never be able to walk into my place in the beyond. She spoke of her beliefs that the almighty was above them and that they would comfort them when they died. It was a difficult concept for me. We spent a considerable amount of time talking about it and all she knew about other beliefs. The idea of life afterlife did not make sense, but I listened, and I learned. I watched behind us often and still saw no one following. It's funny, today we could not have walked the distance we walked without running into hundreds of houses and even more people. Back then, there was nothing but countryside and the animals that lived in the forests and on the plains.

The sun was setting on the second day and again, I watched with utter fascination as the sun set in the western sky. It was not the same sunset the day before. It fascinated me to watch the patterns shift in the sky. The flaming orb changed from illuminating the world into a softly spinning globe that dimmed until only the night remained. Ariana was captivated by my obsession with sunset and sunrise. She stated very simply that she didn't pay as much attention and was now starting to see how the world looked and would appreciate these little things for as long as she may live."

"People take things for granted pretty easily, don't they?" Terri asked. "I mean, I bet you've seen people living next to wonders that really just don't care, right?"

"Just about everything is a wonder if you look at it the right way. When you think about the world and all of the things that make it work, even a blade of grass is a fascination within itself. Having the times I've had; I've done some things that others would think are ridiculous. But in the end, they weren't ridiculous; they were just another expression of beauty."

"Alright, I'll bite," Terri laughed, "give me just one example of something you spent too much time on?"

"Well, you will probably think this is silly, but I spent a year just watching an anthill. Sure, I would stop and eat and occasionally clean up, but for the most part, I stared at ants going in and out of an anthill and all of the interactions that they had. I had never seen ants or really paid attention to them until that time. Their tenacity for taking care of each other and their lives was fascinating to me. If you take the time and watch, there is a unified civilization working together for a single purpose."

"Did you write a book about it or a paper or something?" Terri asked.

"No, I just paid attention. I probably should write a book about many of the things that I've paid attention to, but who would buy it?"

"You don't write a book with the expectation that people will buy it. You write a book to inspire people or teach people or show them a new way." Terri said. "Maybe that's the problem with the world. We are so focused on making money that we don't stop and let people know our experience and vision. In the past day, I have seen the world change considerably, simply from you explaining about your past. In the past day, I feel I have grown a great deal in both my views of the world and my grasp of the reasoning of the world. Still after it's all said and done, what I am realizing every minute is that I know less than nothing about life and the world around me. Think of the possibilities. You have insight into history and human nature that no one else can claim. We haven't talked about it, but I'm betting that you've actually seen things that others in history books have only assumed. I am betting that your story, or at least representations of your story, could open people's eyes to possibilities."

"You forget one very important thing," I said. "How do I explain how I know the things I know? At what point do people start seeing me as a threat to themselves and their way of life? I'll give you a good example. There is probably alien life on this planet right now. There's lots of evidence that says that. But if you were an alien, would you want to tell people that you were an alien based on the movies, books, and the general demeanor of the planet? In my opinion, if an alien came down and said they were from another planet, they would be nuked within 5 minutes. This planet is covered with people but more to the point this planet is covered with bias and emotional immaturity."

"I can see your point. Somewhere in between, someone would start asking questions, and they would either consider you a fraud or eventually burn you at the stake for witchcraft," Terri snickered.

"It's funny you should say that," I replied, "I dreamed about something similar last night. It was a weird dream, and you were in it."

"I know we're in the middle of your past, but what happened in your dream?" Terri asked as she shifted on the stool next to me.

"I dreamed that Magda reassembled herself in the fireplace and came to me in that room I was a prisoner in for so long. Then the fireplace came to life and pulled her back in, and as it did, her face shifted to yours. Then the fireplace chewed her up, and again there were bones in it. It was not my best of dreams," I said.

"It didn't really do me much good either, did it? Being chewed up by a fireplace," Terri laughed. "Is all this talk dredging up old memories?"

"Yeah, I thought the same thing," I said. "Still, it means my mind is chewing on something, and I'm trying to understand what my mind is saying. I've been doing that for hundreds and hundreds of years."

"Let me know if you figure it out, but until then, go on with Ariana," Terri said.

"Getting interested, huh? Ariana and I again found a tree and spent the night nestled against it. On that night, though, we were visited by wolves. They were intent on getting to us, but the long stick I picked up worked well as a staff. My reflexes were fast enough that as each wolf advanced, I was able to dissuade them easily. I was fascinated by these creatures that worked together to attempt to get to Ariana and me. Even in my fascination, I realized how powerful the pack could be and how cautious I should be. When one of the wolves grabbed the end of my makeshift staff, I lifted it three feet off the ground, and the jaws held fast. I swung the staff, and the wolf came free, but I saw how deeply the wood was scarred and knew that a normal person would likely have major issues in a wolf attack. I did not sleep the rest of the night. Ariana slept fitfully and had dreams that we did not discuss the next day."

"People and their dreams huh?" Terri snickered.

"As the sun rose, we began walking and found a larger river. Ariana showed me how to fish with the staff. Once again, I was mesmerized by life, and of course, I was confused by how the images in the water were changed by the water itself. It took some time, but Ariana stabbed a fish with her stick and showed me the squirming animal. She took it to the side of the river and spent some time with grass and leaves and two sticks. I was never shown how to make a fire. As I sat there watching her moving the sticks against each other, they eventually smoldered; she carefully used the smoldering grass to create fire. The area was full of brush, and it was easy to create a small campfire. She showed me how to cook the fish on the end of a stick. We ate well, and later I was able to catch a fish when I finally got the hang of how to sight it in the water."

"I bet you would be good at it now," Terri said.

"I actually got very good at fishing with a spear. Later in life, on the Galápagos Islands, I would fish and eat the fish raw. Raw fish taste just as good if you're paying attention. Many people don't pay attention. Where we were that day so long ago was very comfortable, but somewhere inside, I knew we had to keep moving. We did not have cart nor horses, which meant that Morgan's guards could find us if they got lucky. By midafternoon, we were walking again, heading due east through thick woods and open plains alike. Walking was consistently challenging, and the ever-changing terrain gave way to even more ever-changing terrain. If you look on maps today, you'll see the slight ranges of mountains near both seas, and the up and down chaotic mess of hills and flatlands mixed into what is now Georgia, well at least for the moment."

"Did they ever catch up to you?" Terri asked.

"Not as far as I know," I said. "As we continued to walk, we ran into no one, and no one followed."

"At least there's that," Terri said, "I keep waiting for you to make me jump by telling me that two guards jumped out and Morgan slashed everybody up."

I realized my story was dragging, but I was trying to get Terri to understand what it was like for me seeing the world back then. At this point, I knew that was either going to come, or it wasn't. I continued, "It took us six more days to reach the Black Sea. It was unlike anything that she had seen, either. By modern standards, it is not far from Derbent to the Black Sea but on foot over uneven terrain through woods with potential predators and someone like me who was looking at butterflies with newfound excitement, it took 9 days. As we approached the edge of the great sea, we saw more people. We were soon at a small village. They were very suspicious of us. Ariana was very persuasive and talked to them about food and work. I was a big man, well, you already know that, and the villagers there needed help clearing trees. They handed me an axe, and Ariana goaded me forward, and I went to work. It was actually funny at first as I had never used an axe. There is an art to it and my first few swings were pathetic. After only about 4 swings I realized that rhythm was everything. I noticed the peculiar cut on one of the fallen trees and realized that it was done with purpose. I cut a similar line and felt the tree bend to my axe. Moments later, I watched the first tree fall and noted how the cut guided the tree to a particular location. It made sense, and so I walked to the next and began swinging the axe again.   It was hard work, but it was fulfilling. I would chop down trees as other men worked to saw them and pull the shortened lengths back to their village. It didn't take long for me to actually enjoy cutting trees down with the axe. After the first day, we were treated much better by the villagers who appreciated the extra help. Since I didn't need to rest as much as the others, I became a hit as the "forever worker" and the man with arms of stone. Ariana and I were led to a small hut on the first day, and that night as we lay in the hut, Ariana mounted me."

"I get it," Terri said, "another slut that wants you after a day."

I smiled a little, "To be fair, we had been running for over a week. Also, after 700 years with the same 13 women, you would think it was nothing new. Ariana was different. Although there were times that many of the women took their time with me, it was rare, and the goal was to get me to have an orgasm. As you know, there are many ways to have an orgasm, and the world would probably be a better place if people realized that. Since most of the 13 women had very little interest in my pleasure, I, of course, enjoyed my orgasms, but I hadn't experienced a significant number of other types except when one of them was experimenting. Ariana was slow and gentle and took significant time to bring me to a climax. She did not stop after and walk away but stayed on top of me, and for the first time ever, I fell asleep inside of a woman. That, in itself, is a very unique feeling, and of course, as the male penis softens, it usually falls out. The way Ariana was on top of me, I did not fall out. As the night passed and I became hard again, she brought me to another orgasm from sleep to awake. I was lost in the feelings that were assailing me. She had me six times that night, and it was the most unique feeling I had experienced. She did not speak all night but instead kissed me or held me or put her mouth to all portions of my body. When we finally woke the next morning, she held me tight, and my life actually felt good."

"It sounds like you could have been happy there," Terri said.

"I think for the first time in my life, I was happy. Well, for the first time in the life I remembered, I was happy. It was morning, and there was food being prepared in the small village. Ariana and I emerged and were greeted well and fed, and then the men headed to clear more of the fields. I was given an axe again and continued to knock down trees one after another. Those trees were worked and taken to the village, and although I managed to get ahead, the pace was fast. It became a race for a while between the local men and me who could knock down the tree or clear the area faster. Two men and a cow worked on pulling out the stumps after each tree was removed. Although we overlooked the Black Sea, we were not on it, and I often stopped for a few moments and watched the nearly still waters. It was a magnificent sight in the sunrise, and the sunsets were just as spectacular. We stayed there night after night. Each day was amazing as Ariana and I grew closer. Ariana still talked constantly, telling me about life and about the world, but no one paid any attention to us except for the fact that we were a help to their village. It was good. With Ariana, every night was better than the last. She said she loved me in her language, and eventually, I came to understand and realize I loved her too. It was not easy living then for most normal people, but for Ariana and me each day was filled with hard work, and the village accepted us as one of their own. Every night began with a passionate embrace and Ariana learning more and more about me. I have heard many people speak of love and what it means to them. I have heard many people profess to understand the languages of love. I have read book after book on the subject, and as I did, it only pointed back to the lesson Ariana once taught me. Pay attention to the needs of the person you're with, deliver them with all your might, and be a good person every single day. We could have stayed there forever. Time passed and seemed to last and fade away at the same time."

"How long did you stay?" Terri asked.

"We were there for almost five years until everything changed." I replied. "It was actually a happy time for me. The thoughts of Morgan faded away, and I was no longer concerned with being found. The villagers and I repelled the small raiding parties. We worked together and, using the lumber, built a small barricade. The village grew, and we built several additional dwellings as more families came." I paused for a moment remembering it all. "It was on a day like any other day where I had watched the sunrise over the Black Sea and was working on the fields. Over the past several years, I learned more about life than in the over 700 before. There were wild dogs that were in the area and some in the village that were domestic. I found that animals were naturally very positive with me. Horses, cows, goats, pigs, all of them seemed to have an affinity for me that even I didn't understand. I often wondered if I had not swung the stick if the wolves would have been less aggressive. Perhaps it's because I have no fear of the animals and no fear of death. It is just as likely that their enhanced sense of smell knows that I am different from the others and a different type of respect for me."

"As I worked the field that one day, I saw many men in the distance heading towards our village. The men had crude spears, but they also carried axes, mace, and short swords, which I had not seen so far. As the villagers, Ariana, and I waited, they came and began to burn our village. The men and I fought hard, but these men were hardened raiders riding under a crest of two spears over a wolf. I watched man after man die, and as I used the staff I picked up on our walk to this place as a brutal weapon. I was heavily outnumbered, nearly five to one. On the other hand, the men were having a difficult time hurting me. I was not cut, but each time I was knocked down, I was able to get back up almost immediately. Ariana fought by my side until we were suddenly split up. As I looked on, one of the men with a battle axe swung and took her head. I could see her screaming, still alive, but the man threw her head into the burning pile that was once a house and then threw her body there as well. They all laughed as they saw my grief. I did not know what I was feeling except loss; and then it happened."

"What happened?" Terri asked.

"I got angry," I said. "There were 25 men and all that was left was me and several of the women. I knew I could not save Ariana, and the grief was overwhelming. Somewhere inside me, I knew anger, it was something I did not remember but now it came. I felt determination with the two guards. I felt so many different things. Love, pain, passion, and more. This was different, and I think I went a little mad. I grabbed the nearest man to me, took his spear, and put it through his head as I pulled his sword. I dropped the spear and picked up my axe. I put the sword through the next man's eye socket and felt it go through the back of his head. The men moved in on me, but it didn't matter. I picked up the last man and threw him into many of the others. While they tried to catch him or get around him, I continued my spree of death. I put sword and axe through one man's head after another. I soon realized why it was so easy when I got angry. It was like when I fought the guard who was trying to humiliate me. All of the men seemed to be moving very slowly to me. My senses were keener, and I was moving like an ultra-possessed tornado. One after another, the men fell and lay dead or dying. Several came close to striking me, but at the last moment, I would see their movements and move so rapidly that their blades hit empty air. Fifteen men lay dead around me, and five were wounded mortally. The last five were still fighting, not willing to run from a lone farmer. I felt the rage inside me and moved like a ballerina of carnage. Four of them fell immediately, and the one who was evidently in charge stood looking at me in near terror. I was blinded with uncontrollable rage. I looked at him with different eyes. He took Ariana from me. My anger knew no bounds as I dropped the sword and axe; he smiled only for a moment. I was on him in a second, and my massive arm was around his neck from behind before he could react. He grabbed my arm in panic but would have had a better chance of draining the Black Sea. I pulled and strained and remembered all of the trees I had cleared and all of the things I had done, and I felt flesh tearing as I ripped his head off. I turned it to look at me, and his eyes had lost their defiance and instead only showed dismay and shock. I threw his head into the same fire Ariana had been thrown to and watched it burn for a moment as his head sizzled into a silent scream. My anger was not satiated. I took each fallen man and threw them into the fire as well. Some were still alive and screamed as the fire burned their flesh away. It was not much later they were gone; all of them were ashes."

"The three women who remained and looked upon me in fear. Each of them walked to me and dropped to their knees before me. They referred to me as god and devil both, and I realized that I could never stay there. My temper was fading, and I felt grief now. I looked at the fire and was saddened by the thought that I would never hold Ariana again. It is horrible to think about the death of an immortal, and I wondered how long it took for Ariana to die and felt my anger coming back. I remembered Magda's death and wondered about her as well. The women tried to attend to me, but I sat on the ground between the fires of the burning huts. For the first time, I could easily remember, I cried and was lost in my own despair."

As I finished telling this part of my story, I felt my tears well up. I realized that I missed Ariana and that I did not want to lose Terri. Emotions of grief and sadness fell upon me, and I lowered my head for a moment.

Chapter 16

Terri and I were sitting at the kitchen counter for over an hour. I still had to explain one more piece to her. I looked into her beautiful blue eyes and reached over and touched her face. She smiled at me and leaned in as I leaned over and kissed her. The kiss was gentle, and she was warm and soft and everything I could ever desire.

"What was that for," Terri asked.

"Just because," I said. "It feels good to have someone to be close with."

Terri smiled. It was a pretty smile. "I understand that. I know I'm only 31, and that makes me less than a child to you. People may talk about us behind our back because you look 40 to 45. Having you say how important love is important to me. I have had horrible relationship after horrible relationship and knowing what you went through, I have hope. I don't know how things will go, but I know I feel stronger for you in a day that I have for anyone else in my life. I guess I should as we are stuck together."

"I need to tell you one more thing so that you understand and know enough of my past to feel comfortable with the future.," I said. "If you don't feel comfortable with me, I will happily set you up and show you how to shift from life to life until you finally grow old, and you will never have to see me again. I don't know how long you might live without me being close. I do know it will be a long, long time, and you will have an opportunity to live a life that could be fantastic."

"To be honest, you're scaring me a little bit," Terri said, "what happened after Ariana?"

"That was the problem," I stated as I looked around the room for a moment. "As Ariana became dust in the heat of the fire, I think I went a little mad. I told you I lost my temper. I became angry, and 25 men died in a matter of moments. While I was in my grief-stricken state, I felt nothing for them. I often wonder how I feel and if it is real or if it is something that is just a defense mechanism. It has been so long since Ariana, but after I stared at her charred remains, I took the axe and the sword, a horse from the stable, and I left the women there alone. I rode east. I knew many men were not good men. I believed that good could overcome evil. It was a very basic understanding of good and evil that Ariana explained to me. She convinced me that the 13 women were all evil. She convinced me that I was a gift and that together, we were good. After all, our days and nights were spent making other people happy and then making each other happy. It all made sense to me. A good person goes out of their way for others, and for their partner, they go even further. A bad person only thinks of themselves and lays waste to those around them."

"That makes sense, Adam." Terri said, "What was the problem?"

"As I rode to the east, my anger stayed with me. Actually, I think it grew the farther I rode, and the more I thought about Ariana. I believe I became a bad person for a time. If we have a ledger of both good and bad, for the next 100 years, my ledger was filled with worse than bad. Some might say it was the lesser of "bads." Some might say it was an understood vengeance or even necessary. I can't say that. With my sword and my axe, and eventually a bow and a crossbow, I went on a quest to cleanse the area of raiders. It was not pretty. I felt somewhere inside myself that an immortal life with Ariana was worth thousands of mortal lives. I became known by many names, but they all equated to the evil that hunted men in the night. If there was someone with the same Crest as the raiders who attacked our village, I killed them all. It did not matter if they pled for mercy, nor did it matter if they were a woman or child; if their allegiance was to the Crest, they would die. I'm sitting here now before you with my heart open as much as it can be, for I believe the love we could share is greater than any that I have experienced. I just need you to understand that I have a dark side and that dark side is the terror that so many men fear."

"What do you mean?" Terri asked. "What you have told me is that you sought revenge on people who attacked the innocent. What you have said is that you were imprisoned and treated as a slave for hundreds of years. What you have told me is it a woman showed you the way to love, and you were inspired by it. I don't understand. What is so wrong? You were hurt for the first part of your life. What am I missing here?"

I was stunned by the revelation that maybe it wasn't as bad as I thought. I considered what Terri was saying to me, and tried to accept that in this modern world, she could accept my just cause even though it might be terrifying. Still, I needed to know she understood my concern. "I'm sitting here wondering if I have made too big a deal out of all of this, and then I have the memories. Is it okay with you that I have killed so many thousands of people? Is it okay with you that for the love of one woman, I destroyed so many with the brutality that may well have been the basis for many legends? I don't want you to ever fear me, but I need you to understand that there is a monster in me that I have overcome. That monster is me. No matter how hard I run, it is still there. If something were to happen to you, it is possible that I could become that monster again. When we were at the horse farm, I saw inside you the gentle, intense passion that I have craved for over 3,000 years. I saw inside you something I didn't think existed anymore. Can you live with the fact that somewhere inside me is that horrible monster that took life without consideration?"

"Do you remember yesterday when I got shot? Actually, it was you who got shot, right? If something happens to me, or if someone hurts me, or someone even *wants* to hurt me, it would be my expectation that you will protect me. By that same token, if someone hurts you, or worse, if that is possible, it should be your expectation that I protect you. I think each of us has a monster in this case. Whether it is called justice or vengeance, that is not just okay it should be expected. If something ever happens to me, it's not just okay, I expect you to exact with vengeance because I'm not leaving willingly. It's my hope that nothing ever comes between us."

I was lost in my thoughts for a moment. Here I was over 4,000 years old being schooled by a woman with only 31 years of experience. I told her a long story about my past because I was worried about our future. Ariana's words rang in my ears. She said, *'Pay attention to the needs of the person you're with every day, deliver them with all your might every day, and be a good person every day.'* I remembered her saying those words to me clearly, and now the missing link suddenly made sense. This was not a promise of tomorrow or yesterday, this was a promise of today. This was a litany of what life should be each day. I had watched so many things come and go. I had lived so strongly in the day and in the moment that I had missed the *message* of living in the day and in the moment. Ariana, in her short years, had given me a lesson in life. I should have been living. I considered all of the years. If only I had truly followed Ariana's guidelines, faithfully. I did live for the needs of the person I was with each day, even if it was just me. I did deliver the needs of the person I was with every day, even if it was just me, and I strove to be a good person every day. I did it to make up for all those days that I wasn't a good person, but I should have done it just because it was the right thing to do. I considered over and over. It was uncomplicated. I wanted to slap myself in the head, and instead, I started laughing.

"What's so funny?" Terri asked.

"I have been looking for an answer for so long that was staring me in the face all the time. Here I am virtually immortal, and it took two women who both were less than 50 years old to teach me the importance of living in the moment."

"Well, we women are smarter than you men anyway. It's always going to take you longer; you might as well accept that," Terri laughed.

"Maybe that's it," I said.

"I was just kidding," Terri giggled.

"Still, I was the one that didn't pay attention to the moments. You know, 700 years could have been a lot more fun if I was living in the moment." I smiled.

"Well, those sluts took advantage of you. How many times did you say you had sex? Oh yeah, I'm the one that figured that out. It was over 5 million. That makes you a serious slut too. Maybe if you hadn't been thinking about sex every day, you would have realized what was important. Based on everything you've told me; I think you did find what was important. While you were with Ariana, you learned to love her even though she was a bit of a chatterbox and took advantage of you on the first date. Still, the two of you were good for each other, and if you look at it that way, those five years that you spent with her were worth a lifetime. How long is it been since she died? How long have her bones been dust in the middle of nowhere somewhere near Russia? You have still kept her alive in your heart. You went on a holy crusade, not just because of her but to save the innocents in the area, and to protect other lives. In the five years you were with Ariana, you probably had more love than ever. Well, until now, of course.

I believe in the same thing Ariana said. I believe two people in a relationship should be in that relationship. I believe that two people should pay attention to the needs of the other person every single day. I believe that if anything is more important than paying attention to the needs of the other person, then maybe one of the two people should not be in the relationship. I believe that good people are good people because they want to be. Everyone should be a good person because it is the right thing to do. I also think that sometimes the people that we think are bad may actually be better than the people we think are good. I mean, look at our politicians. They're supposed to be looking out for us, and most of 'em are more crooked than a coat hanger after you try to unlock a car door with it."

I remembered moments after Ariana died and the weight that I put on myself. I remembered the women trying to comfort me as I sat down on the ground and cried. I remember the anger building because for once, I had no control. As I sat there next to Terri, I suddenly felt as though the pressure was gone. As I had thousands of years ago, I put my head in my hands and cried. They were not tears of pain this time. Nor were they tears of anger and fiery righteousness. This time my tears were of relief and the weight that was now gone. I reached over as my eyes cleared and put my arms around Terri again. Before I could do anything else, it was her who reached out to me and kissed me softly, and it was her that held me tight until I felt the lump in my throat start to go away.

"Do you know a lot of people don't realize that the fear of death is what makes life far more meaningful? You just have to come to terms with the fact that it's the fear of other people's death that will make your life more meaningful," Terri whispered.

"Where did you find all this wisdom?" I asked.

"I watch a lot of chick flicks," Terri said with a grin, "and I get hurt an awful lot."

"How about I *not* hurt you," I said to her. "How about I spend every day treating you the best that I can."

"That sounds really good," Terri replied. "How about I spend every day treating you the best that I can."

"I like the way that sounds, too," I said, drying my eyes. I kissed her, and I couldn't stop kissing her. I started by holding her face and sliding her golden hair back as I pulled her close to me, and I just couldn't stop. We were both sitting on stools in my kitchen, making out like teenagers for the first time. It was not awkward. It was tender and kind and loving all at once. As we kissed, my arms rolled down her shoulders, and I felt her warmth. I wanted her, and I knew she wanted me. Not in the easy physical sense that so many people are drawn to; instead, I wanted to be a part of everything she was and everything she would be.

Chapter 17

Our kiss was broken by the phone ringing in my office. Reluctantly, I stood. Terri pulled me down one more time, and as our lips brushed, I felt as though there was nothing in the world I could not overcome. I walked to my office down the hall. Terri followed me and scanned the walls and desk as I answered the phone.

"Hello?" I asked.

"Have you seen the news?" Shawn asked me on the phone.

"No, I haven't," I said. "What channel?"

"Any of them," Shawn said with an undeniable tone that was both urgent and irritated.

"Hang on." I opened the drawer on my desk and pulled out a remote.

I turned on the television in my office. It was a 55-inch Samsung Smart TV and was connected to the local cable and to satellite. I selected cable and switched to Channel 18. A newscaster was repeating a story about two men holding an entire group of people hostage at a bank in downtown Lexington. The story said the police shot at them several times to no avail. Now they were sequestered inside the bank and were threatening to kill hostages unless they were set free with enough money to leave the country. A negotiator had been called in, but there was no update on any demands. The picture on the screen was from a helicopter circling a large building downtown. The Lexington Fayette Urban County Government police force was one of the best in the country, and the officers had the building completely sealed off. I was instantly concerned with the potential outcomes and how they could affect both me and Terri.

"You seem to have them cornered," I said, "Why call me?"

"Easy," Shawn said with significant frustration. "The negotiator has been in contact with them several times now. The two boys have stated over and over they will only negotiate with you face to face. They were very clear it had to be you and absolutely no one else. Adam, you need to be straight with me. Why are they asking for you?"

"You know exactly why they're asking for me," I said, "Those are the boys that attacked me, and those are the boys that I hurt. It should have been critical, but I suppose, there's been a mistake."

"Don't bullshit me, Adam," Shawn barked, "I've seen these boys through the scope. They both have arms and they both have jaws. Whoever you hurt is missing one or the other of each."

"Shawn, I really can't explain this right now without you becoming very agitated," I said. "If I promise on my word of honor to tell you after this is over, will you allow me to resolve this issue?"

"What are you talking about, Adam?" Shawn yelled into the phone. "What is all of this word of honor and resolve the issue stuff. You've helped us with dozens of cases, and I know you very well, and you're telling me now there's something I don't know?"

"There's quite a bit you don't know about me," I said in a calm voice, "but if you trust me, I will share with you what's going on after this is done."

"Why not tell me right now so that I have some idea of what's going on?" Shawn said. His voice was not only agitated, but he was clearly very angry.

"If I try to explain now, it will confuse the issue, and you may well take me to an insane asylum even though they don't exist anymore," I said. *"You know me,"* I emphasized the last part very heavily. "You know that that I always try to do the right thing, and I'm sorry that this particular event is so complicated, but if you let me, I can solve the issue. You just have to trust me."

"Trust you?" Shawn said. "You are telling me to trust you because you haven't shared with me before. That kind of negates the idea of trust, doesn't it? I thought I knew everything about you, and now this? What are you, a secret agent or worse, a Russian spy?"

"I am not a spy, and I have nothing but the best intentions for you and this situation. When I explain everything to you, it may change our relationship forever or it may just make it different. If you give me the leeway that I think you really owe me, I can solve this. You have to decide if you can trust me or not. I'm putting myself out there for you and putting myself at great risk. I'm willing to come down right now and be there to negotiate an end to this. When it's all said and done, it will be over, and then you can come to my house, and we can discuss in private something I have considered telling you for quite some time. You may still think I'm crazy, but it won't interfere with this very difficult issue that you are facing right now."

"This kind of feels like I'm in between a rock and a hard place," Shawn said in a calmer voice. "How long will it take you to get here?"

"We can be there inside of 20 minutes," I said.

"We?" Shawn asked.

"Terri will come with me. She'll stay with you but if I need her, you'll have to let her in as well. I know this is a lot, Shawn. I know this is more than you ever want to deal with but trust me, it'll be better if we wait until after this is over to talk."

"Get down here right now," Shawn said, "I will make some kind of excuse for you. I don't know what that'll be right now. Damnit, if you don't keep your word Adam I swear I'll..."

"I will keep my word, Shawn," I said. "I owe you that much and a lot more. It will be up to you where we go after we talk. It will all be up to you."

"I like the sound of that a little better," Shawn said. "Hurry up and get down here, I don't want any hostages dying, and I damn sure don't want another cop dying."

"Me either," I said, "We're on our way." I hung up the phone and stared at my computer screen. I opened my contacts and scrolled down. There was a number for emergencies. If I called it, my identity would start to shift, and all of my things in this house would be packed and gone within a day. I looked at the number, then looked up at Terri."

"Things are bad, aren't they?" Terri asked.

"Really bad," I said. "I have some tough decisions to make. Correction, we have some tough decisions to make."

"What's the decision?" Terri asked.

"You heard me agree to go downtown and negotiate the release of the hostages. Right now, those boys will regenerate if they are shot or if someone does something to them. There are television cameras and snipers everywhere. If I kill them, it will be brutal, and the only way I know how is to decapitate and burn them. That's not exactly what the viewing audience would like to see on national television."

"You must not watch NASCAR," Terri broke in.

I smiled. Even in this tense situation, Terri was still in control. I continued. "If they're captured, it will all come out, and the world will know about me. It will probably be on national television as well, then the internet, and who knows what else. There are very few possibilities here where there is a win. The number that I am considering calling will move everything in this house to another home that I own in another state with another identity, and after this is over, we'll start fresh. I like Lexington, I like living here, but I can't take the chance of being found out. Now that affects you. I feel like I'm stuck, and I had to add an extra wrinkle. You heard me promise to tell Shawn the truth. He is a grassroots police captain, and I have no idea how he will take it if I tell him the truth. Which puts us back at the same place. Either I will be on the front page of the morning paper or in the news, or I will be in a lab somewhere being dissected on live television as the cure for aging. I could even end up on an infomercial at 3:00 AM with the secret to eternal life."

"There is the other option," Terri said. "You could tell Shawn, and he could believe you and still be your friend. You might be able to trust him and never have a problem again. He is a reasonable person, and if you let him, he may be somebody that could help you even more."

"There's always that possibility," I replied as I considered Terri's wisdom. "I do have to make note that with the exception of you and Ariana, everyone who has known about me has tried to capture me and make me into a commodity. It was a huge decision to give you some of my blood, which changed you forever. It would have been easier if I was a vampire or some mythical creature that has a critical weakness and could die as easily as I live. I've taken a grenade at close range and lived from it, and something tells me I'm not going to die easily. Telling someone that you almost certainly would become nearly impervious and immortal if you get a little bit of my blood or I have sex with you or change bodily fluids with you in some way, well, I don't have as much faith in the world as you do."

"You don't need faith in the world. You have faith in me. You have faith in Shawn. You also have faith in Micah. Why don't you see if your faith in Shawn is well-founded? Why don't you give him a chance and then maybe decide over a cup of tea if he reacts poorly?"

I pondered for a moment. There was so much going on in my mind it felt like my brain was on fire. I looked into Terri's eyes, and again I smiled for just a moment. I had an idea. "We don't have much time, help me in the kitchen," I said.

Terri and I quickly made a large Pyrex container of hot water. I got a large thermos and a tea strainer and mixed the tea that made people forget. I made it a larger dose that would take several days from the boy's memories. We poured the hot water into the thermos, dropped the strainer in, chain and all, put the top on, and rushed to the garage.

"Did you turn the stove off?" I asked.

"Yes, I turned the stove off," Terri replied. "I'm actually very good at that. I always turn the stove off, and then I always double-check turning the stove off because I left the stove on once. Because of that, I know I turned the stove off."

The Impala was uncovered, and we both got in as the garage door opened. I pulled out of the garage and slowed as the gate opened, leaving the driveway. Looking in the rearview mirror, I saw the garage closing and the gate closing as well. I pressed the gas pedal on the very powerful Impala.

Terri pulled down the mirror and began checking her makeup and making sure that she looked good. I looked over at her and smiled, and simply said, "You can't improve on perfection; what are you trying to do?"

"Hey," Terri said, "I don't tell you how to live forever, you don't get to tell me how to look amazing."

"You look amazing all the time," I said.

"You are so sweet, and that's one of the reasons I love you," Terri said, "but a girl's gotta keep herself looking great when she's got a good chance of being on television."

I laughed and smiled at the same time. "You love me?" I asked.

"Of course, I love you, you idiot," Terri said. "I loved you the moment we met, but it's not like I'm going to tell you right away. I loved you before you saved my life, but saving my life is really a good way to make somebody love you. I loved you before you told me about the 13 sluts and the woman who opened your eyes. I still loved you after you told me you had had sex over 5 million times already. Now that's a lot of love don't you think?"

I smiled as I was driving. As the light turned green far in front of us, I floored the car, and it jumped like some angry beast wanting to reach fleeing gazelle.

"I know you probably can't kill us in a car accident, but I'd rather not have one," Terri said. "Do you think it would hurt?"

"Don't worry, I won't kill us." I laughed as I took a corner and drifted with it. "I was a professional racecar driver for a while on the circuit. I made sure that I never won too much, but it was a lot of fun."

"I get it," Terri laughed, "but I'm wondering when my pancreas is going to fly out of my body as you're taking these corners. Don't they have big giant harnesses in race cars?"

"Your seatbelt is on, isn't it?" I laughed.

"Absolutely," Terri said, "I always wear a seat belt."

"See," I said, "Safety at work. We're almost there," I said as we turned on Vine Street. "The bank is in its own building down where Prudential used to be. Worst case, the building isn't attached to anything else, and I don't think that there are any other tenants. There weren't a few months ago." I considered for a moment and glanced at Terri, then touched her arm for a moment. She looked up at me. "I will try to reason with the boys and if I can get them to drink the tea with me, it will be okay. It could get ugly, and it's hard to know how ugly it could get. I will try to avoid that."

Police were everywhere as we neared the bank building. The area was cordoned off, and police officers manned yellow lines that kept out both reporters and bystanders. I saw Shawn scanning the area, and he saw the Impala pull up. I moved the car forward as he waved towards me and lifted the yellow police tape. Another officer got to the other side and waved me through as well. Once I was just beyond the line, I stopped the car and got out. Terri got out of the other side. Shawn glanced at her and nodded.

"It's about time you got here," Shawn said. "You're late by 5 minutes. Fortunately, I told them thirty minutes to give you time to get here. I expected traffic or some grandmother to be crossing the road somewhere because that's just my luck right now."

"I'm here. I'm ready to go. Do I need a radio or something?" I asked. "How about body armor?" Terri glanced at me and raised an eyebrow.

"No, they said they're going to check you when you get in, so a radio will definitely not be in the cards. Take your cell phone and once you're inside, if you get anywhere call me. They will allow the cell phone; I am pretty sure. Don't be a hero. You're not trained to handle anything like this, and I have no idea why they're asking for you. I am sure you do, and I am expecting I will be briefed afterwards."

We started walking towards a mobile command center that was set up in front of the door. It was a large trailer that was heavily armored and had cables running from it everywhere. Men were walking in and out of it at a frenzied pace. I stopped and said, "One second." Then I turned and ran to the trunk of the Impala, opening it as I approached with the key fob. I reached in the trunk and grabbed two hand grenades magnetically mounted to the inside right of the trunk. I slipped them into my pocket, then opened the door and grabbed the thermos of tea. I jogged back up to the two of them and looked at Terri, "I almost forgot the tea."

"You brought tea to a hostage situation?" Shawn asked. "That's a new one on me."

"Tea can calm people, and it may allow me to talk to them a little bit longer," I said. "Trust me, I have been in a lot of difficult situations before, and the tea and I may be able to help you more than you think."

"I've done my diligence on you, Adam," Shawn said, "Remember? When we first allowed you to help us out. I had to look you up. You have no training, and there is little to nothing special about you. You didn't do very well in school, you didn't do very well in college, and except for having some money that your parents left you, you really haven't done much of anything. To me, it looks like you've done everything in your life to stay out of the limelight and take zero risks; so why would I believe that you could help me with a difficult situation? I know you've been able to help with these cases, but it's almost like a game to you. I really like you as a friend, but I'm not sure about everything else."

I laughed for a second. "Would you like me to tell you exactly when you ran the background check? How 'bout I hand you the recordings for every person you called about me? Maybe you would like to know what your background check says? I'm not here to compare the length of anyone's wing wang, but I already told you I'd tell you the truth after this was over. Do you think you could set all this aside and trust me for a few minutes? Would you rather I just go?" I was taking a chance pushing Shawn this hard. I was hoping that he would draw some incorrect lines and think I was an ex-government agent or someone in witness protection that had more skills than he was aware of. I could see that he was pondering what I had just said to him, and I wondered how he was approaching it. For all I knew he, might be thinking I was crazy right now.

Terri was right, I did have faith in him. Apparently, I had faith in a lot of people that I still kept at arm's length. I laughed to myself that a thirty-one-year-old girl was teaching someone as old as me.

Shawn stammered for a moment; I had never seen him at a loss for words. "You know that's the most aggressive thing you've ever said to me. You are always a little bit of a wimp for such a big guy. It kind of gives me a little more faith in you. I'll call them and tell them you're coming in."

Terri looked over at me and smiled. She leaned close to me and put her lips next to my ear, kissing it lightly. "I told you so," she whispered.

Shawn walked back over to us, "They said for you to go ahead and go in. Be careful Adam, you're not Superman, and they have already hurt people. I don't want you to be on that list."

I smiled and hugged Terri. I then began walking towards the front door of the bank with cameras, helicopters, and about 40 police officers focused on me. As I walked, I skipped a little and then looked back at Terri who had her face in her palm. I reached the door and pulled it open. I was inside. In the atrium, I could see the hostages. It looked to be between 15 and 20 people with the two boys standing near them, guns held at arm's length. I saw some bloodstains on the one boy's shirt and some holes in the fabric and knew he had been shot. It was clear that the shot did not hit anything important or slow him down at all, as he was fully focused on both the prisoners and me.

"Hi everyone," I said. "My name is Adam."

The boys pointed their guns at me, "Yeah, we know, Adam. We know you from yesterday, remember?"

"Why don't we let some of the prisoners go?" I asked. "In fact, why don't we let all of the prisoners go so we can talk frankly among the three of us. We have a lot to talk about, don't we?"

The two boys looked at each other and whispered to each other with nervous energy.

"How do we know we can trust you?" one boy asked.

"If you remember, I was the one trying to give you every chance to walk away yesterday morning," I said. "I didn't want anyone to get hurt, and I definitely don't want to hurt either one of you."

"You can't hurt us now," the other boy said. "We can't be hurt at all anymore."

"Of course, you're right," I lied a little. "So it's just two to one. Why don't you let all of them go, and we'll settle this like real men? We'll talk it out over some tea. I even brought hot tea."

"Tea," the first boy said again, "real men settle things over beer. Did you bring any beer?" The boy chuckled.

"You haven't made it that far yet, have you," I said. "You won't be getting drunk ever again or you'll have to spend a whole lot of money to do it. No more getting drunk, or high, or really anything except high on life."

"What did you do to us?" The second boy asked.

"Let's let the hostages go free, and we'll sit down and talk this out. Isn't this better if we talked about it alone? Good or bad, don't you want this to be your secret?" I played on their vanity and their need to be superior. "You don't want to end up in a lab, do you?" The two boys seemed to be contemplating what I said. They moved over to the side, still holding guns on the hostages, and began whispering.

Two younger women whimpered in the front, tears falling and smearing their mascara. A man towards the back, wearing glasses, had blood running down his head where something had struck him. I scanned all of the hostages, and they all looked in good health; just afraid and a few of them a little battered. One man locked eyes with me for a moment, and I could tell he was military. He nodded imperceptibly, and I winked at him while shaking my head 'no' very slightly.

"Okay," the first boy said, "we'll let the hostages go, but you have to promise to stay here with us. Don't be lying to us."

"I promise I'll stay here with you until this is resolved." I smiled. "Should we order some pizza?"

"Yeah, pizza sounds really good," the first boy said.

"What kind of pizza do you want?" I said, "I like Donatos, and they're close, up by campus, but I also like the Domino's meat lover's pizza. It's pretty yummy. Still, Donatos has those little squares. Their pepperoni is so awesome. Maybe that's the better choice. What do you guys think?"

The two boys looked at each other and were clearly unsure about me. All the better. They had not bothered to search me at this point, and of course, the more I made myself harmless the more that they were likely to drop their guard. As I watched the two boys talking to each other, I thought back to thousands of years ago when the two guards were talking to each other, getting ready to try to humiliate me. Everything was unpredictable at the moment, and I had no idea how this was going to turn out.

"Donatos is good," the first boy said. "We'll let them go, and we'll get some pizza in here, right?"

"I'm going to reach in my pocket and grab my cell phone, it's all I brought with me," I said and slowly reached into my pocket and pulled out my cell phone. "Do you want to listen, or do you trust me?"

"We want to listen," the second boy said.

The phone rang once, and Shawn picked up, "What's the story?"

"Well, hello to you too, Shawn," I said. "The guys and I have been talking in here. We've decided to let the hostages go, and just the three of us talk for a little bit. I hope that's okay with you. We also decided we'd like a couple of large Donato's pepperoni pizzas. Do you think you can do that for us?"

"Yeah, I think I can do that for you, do you want any of those breadsticks or just the pizza?" Shawn asked.

"That's a good idea," I said, "how about you get the breadsticks too? You know, just in case we want them with some of that marinara sauce. Maybe a garlic sauce too."

"When are you going to send the hostages out?" Shawn asked.

"We have some serious talking to do, so as soon as I hang up the phone, the guys will send them out," I said. "No tricks now, and keep those guns away, we don't want anybody getting shot."

"No tricks," Shawn said. "I'll make the call and the pizza will be here within 30 minutes."

"I noticed you were putting on a few pounds, tell me it isn't Donatos," I laughed.

"Hey, you know I like the thin crust with those little pepperonis," Shawn said. "Give me a break. I work out more than you do."

"Shut up," the second boy yelled. "Get the hostages out of here so we can talk."

"Gotta go, Shawn. We'll send the hostages out, and you get me some pizza," I said as I hung up the phone. "Okay, we've got pizza coming. Let's get rid of these people so we can talk. You're going to have a lot of questions for me."

The two boys looked at each other and then waved their guns at the hostages, "All right, all of you, stand up," the first boy said. "We're going to walk single file out of here, and once you're outside, you walk to those police and don't say a word about anything, or we'll shoot you."

The group stood and started walking towards the door. I hung back behind the boys. I tapped the side of my pocket and felt the weight of the two hand grenades. I was hoping that I wouldn't need them. The man who locked eyes with me earlier was now staring at me, wondering if he should do anything. I shook my head 'no' imperceptibly again, and he walked out the door with the rest of the hostages. As each hostage reached the outer door, they shuffled faster or ran to the police officers waiting outside for them. One by one, they filed out until it was just the three of us. The two boys closed the inner door, locked it, and came back to me.

"These guns won't do much to you, will they?" the first boy asked.

"No, but keep them up. The police don't know anything about the three of us," I said. "Before we get started, I know one of you is Jimmy and one of you is Cal. Which is which?"

The first boy spoke up and said, "I'm Jimmy."

I looked at the second boy and said, "That makes you Cal, right?"

"Yeah, I'm Cal," Cal replied to me.

"Well," I sighed; "first I have to say I'm sorry I hurt both of you. I know it hurts just as bad when it comes back, so I can't really blame you for being so frustrated."

"Yeah, why did you have to go and hurt us that bad," Cal said, "I mean, what did we do to you?"

"Oh, I don't know," I replied; "you just tried to kill me and the girl I was with."

Jimmy laughed a little and sat down in the chair, "Yeah, we did do that," he said, "but it was all Sam. You know it was all Sam."

"Yeah, I know it was Sam," I said. "But you guys sure wanted to hurt me pretty bad. If I remember correctly, I got belted with a baseball bat a few times."

"About that," Cal asked, "why didn't we get stronger like you?"

"Doesn't work that way," I said. "It'll come but it takes a lot of time. You guys have already started moving too fast and are burning it away."

"What do we have to do to get out of this?" Cal said. "I know the police aren't going to let us out of here, and you won't want to let us out of here either. The way I figure it, if we go to the police or the press, it'll make a lot of trouble for you and for us. We kinda screwed up with all of this, but when the police broke into the house, he shot and it just happened. He was surprised when I didn't fall down. I picked up the baseball bat and just got angry. I hit him over and over until I calmed down."

"Yeah," Jimmy said. "Can you give us some money or something, and we can just disappear; or are we gonna die here today?"

"That depends on you," I said. "I came in here 100% ready to kill you both. But there is another way."

The two boys looked at each other and nodded, "I think we'd like to take the other way if we could, Sir." Jimmy said.

"I really don't want to die right now," Cal said. "I was getting really close to graduating. I'd like to graduate, get married, and grow old. We shouldn't have listened to Sam, but I didn't know what else to do. Scholarships cover a lot, but they don't make ends meet like they used to, and it's a struggle to eat sometimes. Do you think you can help us?"

"It's going to be tough. I've gotta level with you," I said. "I'm sure you guys didn't want to make trouble but there is trouble now, and it's all because of Sam. I get that, but it's also because of you." I set the tea on top of the table. "What I have here is a way out for you. If the two of you drink this tea, you will forget all about the last two days. If we do that, we'll come up with a story together that will work where you didn't kill the cop, and you didn't know what was going on. We'll come up with a story where the two of you were told that if you didn't come to this bank that they were going to kill you."

"Yeah, maybe that'll work, but I don't think I'll last if they start screaming and yelling at me." Jimmy was noticeably agitated.

"You let me handle that. If you drink the tea, you won't remember any of this. You won't remember getting hurt, you won't remember coming here, and if they put you through a lie detector test, you'll pass with flying colors because you just won't remember. Sometime after they release you, and they will eventually release you, I will come and straighten this out with you even though you won't remember me either."

"How do we know you won't lie to us?" Jimmy said.

"Well, you won't," I said. "I will give you my word that what I'm telling you is true, but once you drink the tea, you won't know. I will tell you that I'll have to do something because otherwise, you'll freak out the first time you cut yourself."

"Cal, I think we better do as he says," Jimmy said.

I pulled out the tea and opened it at the table where we were sitting. I also pulled out the two collapsible cups I put in my pocket and opened them as well. I poured the tea into the two cups and set them in front of the boys. The boys looked at the tea, then looked at each other and smiled.

"You really didn't think we were going to drink that tea did you," Jimmy said. "We were just playing along see what you were going to do." Both boys picked up the cups of tea and poured them out on the ground. They then slapped the Thermos, and it bounced with clinks and clangs across the floor and into the wall. I glanced at my watch and noted the time to myself. I felt bad about everything that was going on. But I knew what I was going to have to do.

"Actually, I didn't think there was any chance in hell you were going to drink that tea," I said. "That's why you just threw away some good tea and nothing else. There are people out there keeping an eye on things, and pretty soon, I won't have to worry about you anymore."

"What do you mean you won't have to worry about us and who's watching us?" Jimmy yelped.

"Why a sniper, of course, and he has a special bullet that'll take you both out," I lied. "You see, if you had drunk the tea, it was going to be a sign to them that you were cooperating. Since you didn't drink the tea, the government group that I work for isn't going to be kind to you."

"The government," Cal stammered. "You see, Jimmy, I told you it was the government. This is one of those government experiments and now we've just messed it up. They probably know about the other people we killed today, and they're going to take us in and do experiments on us. Damn it, Jimmy. We could have just laid low, and nobody would have known, but you had to go out and do shit."

I looked at the window and then looked at my watch again. "Boys, if you want to talk anymore, we better go to the vault. We've only got about 3 minutes before those big bullets start coming in here. They won't be able to penetrate the vault. They won't be able to have cameras in there either, so you'll be safe to talk, and then maybe I can work something out."

"Shit," Jimmy said. "Let me think. No tricks right," Jimmy said.

"No tricks. I'll walk right into the vault with my hands up, so you know I won't be pulling any tricks on you," I said.

"Let's go right now. I don't want anybody shooting early at me," Cal said and pushed me forward. "It hurts when they hit you."

The vault was open as was normal in banks during business hours. All of the important items were locked behind either bars or inside safe deposit boxes. As such, the outer vault door just kept all of the inside stuff safe. When vaults were invented for banks, the safety deposit boxes were supposed to be as safe as the vault. I found that out in the 1920s when I tried to drill open a safety deposit box and broke ten drill bits in the process. We walked into the vault, and I pulled the door back towards us.

"I don't think we have to close it. We just have to make sure they can't see us," I said, putting my hands down. "What are you guys going to do if you get out of here?" I asked while putting my hands in my jacket pockets.

"Pretty much anything we want, right?" Cal said.

"You're just going to have to stay one step ahead of the government because they will be coming for you," I lied. "I might be able to get you a car and some money, but they're going to find you eventually unless you hide really well."

"Don't you worry about it, Mr. Adam," Jimmy said. "We're going to go into the deep hills and disappear."

"That will probably work," I said.

I looked at my watch again then put my hand back in my coat pocket. I heard a knock at the door, and the two boys jumped up. I looked out and saw that Shawn was at the door. He was holding two pizzas. I started to walk out of the vault.

"Where are you going?" Jimmy asked.

"It's just the pizza," I said.

Both boys moved towards the vault door and looked out towards where Shawn stood with two pizza boxes. They both looked hungry, and as they turned back to me, they nodded and motioned towards the door. The two boys were looking at me as I pulled my hands from the pocket, my thumbs in the pins of the two grenades I brought. I pushed the grenades forward so fast I couldn't be seen easily and jammed one into each of the boys' mouths as I pulled the pins out of both. With the pins still in my hand, I dropped to my knees and punched both boys in the groin. Both of them fell forward with the grenades lodged inside their mouths and blood drooling outside of them. I opened the vault door and then slammed it while running towards Shawn.

Shawn dropped the pizzas, drew his Glock 43, and rushed to the door. The inner door was locked. He shook it and then fired the pistol twice at the glass of the door.

I screamed, "Get down!" as I jumped to the floor. We both heard the explosions almost immediately. The explosions were so powerful they shook the building and the floor. The grenades were doctored with the heaviest charge I could fit inside of them. I had them made in the 1940s when I found that some strange things happening that could have been attributed to someone like me. It all turned out to be a hoax, and I'd never had to use them until today.

Dust fell from the ceiling and alarms sounded all over. The explosion was over. I stood up and looked at the Armormax glass door and the two embedded bullets from Shawn's gun. I turned the knob on the inside door and opened it as Shawn walked in with his gun still drawn.

Shawn immediately asked me, "What was that? What happened?"

"They said they were going to kill me and kill themselves. They had grenades. When they pulled the pins, I kicked one of 'em in the nuts and ran out," I said.

"Those weren't normal grenades," Shawn said. "I have thrown enough grenades to know what they sound like, and that was more like a few sticks of dynamite."

"I wouldn't know," I said, "but they looked like older grenades, so maybe they were a little more powerful."

Shawn walked with me to the vault door, and we pulled it open. Inside it was a scene out of a horror movie. Many of the safe deposit boxes had been dented, but it looked like most of the safe had held strong. The boys, however, were in so many pieces that it looked like they had been blended and poured into the safe. Nothing moved, and everything was okay in the back of my mind. I still had to arrange for someone to clean this up, and make sure no one was infected by me again.

"I'm sorry, Shawn," I said. "I wanted to save them, I really did, but they wanted to die. They said they knew the police would either kill them or put them in jail forever for killing an officer. They said they killed other people today and just couldn't live with it anymore; they wanted me to die with him. I'm so sorry I couldn't keep them alive for you to put on trial."

Shawn was looking over the mess, shaking his head. Finally, he turned to me and said, "It's not your fault. You got the hostages out, and that's more than anybody else could do. We'll clean up this mess; you take your girl home."

"Thanks, Shawn," I said. "Will you be coming over later to talk?"

"You know what? I think I'm gonna let you keep your secrets," Shawn said. "While you were in here, I was considering that you might die. Watching Terri pay such close attention to you, I realized that you had been nothing but honest with me. We both know you try to help me all the time. It was just like you said. I was just caught up in the moment.

You keep your secret, and someday when you're ready, tell me. I really appreciate you coming."

I put out my hand and Shawn took it. As we were sitting there shaking hands, he pulled me close and hugged me for a moment and then let me go. "You do owe me a golf game for all of this," I laughed.

"I thought you were the big dude that kept all the great greens fees up," Shawn laughed. "Maybe it's you that owes me a golf game."

We both laughed for a moment. I walked out of the bank as cameras, cell phones, and videos focused on me. As I got to the edge, Terri ran up to me and put her arms around me. "Are you okay?" she asked.

"I'm a little sad, I suppose," I said as we walked to the car and got in. "I thought I could save them. I thought they wanted to do the right thing, and they were good kids at heart. For whatever reason, they were cold-hearted and wanted nothing more than to exploit the world. It's my fault they got that way, you know, like me, but still, I didn't make them into killers. While I was sitting there, they confessed to killing a lot more people than just the police officer. I don't know. I almost had them drinking the tea, but it was all a game to them. In the end, I didn't feel as sad when I killed them."

I started the car and an officer guided me out of the taped-off area. Soon I was on Main Street heading back to the house. I was quiet and so was Terri for a few short minutes. "How did you kill them?" she asked.

"I took in two grenades as a backup plan. If the police follow standard operating procedures, they'll be very careful with the cleanup and run standard tests. Nothing genetic will be done, and there won't be any intense testing of the tissues. Most of the tissues will be cleaned up, eliminated, and because of all the blood-borne illnesses, no one will dare touch any of it. I'll also call Phillip and see if he knows anyone on the team that will do the final cleanup since they'll only take samples. If he does, he'll be able to clean it up and dispose of it as a biohazard which means burning it down to nothing. Either way, the risk is low, and the police here are very thorough and follow processes and procedures to the letter."

"Well, not exactly to the letter," Terri said. "After all, Shawn just let you go without a full debrief. Usually, things are tied up for quite a while."

"Yeah, I know," I replied. "Shawn said that he wouldn't be asking me any other questions and that he was a little too aggressive and out of line today. It is not normal for him, but who am I to question it? I think he just wants perfection and doesn't always get it," I said.

"What now?" Terri asked.

"Well, we go home and try to build a good life together," I said. "This little adventure is over, but we both know there will be another. We will take our time and make every single day count."

Chapter 18

We talked about everything and nothing on the drive home. It was apparent to me that Terri was a little upset the two boys had died. We were stuck in traffic for a while again and not making good headway. Terri finally asked, "Was there any other way? Doesn't it get tiring to have eternal life and be around death so much?"

I thought about her question for several minutes before I answered. I wasn't sure the best way to approach it as every avenue made me seem selfish. Finally, I admitted, "There probably could have been. I walked in thinking there were only two options. Either the boys drank the tea and later I moved them and explained a little more, or they were too far gone, and they had to die. Thinking about it now, I could just as easily have been wrong. To be fair, this is very complicated right now, and I haven't been this close to compromised since I was in Spain during the inquisition."

"There are always other choices even in complicated situations like this," Terri said. "I know I'm barely a fraction of an itty-bitty percentage of your age, but I would like to think that life has meaning and that taking a life is the last choice that any of us should make. Who cares if we would have had to move? If the boys were out of line, so what if they became test subjects? It didn't have to affect us. If you really care about me, and I know it's early, you should consider that life is important. I know you have a vastly different view of what life is, and what humans are in general, but are we all that bad? Is our life so meaningless that we can snuff it out in an instant to protect where you live or your comfort level?"

"No," I said. "I understand your point of view, and I have to admit I have always chosen the more violent path because I felt I was given no choice. When Sam came at you, he wasn't trying to just hurt you or embarrass you, he was trying to kill you. I restrained myself at your request, and as Sam died, I felt regret. I am not the Angel of Death, nor am I someone that loves to kill or even likes to kill. I am sometimes forced to kill by the situations that I am in. If it means anything, it has been a very long time since I hurt anyone as bad as the last two days. It has been a long time since I have been in a complicated situation, even a little like this."

"Of course, it means something," Terri said. "The fact that I'm talking about this means that it means something. I know you were forced into a difficult situation, and I know there was probably no other choice, but still, I don't know what I don't know. You promised me before not to hurt anyone, and you followed that to the letter. I'm hopeful that our relationship will be based on trust, and you and I trying to take that higher ground."

I sat quietly again for a few minutes. How could I tell Terri that I always tried to take the higher ground? How could I explain to her the destruction the two boys could have done with their attitudes and their new ability? Anything that I could say would instantly be turned against me, and anything I tried to explain could be seen as condescending. I knew I was in a no-win situation, so I simply said, "I will always try to take the higher ground. I can't promise that will always be the winning strategy, but I will always try."

Terri slid over on the bench seat of the Impala and hugged my arm. "That's all I ever wanted."

We pulled into the driveway, and the gate opened, followed by the garage. As the gate closed behind us, I drove into the garage into the slot for the Impala. I pressed the button, and the garage closed as I turned the engine off. We got out of the car, and I considered putting the cover on but decided against it. Terri came around to my side of the car and put her arms around me. "Quiet night at home tonight, maybe?"

"Sounds great to me," I said.

We walked into the house together and around into the hallway. Terri was in the lead, and I followed behind closely feeling good about our talk, and the future before us. As we walked into the large den, I turned on the lights, and there was a rapid flash. Before me, Terri fell to the ground. Another flash, and I felt the sting of a dart in my chest and pulled it out, looking for a source. I saw none. I fell to my knees and checked Terri. She was alive but out cold. I felt dizzy and disoriented, but I held my ground, looking around the room. Still, I saw nothing.

I struggled on my hands and knees, holding on to consciousness with a thin thread. My eyes blurred for a moment, and I tried to crawl towards the cases filled with a multitude of weapons. There was a voice behind me, "That's it. Just keep struggling let the sedative work its way through you."

The voice was familiar, but I couldn't place it. I flipped to my back and looked up. A red dress sparkled in front of me. I slowly scanned up the well-built figure, the slit of the red evening dress was out of a Hollywood gala. I shook my head and saw the raven-black hair and finally the blue eyes looking straight at me. It was Morgan.

"Should I call you Adam now? That is the identity you have taken, right?" she said, "How long has it been lover? At least a few 1,000 years, I would say. You are a hard one to find, and I am sure I have come close many times. I couldn't believe my luck tonight. I was in Cincinnati for a museum benefit when your picture ended up all over the television. What was that? An hour ago? My goodness," Morgan said as she stared at me. "You haven't aged a day. You don't know how I've missed you. I've filled my time with so many other hobbies and pursuits. I've had a few flings but none as exciting as you. My flings have always had to end with a bang, or in most cases, a beheading and a crematory. It has made it easier in the last few years. It is truly a gift to be able to enjoy a man until he annoys me, then behead him and turn him to ash in a short time. I may even start turning them into diamonds now and making a necklace of lovers. What a great idea."

"How are you still alive?" I asked while trying to regain my control.

"Well," Morgan walked the room, visibly unworried about me. Terri was still on the ground, out cold. "It appears that you're a little more potent than we thought. There was a study in the last 10 years that noted when a man and a woman have sexual relations, parts of the woman's DNA is changed just by that interaction. You men aren't as lucky. You just get to go around dropping your seed everywhere. Apparently, the 700 or so years that we were together has allowed me to live this long pretty easily. I've found a few of the other women who are still alive as well. I have to say I fared much better than those that I located." Morgan picked up an artifact on one of the shelves in the room, then dropped it casually to the floor. "The ones I have found so far are living in exile and have forgotten who they could be. Magda would not have been so frivolous with an immortal life. I am glad she is gone." Morgan looked at the wall of swords and touched the blade of the large broadsword in the center. She licked her fingertip, and I assumed the razor-sharp blade cut her. "I also found out that a little bit of blood works a whole lot better on normal people. I have made a few almost immortals, accidently, when I was testing the pure blood. It happens fast, and you get an immortal within a few days." She noted the concern on my face. "Don't worry, they were quickly eliminated. I really don't like competition."

I shook my head again and could feel the effects of the drug. At the same time, I could feel my body removing it. If I could get to a drawer that had adrenaline in it, I could reverse the effects. I looked side to side for anyone else in the room. I needed time. "How would you be able to test?"

"That's a good question. I am glad you asked. I accidentally found out there's more than one of you. I found an English gentleman as I tracked different people looking for you. He was a popular discussion among many people in the area. The rumors were that he looked like his own grandfather, and his great grandfather, and so on. I thought maybe it was you. I was a little disappointed that it wasn't, but as I looked at the pictures, I realized they were right. I tried to get close to him, but he was elusive and allowed no one near him. You took a much different tact with stealth. He took a more direct approach with guards and dogs and servants everywhere. Eventually, I was able to get close to him, and one night, I slipped into his bedroom and had my way with him. I have found interesting ways to take a man easily, since you. I digress."

After I had him, I felt the charge in my body. It did not make me anymore beautiful. It doesn't work that way. I found after bedding Magda's man and, of course, you that you can feel it afterwards if you pay attention. The guards and estate were easy. I was his new wife, and they fell in line rapidly. He became a toy for me. I would still have him around if he hadn't thrown himself into a fireplace. I guess he didn't like me as much as I enjoyed him." Morgan paused, perceptibly pleased with herself. Her nature was crueler than she had been previously. "You know, when I threw Magda into the fireplace, I didn't get to relish that moment. When Nigel jumped into the fireplace, I saw him regenerate over and over until the fire got ahead of the regeneration. He finally died. I wasn't sad; I just knew I had to keep looking for others. I knew there were more of you and that you were probably still out there."

"What do you want?" I asked.

"That's a tough question," Morgan said. "I thought about just taking the girl when I considered you must have made her young. I could have kept her for perhaps thousands of years as my failsafe. It is apparent to me now that she has not turned. My security team ran her bio on the way here. She is only 31. How do you explain not sleeping with her? You really hurt my feelings when you left me, and I've thought for years of how I could hurt you."

"I think you did a pretty good job of it before," I said.

"Oh, I'm sure you do," Morgan walked around the room. "I'm sure you think that I was the most terrible prison guard ever. Remember me teaching you all the things I taught you? I had always planned on it being you and me eternally, forever. You ruined it for me. Maybe this girl was going to be yours. Do you have feelings for her?"

I was still groggy, but it was evident that Morgan didn't know as much about my physiology, and I felt my energy coming back. Terri lay still, having taken two darts. I was watching Morgan in her bright red evening gown and bright red high-heeled shoes, walking in circles around the two of us. I knew time was growing short. "You still haven't told me what you want?"

"Still focused," Morgan said, "I like that. I knew you were going to be intelligent. You were so curious. You were also so malleable and eager to please. What have you done all this time? Hide? Collect the antiquities of things that you wanted to do? Found another rock? Have you been waiting for me to come to get you?"

"To be honest, I've thought very little of you over the past thousands of years," I said as I realized I was under the desk. I glanced up at the bottom of the desk and saw the magnetically mounted pistol. Then immediately looked back at Morgan. She was oblivious and felt she was in control. I didn't know if the pistol would do anything, as it was minimally effective on me, but I did know that Magda and the boys did not regenerate as quickly. She continued walking around the room, paying very little attention to me and no attention to Terri.

"That's so hurtful," Morgan said. "I would have thought you were constantly thinking of me. It saddens me to think that you didn't pine over me or want me or desire to be with me one more time."

"I'd rather not," I said, "I'm kind of tired of old women."

"Old?" Morgan said as she knelt down. "Do I look old to you?" She leaned down and grabbed my hand. I stayed limp, feigning that the drug was still affecting me. She put my hand on her breast. "Does this feel anything less than perfect?" She threw my hand down to the ground, and I let it fall hard and bounce to the side. "What a waste. We could have had all this time together, and instead, you are nothing; maybe less than nothing. How did you even get any of this stuff? You have no skills. You have no way of making money. Is this someone else's house?"

I wondered why Morgan was so ignorant about my past. I patted myself on the back internally, knowing that I had done a good job of hiding my tracks, just like when Ariana and I escaped.

"Maybe you need a lesson in pain again," Morgan was ranting. Perhaps she had found a way to escape aging, but she sounded quite mad. Morgan kicked Terri over onto her back. In a swift motion Morgan grabbed a golden-hilted sword from the wall and plunged it into Terri's stomach. I screamed and started to move as the blood pooled on Terri's clothing.

"I think I will leave the woman to die, and you will wonder if you could have saved her. For now, I will take you, and turn you into my dog again. Maybe I'll find a way to synthesize the proteins, and I won't need you anymore as my safety net. Don't worry, I still won't let you go." She snapped her fingers, and two men walked out from the hallway wearing all black and carrying tranquilizer guns. "It's so sad. Two men couldn't take me down on their best day, and here you are, laying on the ground, ready to pass out from a low-dose drug. Pathetic."

Morgan leaned down to me and looked me in the eye. She was quite beautiful, but I knew how ugly she was inside. I remembered how she killed Magda and how she sold me to the 12 other women for her own gain. She grabbed my jaw and squeezed it together. "We're going to have fun together again, lover." She kissed my lips and I felt sick. She looked up at the two men. "Take him. Leave her. He won't give you any trouble," she looked down at me. "Will you, sweetheart?"

I reached up and grabbed the pistol and felt it fall into my hand perfectly. Grabbing Morgan by the hair, I put the pistol into her eye socket and pulled the trigger three times then threw her to the side. Blood sprayed everywhere, and I could see pieces of her brain across the room. I didn't stop. I aimed at the two men. Before the first could react, I shot him between the eyes. He fell fast and hard to the ground, and his body convulsed in the throes of death. The second man was swinging his tranquilizer gun at me, but I kicked at it as I shot him twice in the head. My ears rang, but through it, I could hear Morgan screaming.

"You ruined my makeup," Morgan screamed, she was looking at me with one eye, and part of her face and skull was missing, but she still stood. The skin was trying to seal but it was very slow. I fired three more times into her chest, and then the slide on the gun locked back. "Bullets? Really?" Morgan seethed in undeniable pain. She turned with her good eye and looked at the bookcases, grabbing and pulling them down. The bookcase fell on me, and Morgan cackled like an evil witch out of a bad movie. I struggled to move the bookcase, no longer feeling the effects of whatever drug they had used on me. Morgan stood over me. Her skin was slowly folding in upon itself, repairing. "Do you know how much this dress cost?" She looked at the holes caused by the multiple bullets.

Morgan looked at the wall, walked a few steps, and grabbed a battle axe. She walked back to me. I was still pinned by the heavy bookcases, struggling to get out.

"I think I may just take your head and see if you grow back from it." Morgan cackled again.

I pushed hard, but her foot was on the bookcase, and I had no leverage. She raised the axe, and her arm came off on top of the bookcase.

"Do you have any idea how bad it hurts to have a sword put through your gut?" Terri said as she panted and held the sword like a cane before her now. The golden hilt shimmered in the light, and blood streamed down the blade where she had taken Morgan's arm.

"You!" Morgan cried. Morgan looked at her arm and the woman holding the sword next to her. There was a momentary look of panic in Morgan's eyes, and I believe she knew she had miscalculated. She pushed Terri hard with her remaining arm and knocked her to the floor. As she ran to the halls she reached down and picked up one of her men's weapons, firing wildly at us.

There was smoke and silence for a minute, and I called to Terri. I was done and pushed with my might throwing the bookcase to the side of me. I stood and looked around the room. Morgan was gone. I heard the door to the garage slammed shut and ran that way as fast as I could. As I got to the laundry room, I grabbed a broom and broke it off so it would work as a makeshift staff. I opened the garage door and saw nothing. I turned on the bright overhead lights, and I still saw nothing. The garage door was open. Morgan was gone.

I looked at the door handle and saw blood and knew Morgan had used the door. I hit the wall control and made sure that the garage was secure. Satisfied, I ran back into the house. Terri met me in the hall, limping.

"What just happened?" she gasped.

"We were ambushed," I said.

"No kidding, so that was an ambush." Terri smiled through her pain as we walked back to the den. "Remind me to avoid swords in the gut for a while. They sting. Who ambushed us?"

"You won't believe this because I sure didn't," I said. "Morgan saw us on television and was in Cincinnati. In the time they aired me going into the bank, she had found out who I was, where I lived and was waiting for us here." The room was a mess, so we moved to the bedroom, and both of us fell onto the bed.

"Morgan is still alive?" Terri sighed. "She looked good for an old broad, and I liked her dress. Think I would look good in a red dress? It would match my sword." I realized she was still holding on to the broadsword even as we lay on the bed.

"She is very much alive, and she found another person like me, and killed them. She spit out a lot of information, and my effect may be almost permanent. We will have a lot of work to do." I tried to sit up and was still sore as my body was catching up from all the trauma. I pushed myself, got up, and pulled out my cellphone. "I know you don't have much but pack what you have, and we'll go to a random hotel."

"Another question, did I see two dead men in the den?" Terri asked.

"They were the two men with her, and they were going to take me. She actually spit out a lot of options and sounds quite mad. Maybe I wasn't the first person to scramble her brains with a pistol."

Terri tried to stand up, "Just when I thought the day was going to be good. I guess I need a suitcase. Maybe I need a nap first." Terri lay back down on the bed and closed her eyes while holding the broadsword. She fell asleep in moments.

I went to the den and covered the two men, then got another magazine for the 1911. I dialed Shawn.

"Hi," I said.

"Adam," Shawn said, "I am still downtown, cleaning up."

"Shawn," I said, "I think I need you here, and I am going to tell you a story when you get here. Apparently, I don't have any choice."

"Are you okay?" Shawn asked.

"Well," I said, "for someone who was just about killed, I think I am pretty good. Can you come out to the house? We will wait for you but we will be going to a hotel later."

"I'll be there in twenty minutes," Shawn said.

"Twenty-five," I laughed as I hung up.

This was going to be a long night.

Chapter 19

Terri was still asleep when Shawn arrived. The gate was closed, so he called and let me know he was waiting. I opened the gate and walked to the garage and watched him drive up in his unmarked Charger. I didn't know how the next few minutes were going to go, but I hoped that Shawn's trust in me was enough to get through this shock.

"You certainly left a big mess downtown," Shawn said. "We will be writing paperwork and sifting through body parts for some time."

"Shawn," I began, "you've been a good friend to me. I've known you for a long time."

"I'm not sure I like where this is going," Shawn said. "Maybe we should sit down with a drink before this talk happens."

"Maybe," I said, "but in this particular case, I wanted to be out here for a moment so I can remove all doubt before we talk."

"I'm not sure I like that much either, but let's get this over with." Shawn was cautious, but his curiosity was what made him a good detective.

I took a deep breath and looked Shawn in the eye. "I've spent the last two days with Terri trying to make sure she understood the implications of who I am. I don't have two days right now, but I know that you and I have known each other long enough that you will understand far more than she would. After all, she and I just met. Shawn, I don't know what I am for sure, but I have been alive for a long, long time. My first memory was in what you know as 2,200 BC. I am pretty sure I am far older, but I don't have any memory before that time."

"What kind of game is this Adam?" Shawn asked. "I know you think you're serious, but what you're saying is very difficult to believe."

"I knew you'd say that, which is why I wanted to be out here first." I picked up a rag from the clean rags bin, then grabbed the screwdriver from the toolbox and said, "Pay attention, I really only want to do this once."

Shawn jumped as he saw the screwdriver stab my hand. There was some blood for just a moment that I wiped off as I pulled the screwdriver from my palm. I put my palm out face up to Shawn so he could see it as though I was waving "Hi."

As expected, the hole began folding in upon itself, and the tissue sealed almost instantly. In just a few seconds, the hole was gone, and my hand was clean where it had been rebuilt but still had blood around the edges.

Shawn's eyes were wide in disbelief. He stepped forward to me and grabbed my hand, turning it over and looking at both the palm and back of my hand. "I don't believe this."

"I have a lot to tell you in a very short time, but if you don't want to hear it or if you're afraid or you just don't think you'll believe me, then you need to go right now. I will be giving you a very short version, and I hope sometime in the future we can talk in more depth, and I can let you ask questions."

"This I have to hear," Shawn said. "How did this happen, and what exactly, are you?"

"I'm as human as you are," I said. "There is something different about my body that not only repairs itself but allows me to live potentially forever. I have no idea how old I am or how old I will become. Before you ask, I am not a vampire or any mythical creature you may have heard of from books or movies. As far as I know, most of those do not exist. I am just a man who is different, and even though I have thousands of years of experience, I am still just a man. I found out only tonight that there was at least one more of me. I have had no contact with any others except those that I have accidentally created, including that one."

"Accidentally created?" Shawn asked.

"Yes," I said. "I apparently can give this gift in some form to others."

"How do you do that?" Shawn asked.

"Originally, I thought it was only from having sex with someone, but I eventually found out that my bodily fluids, including my blood, will pass this trait to other humans. When it was discovered the properties of my sex, I was held captive for 700 years by 13 women in what you would consider ancient times. I was not treated poorly but I was used to allow them youth and longevity."

"Sounds like every man's dream," Shawn said.

"A lot of people would think that," I said. "Looking back, it was just another word for prison. I was chained or bound most of my first 700 years of memories and had sex fifteen to twenty times a day or more. I escaped with a slave girl and, for a short time, had a good life. She was killed, and until this week, I have been mostly alone for nearly 3,500 years."

"This is a lot to swallow," Shawn said. "If I hadn't seen your little trick, I would be putting cuffs on you and taking you to the Ridge."

"I understand," I said, "but you have to understand something else. The same thing that gives me my magnificent healing properties gives me strength. I'm sorry that I lied to you, but I punched Sam in the chest and that's how he died. If you want to take me in for that, I understand but I don't think I can let you right now because my entire world has just been turned upside down."

"That too is a little bit difficult, and that particular case has been closed as a hit and run. Still, I have a duty to uphold justice," Shawn stated.

"That's why you're here," I replied. "When I came home tonight, I was ambushed. The fact that I was ambushed could be a normal situation, but the fact that I was ambushed by the leader of the women who kept me captive makes it something entirely different. There was a woman called Morgan here tonight and my first memory begins with her as an old woman. She had sex with me and became young and beautiful again, but she is quite evil and tried to kill Terri and kidnap me again to become her slave forever, if not longer. There was a heated fight inside my house, and the situation is far more complex than is covered by current laws. If my abilities were to be discovered it is likely I would be imprisoned, dissected, and used for even more evil purposes. I am trusting you, Shawn because I honestly believe you are a good man and can see past the law to a greater law."

"Where is this Morgan now?" Shawn asked.

"She escaped," I stated. "I put three bullets into her head and at least five into her body, and she healed not as fast as me but fast enough. She was about to take my head with a battle-axe, except Terri cut off her arm with a sword. I know this sounds crazy as all get out, but I swear it is all true. Worse, now that she knows I am alive, she will be coming for me and Terri. I have to go on the run."

"I am assuming Terri is good with all of this?" Shawn said.

"What I didn't tell you yet is that Sam shot Terri before I punched him, and she was dying. As she lay dying, I made the decision to save her by using my blood, and now she is similar to me."

"That explains some things," Shawn said, "like why you delayed and kept her away from me. I'm assuming this doesn't happen instantly."

"No, it was quite painful for her, but I thought it better than her being dead," I said. "If you can accept that I'm still the person you knew and I'm still your friend, let's go inside. If you can't, you can go, and I will be out of the city by morning."

"This is all a little hard to believe," Shawn said. "I'm not sure I believe everything you're saying, but I believe you believe it, and I have seen a lot today that I can't easily explain. Above all, I am your friend and an officer of the law. I have no clue what to do except see what's here and make the best decision to uphold the law and our friendship. I want to believe you. Let's see where this goes, and if necessary, I will help."

We walked up the stairs and into the house. I closed the garage, and we walked down the hall to the den. The two men were still there lying on the floor, dead.

"I guess they are not immortal," Shawn said.

"No, they were guards for Morgan. She kept guards all the time that she had me captive. As far as I know, only one was ever given the gift. She said tonight that she played with it and several people but then killed them afterwards. She doesn't want anyone to potentially challenge her power, and that includes me."

Shawn was checking the two men and noted that they were both dead.

"I should report this," Shawn said.

"I know this is a lot to ask, but can you let me take care of it?" I asked. "I have someone that will make sure there are no traces, but I needed you to understand what I was up against. If you can, take prints and try to find out who her thugs are, but not officially."

"Should I be worried that you've killed a bunch of people," Shawn asked.

"No," I said, "I've not killed anyone in a long time until this week. I have tried to avoid any situation with conflict unless I am part of the conflict. I was involved in several wars and have been in countless battles over time. After tonight, I know I am not the real monster. The real monster is out there, and who knows the depth of her power and influence? Where I hid in the shadows and stayed low, she apparently is in the limelight and involved in many levels of society."

"What do you want from me Adam?" Shawn asked. "It seems like you're going to take care of everything."

"I need someone I can trust, and right now, you're one of only a few that I actually believe in. I'm going to have to evade Morgan or end up as her slave again."

"That's not happening," Terri said as she walked into the room. "I think you're going to be stuck with me for a long time, and I'm not into sharing."

Shawn looked at Terri. He then looked at her shirt and the tear in the center. "What happened?"

"The slut put a sword through me," Terri said. "So, I did the only thing I could and cut her arm off when she tried to cut off Adam's head." Terri picked up the arm that still held the battle-axe. "I suppose this would make a cool souvenir if you wanted it, Shawn."

Shawn looked at the arm and shook his head. "Of course, I'll help you, Adam. This is so far out there I'm expecting Bigfoot to bring you a telegram or a vampire to fly in the window."

"He keeps telling me there are no vampires," Terri said. "But I haven't asked him about Bigfoot, and he won't say anything about werewolves. I'm betting he's still keeping secrets from both of us. I think I'll spend a few 100 years getting those secrets out of him."

I went to my desk and opened one of the drawers. I pulled out two cell phones. I handed them to Shawn and then opened another drawer and pulled out an envelope. "The cell phones are pay as you go and have 100 minutes on each. I wouldn't keep them on you, but occasionally I will reach out, and we can talk. They are scrambled and have no voicemail or text. In theory, our discussions will be fairly private. In the envelope is fifty thousand dollars. If I need something or we need to get together, this will allow us to talk with no questions. I would get a safe deposit box and put this away, so you don't have anyone looking over your shoulders."

"Are you trying to bribe me?" Shawn smiled as he walked to my desk and rummaged through it to find an ink pad and piece of paper. Shawn went to the two bodies and took prints from the two men as I continued.

"No," I laughed, "I just want to make sure that you can get to me if you need to. Terri and I will find a place or stay mobile for some time, and this house will be packed up and stored. I'll miss the house, but I need to keep Terri safe."

"Well, I need to keep him safe too," Terri said, "after all, he let a slut in a red party dress kick his ass tonight, and I, a mere girl, had to save him."

Shawn nodded with a wry smile. "I'm sure that's how that happened."

"Thanks, Shawn," I said.

"I think I want to say nothing and walk out of here right now, and I guess I will," Shawn said as he folded the now dry prints and put them in his pocket. "I'm assuming I can use your same phone number for a while?" He handed me the inkpad.

"Absolutely, until we are far away. I'm pretty sure Morgan will have me tracked pretty quickly. I'm also pretty sure that by morning she may be back here. I would appreciate it if you could keep an eye on things as I don't think she wants to be in the limelight of the law. I know she will not find my assets nor my other homes."

Shawn walked over to me and hugged me. He had never done that before. As he hugged me, he simply said, "I hope we see each other again. Let me know where I can visit you someday."

"I know we will, one day," I said as Shawn walked down the hall, shaking his head.

"That went well," Terri said. "Maybe we should have company more often."

I smirked. "We need to pack and get out of here. We'll have to switch cars since all the ones in the garage are registered to me."

"How will we do that?"

"I would say it's time to take some cash and buy a vehicle first thing in the morning. For now, let's just get out of here."

Chapter 20

It has been six months now. I've made the phone calls, and my magnificent house on Parkers Mill Road has been packed with great care and moved to an undisclosed location. A team also went to Terri's house and carefully packed all her belongings and sent them to the same location.

Shawn has proven himself to be a true friend and a valuable asset to Terri and me. We have met twice. Both times we were in Las Vegas. The masses of people and over-the-top security allowed us to meet without much distraction. Shawn is considering retiring and putting his full-time work into finding Morgan and the others like her. When we met the first time in Las Vegas, he had a list of questions that took almost six hours to answer. Most of his questions had to do with the doctor I told him about. In Shawn's investigation, he now questions what happened to the doctor and to all his research. He has found abnormalities in both the stories and the evidence chain, and as he looked into it, he ran into a strange roadblock that kept him distanced from the truth.

Shawn was unable to trace the two men who died in my Lexington home. The prints came back as two men in the English military, but those men had been dead for many years. In contacting family and friends, all confirmed the men were dead and buried after a horrible crash. Shawn was sure this meant they were very highly paid mercenaries but had no way to trace who they ended up with, and each time he tried, he ended up at a dead-end.

During his second visit, he brought us news about another potential lead in Alaska. Terri and I are considering following up after we take some more time to be prepared. Terri continues to surprise me. I have enjoyed every moment of the last. When I asked her if she was okay with all of this, she always says, "You waited your whole life to find me, and I only had to wait a few years. Of course, I'm okay."

Morgan has been elusive. Shawn located a picture of her at a gala ball in Cincinnati. It was unmistakable it was her with the long red dress and ebony hair wearing heels and in the middle of everything. Shawn contacted the nonprofit that sponsored the ball and they stated Ms.

LeFay was the widow of a prominent English socialite. They had no permanent address for her but stated simply she was somewhere in the Mediterranean on her 100-foot yacht. Shawn spent a significant amount of time trying to trace anything about the yacht or Nigel LeFay and found that most records were obscure. Although to me, it was unmistakable that the woman in the picture was Morgan, she was very careful not to have her face photographed.

As a parting gift at our second meeting, Shawn gave me a license to carry a weapon and kept it pretty much off the books. It will not hold up under intense scrutiny, but it is enough that the pistol I now carry will no longer be questioned.

I told Micah I would be traveling for a while with Terri. I talk to him often but about nothing in particular. He continues to tell me that when Terri tires of me, she should come to stay with him. Terri and I both laugh. Micah has added eight more people and has opened up a small branch in Cincinnati now. Someday he will get a copy of the death certificate that will ensure there are no questions, and the company will be his forever.

Garret found his way home and mourned his two friends. I sent anonymous flowers to their funerals and made sure everything was paid. The families were saddened, and all of Lexington mourned the two boys. I was glad they would never know the truth of the line the boys had crossed because of my mistake. Sometimes ignorance can create more happiness than the truth.

For the moment, Terri and I live nowhere. We're wandering vagabonds right now as we watch the news and try to see some indication of Morgan or any of the others. With the minimal information Morgan gave me, I also know there may be more like me if only, I can find them. I do not know if we are part of another race, or a genetic fluke.

This is now a battle of wills. I know Morgan is alive, and that means that 11 other women might be alive and potentially looking for me. Today is much different than I intended. Instead of a stable life, Terri and I are truly on the run. Until I can find a way to ensure Terri's safety we will keep moving.

Terri and I now travel in a small motorhome and continue to go from town to town doing what we can and looking for clues on the Internet. Mostly, we enjoy each other and find a passion that most people will never see. As we drive each day, we watch the sunrise and the sunset and will take nothing for granted. We know that Morgan is still out there, and I am sure she is looking for me as hard as I am looking for her. When the time comes, and I find her, I will take the fight to her in a way she will never expect. When the time comes, I will make sure that she can never harm Terri or me again. My quest to find her is eternal, forever.

ACKNOWLEDGMENTS

An amazing thank you to all the people who have guided this book. The city of Lexington, Kentucky was my home for a great many years and is a fantastic place to visit. If you get the chance go there, see the sites, drink the bourbon, enjoy Keeneland, and see the magic this city holds.

I also would like to acknowledge Pages Promotions and Diana Kathryn Plopa for assisting at the end of this book. Her editing skill was terrific and found numerous issues that are now resolved.

ABOUT THE AUTHOR

Andrew Allen Smith was born in Anderson, Indiana. Until the age of 15 he moved at least once per year and finally settled in Lexington, Kentucky. Andrew spent a significant amount of his teenage years reading and writing short stories and poetry. He published his first book, "A Slice of Passion," in 2005. It was a book of poetry that had been compiled from dozens of years of work. In 2015 he published "The Theft and other Short Stories" as a collection of some of his favorites after he was challenged to self-publish a book. In 2016 he published his first novel, "Vengeful Son," and began building a franchise with that book. The Masterson Files (the series containing "Vengeful Son") now contains five books and has 15 in outline form. Andrew's work as a quality engineer and system architect also gave him credit for a series of instructional manuals for site relationship management systems and a variety of quality documents and development lifecycles. In Andrew's spare time, he has a passion for a considerable number of hobbies and his family, which he considers paramount. For more information about Andrew, please visit andrewallensmith.com.

Other Books by Andrew Allen Smith

Fiction

A Slice of Passion

A Slice of Fear

The Theft and Other Short Stories

The Masterson Files Series

Vengeful Son

Sinful Father

Deadly Daughter

Fateful Friend

Silent Sister

Non-Fiction

What NOT to say to People Who are Grieving

Books Containing Andrew Allen Smith prose

Monster Hunter – Intern

Simple Things

Coming Soon

Burial Ground

Curious Cousin

Another Slice of Fear

Stealth Drive